CHAPTER ONE

The only thing missing from Della's nearly perfect life was a mother. All the other little girls she knew had mothers to love them and provide guidance on how a lady should behave. Which may have been part of the reason Tilya, her nursemaid, was always telling her that she was too unruly, yet wonderfully resilient. It was also why the news of getting a new mother *and* two sisters was so exciting.

"A mother!" Della cried out, twirling around the room.

"Come here and let me finish getting you ready, Little Lady," Tilya, her nursemaid, sighed in frustration.

Della couldn't sit still. She continued to dance around with her hair half combed. Her dress slipped off one shoulder, its undone laces swinging wildly against her exposed back. She almost tripped over the corner of the large four-poster bed. Tilya clamped firm hands on her shoulders, stopping Della mid-twirl.

"I'm happy for you, Little Lady. Great Cliffs knows if any seven-year-old girl needs a mother it's you. Now sit still a minute."

Tilya pulled Della across the room and plopped her down on the cushioned stool before the dressing table. The nursemaid smoothed her mousy brown hair in exasperation, despite it already being in a perfect, tight bun. Tilya was old enough to be her mother and Della loved hugging her comforting plumpness. She would have turned around and hugged her now, but it would only have made Tilya more exasperated.

"You want your new mother to like you, don't you? You need to look like the lady you are." Tilya made quick work of the laces on the dress. She picked up the brush sitting on the dressing table.

Della tried to keep still as Tilya did her hair, but her foot tapped the leg of the stool as the nursemaid wove the golden waves into a tight braid around the crown of her head. She didn't bother to stop the smile tugging up her rosy lips, making her blue-green eyes sparkle with joy. Her fair cheeks were still flushed from twirling about the room moments before. Della made an impish face in the mirror and Tilya caught sight of it out of the corner of her eye, startling her into a gasp. Della laughed with delight.

"Little Lady! You aren't a monkey at the market, don't behave like one."

"What do you think it will be like to have sisters? I think it will be like visiting with my friends, only *much* better. That's because none of us will ever have to go home! We can play together all day." Della swung her legs around in excitement and threw her arms out.

"I'm sure it will be lovely. Now sit still so I can finish this," Tilya ordered. Deft fingers pinned the ends of Della's hair into a firm bun, a hairstyle that might last long enough for her new family to arrive.

"Are you satisfied now?" Della shifted her feet with impatience.

Beneath the Cinders

Copyright © 2023 by Alice Rosegold

All rights reserved.

Beneath the Cinders

A Cinderella Retelling

ALICE ROSEGOLD

CONTENTS

Dedication

To all the children who were ever scared in their own home, but didn't know how to leave. To the little girl I once was. I promise you that you can make it out alive, and that it gets better.

"Yes, you look lovely. Now wait just a minute, you can't go rushing outside! You'll ruin all my hard work. No, don't argue—I know you, Little Lady. You wait with me inside the manor until they are close. You can watch from the window there."

Della fiddled with the curtain while she waited. At long last, a carriage appeared on the road. Everyone lined up outside just down from the steps—the manor servants in a row on one side, Tilya and Della on the other. Though Tilya gripped Della's hand in an attempt to keep her in place, Della still bounced on her toes. It seemed to Della that the carriage rolled in with agonizing slowness as if time itself had slowed down. Finally, *finally* the footman opened the carriage door. Della's father came out first. His flaxen hair shone in the sunlight and Della was reminded of just how tall he was. He moved aside and the footman handed down one girl, then another.

Della's eyes widened at the soft brown hair flowing down the taller girl's shoulders. She stared with admiration at the younger girl's equally rare hair, such a dark brown it verged on black, that swayed as she stepped closer to her sister. Most Aleecean's hair was fair, but perhaps in Tamaria darker locks were more prevalent. Their fair skin and pink lips matched Della's and she wondered if it would be enough for people to think she and her new sisters looked alike. Della waved at them. The taller one maintained her regal posture while the shorter one gave a smile and small wave back.

Della's father took over for the footman and helped Della's new mother down from the carriage. She reminded Della of a wine glass—tall and dainty, but with curves in all the right places. Her full lips formed a delicate pout and her dark hair was swept up into a chignon—a hairstyle Della had only seen on those visiting from the western country. The cloying scent of her perfume was strong even from a distance.

At last, Della's father came to her and whisked her up into a spinning hug. They both whooped and Della thought she saw her new mother cringe as they spun past, but Della dismissed it instantly. Who wouldn't want to be spun around by her father? She had probably imagined the wince.

"I have missed you, dear one," her father told her fondly. He set Della down. "Now, introductions! This is my Della. Della, these are your new sisters Marien and Eleonora, and this is..."

Her father trailed off as if unsure how to introduce his new wife to his daughter. The woman stepped forward and wrapped her arms around one of his.

"I'm Duchess Mariel DeVoss—or rather Caspari now." She let out an amused giggle at the slip. "I suppose I shall have to get used to that."

"How do you do?" Della bobbed a curtsy.

"How charming," she cooed in an almost too sweet voice.

Della frowned at the false note, but smiled again a moment later. This was her new mother!

Della's father quickly introduced her stepmother to the staff, before turning back to Della. "I know I've been away for some time, but I have business I must attend to now that I've returned. I will see you at supper."

He pressed a quick kiss on her head and strode past them, making quick work of the front steps before disappearing indoors.

"Well, let's go inside and have some tea," Della's new mother said.

"The sitting room is this way," Della said, eager to be useful. She ran to Tilya and tugged her hand. Tilya had been giving

Della's new mother an odd look, but swept into the house with her charge.

Della bounced on her toes as she led them across the hall into the sitting room. Della's new sisters sat together on one of the settees in the room. Large windows with gauzy curtains let sunlight flood the room, highlighting the soft blues and creams that decorated the room. Della towed Tilya toward the settee across from her sisters.

"That will be all. You may go." Her new mother dismissed Tilya with a wave of her hand.

"But I always take tea with Tilya!" Della protested.

"Take tea with the help? I think not! I see I shall have my work cut out for me teaching you proper manners." Her new mother looked aghast.

"It's alright, dear," Tilya whispered. She patted Della's hand before leaving the room.

"Now then, we should discuss something so that we may have a proper start. I don't expect to replace your mother and therefore you shouldn't be forced to call me mother," her stepmother told her.

Della wilted slightly at this. Did that mean she wouldn't be a mother to her? Della ached to ask her, but for the first time in her young life her courage failed her. "Then what should I call you?"

"Duchess Mariel will do fine," her stepmother told her.

"Duchess Mariel?" Della queried, testing the word on her lips. It felt odd to refer to her so formally.

"Yes, that's right," the woman purred. Her lips curled up in a way that reminded Della of a barn cat about to pounce on a particularly fat mouse.

Supper that night was not the lively affair Della had envisioned. Her stepmother sat on the right side of her father and Marien sat on his left with Eleonora and Della following. Della felt oddly displaced by this new woman. She supposed her new family were to sit between her and her father so they could all get to know each other. The duchess spoke softly with her father, capturing his attention most of the night. Della was too far away to talk to him without raising her voice, for which her stepmother would surely give her a disapproving glance like the one she had given her for skipping in the hallway earlier. Still wanting to find her way into the woman's good graces without disappointing her too much, Della decided it was best to refrain. So, she turned instead to her new sisters, determined to make a friend by the end of the evening.

"Are you from Aleece?" Della asked the sisters sitting to her left.

"Obviously not," Marien sniffed.

"I didn't think so—because of your hair—but you never know," Della said, trying to keep the conversation going.

"We also don't have a ridiculous accent," Marien scoffed.

Della frowned. She didn't have an accent, did she? There were so many travelers in Aleece, especially here in the capital, that accents were common to the point that she didn't really notice them anymore.

"We're from Tamaria," Eleonora murmured.

Della squinted her eyes as she recalled the geography Tilya had taught her. "That's to the west of here."

"Yes, and it was a dreadfully long journey, so we should like to rest," Marien said pointedly.

Duchess Mariel looked at the girls. "Are you tired? Oh, my poor dears. I should have thought of the toll the journey would take on you."

"Yes," Marien replied quickly, though Eleonora looked disappointed.

Her stepmother turned to her father. "The girls should really go to bed now, darling."

"So early? Er—but of course," Della's father quickly acquiesced when the duchess frowned at him.

"Della should get some rest too. It's been a taxing day," she continued.

"Oh, that's alright, I don't feel tired at all." Della's insides warmed at the thought of spending the evening with her father as they used to when he returned home from his trips.

"You really should rest as well," her stepmother turned to Della. She smiled, but the look was frosty.

"It's alright. Della can stay up. We always stay up late the night I return."

Della beamed at her father.

"Am I not the woman of this household now? How do you expect Della to respect my word if you undermine what I say?"

"Well... I suppose I see your point," Della's father said with a sigh.

"Off to bed, Della," Duchess Mariel told her.

"Fine." Della slumped back in her chair. Her stepmother motioned at her so Della pushed back her chair. It made a horrible scraping noise when it slid off the rug and onto the floor.

The woman pursed her lips. "You should address people when you speak to them. It shows respect. Try again."

"Alright, Duchess Mariel."

"Della! There's no need to be rude," her father scolded her.

"No, no, it's alright. I told her she could call me that, as I don't expect to replace her mother." The duchess gave him a disarming smile.

Her father frowned, but didn't argue.

The duchess ushered the girls out of the room and off to their respective bedrooms. Tilya came to Della later than usual as the duchess had pulled the nursemaid into her daughters' rooms first. Della watched through her cracked door as Tilya left Marien's room and moved on to Eleonora's. Her stepmother entered Marien's room. As Tilya left Eleonora's room, her stepmother slipped in.

"Della! What are you doing there?" Tilya demanded as she swung Della's door open.

"I was waiting for you," Della gave her the half-truth.

Tilya shut the door firmly behind her and turned back to Della. "You were spying, Little Lady. No more of that. Now, let's get you into your nightgown."

A few minutes later Tilya tucked Della into bed. After her nursemaid left the room, she waited expectantly for her stepmother to come say goodnight. She waited. And waited. And waited. Finally, the young girl dozed off, still sitting propped up against her pillows.

She woke a few hours later as her father shifted her down into a more comfortable position. He smoothed her hair.

"I missed you, my dear child."

"I missed you too. Please don't leave again anytime soon," Della begged.

"It is so hard to leave you each time. Now you have a new—well, two new sisters to play with. You won't be half as lonely when I'm gone. If you ever do get lonely, just look to the stars. I will be spending the night under the same stars as you. Your mother is looking down at you from the stars as well. I know she wishes you every happiness."

"Will she try to come close to me tonight?"

"If you see a shooting star you know she is coming as close as she can. Don't forget to make a wish. If she catches it, then it will come true. I knew your mother to be excellent at catching things. After all, she caught me."

"Aunt Osanna describes it as the other way around," Della corrected him with a giggle.

"Well, your aunts are very wise. All eleven of them. If you know nothing else, then you can be assured that you are well-loved, dear one. Now, go to sleep and dream of delightful things." Her father planted a kiss on her forehead and left.

Della burrowed down in her blanket, but sleep didn't come easily. She puzzled over the day's events, her excitement long gone. Would she be taking tea without Tilya from now on? She swallowed a lump in her throat. Della brightened as she realized it might give her a greater opportunity to get to know her new sisters if she only talked to them during tea time, rather than Tilya. She hadn't had much time to speak with them and she realized she didn't even know if they liked horses or picking wildflowers or watching the troupes perform. Did they know not to wander too far in the woods? She resolved to tell them. Surely the three girls would find something they all liked to do together.

Her new—Duchess Mariel confused her, though. She had been so excited to have a mother around. All her friends had them, and while they could sometimes be strict, it was still fun to go shopping with them. The duchess had looked fashionable, perhaps she would take them into the city to go shopping soon. Why hadn't she come in to say goodnight to her? Perhaps Duchess Mariel had worried she didn't like her since Della had been a bit rude at dinner. She must look for a way to repair things. She would assure the duchess that she would try her best to learn to be a lady, and that they could get on well together. Della fell asleep dreaming of her new stepmother reading her stories and braiding wildflowers into her hair.

CHAPTER TWO

The next afternoon Della bounced with excitement. Tilya had heard there was a new troupe visiting Delemy and had told her as much while they worked to tidy Della's room. Della dumped an armful of dolls and wooden toys into a small chest and shut it. Tilya arched an eyebrow at the young girl's haphazard cleaning. Della gave her an unrepentant grin and Tilya sighed as she straightened the bed.

"I hope they sing songs from across the lands. Those are my favorite!" Della picked up a pillow and threw it onto the bed.

"I'm sure they will. They usually do, though they may be ones you have already heard before." Tilya fluffed the pillow before placing it at the top of the bed. "There, now that's done. Would you like to go?"

"May I invite my sisters? I'm sure they would enjoy the show as well," Della asked.

"Of course you may. Go on then," Tilya told her.

Della found her sisters taking tea in the sitting room. She hesitated in the doorway. She took a steadying breath and approached them with a smile. "Would you like to come see the new troupe in the city proper?"

"What's a troupe?" Eleonora cocked her head, curious.

"They're a group of performers. The city has a few stages for them to do their shows on, though we usually go to the one at the market center right before the palace since only the best can present there. Troupes travel all over the continent and perform. They always have new songs or acts to show off. It's quite exciting," Della explained.

"They travel all of Meliorate?" Marien crossed her arms and arched a brow.

Della nodded with enthusiasm. "Yes! The whole continent! They bring back so many wondrous acts from each place."

Eleonora set down her teacup. "That does sound exciting!"

"You want us to go watch street performers? That doesn't seem like a suitable activity for a young lady," Marien scoffed. She sipped her tea primly.

"On the contrary, many lords and ladies stop to watch them. My father takes me when he has the time." Della frowned.

"I think we'll stay here," Marien said with her nose in the air.

Eleonora glanced between her older sister and Della, the latter giving her a genuine smile. Eleonora bit her lip and considered.

"I'd like to go," she said shyly. Marien choked on her tea.

Della grinned and grabbed Eleonora's hand. She pulled the youngest sister out of the room.

"Eleonora!" Marien spluttered, her voice fading as Della led Eleonora through the house before she could change her mind.

Tilya fell in behind them at the door and the three went out into the waiting carriage. It was the other carriage they had, one with an open top. Della enjoyed the wind whipping her hair as they traveled into the city proper. She grinned at Eleonora, who was using both hands in an attempt to hold her dark locks out of her face which held a smile that made her eyes twinkle. Tilya's headscarf kept her tight bun protected from the wind.

Della loved their manor, set amongst the many trees outside the sprawling capital city. It was still considered part of the city, though it lay outside the gates. Many of the nobles had manors in the surrounding lands. Even with all the trees that had been cleared to make the enormous city, it wasn't enough to keep up with the ever-growing population. Those who could afford the cost of clearing a portion of the forest often lived outside the walls in the surrounding area, so it was considered an expansion of the great city despite being outside the walls. Della's mother had been granted this land when she was given the title of duchess and the crown had paid for the trees to be cleared and the manor to be built. Della's father had then funded more tree removal to have room for pastures and training rings for the horses he bred, trained, and sold.

Their manor was *home*, but Della loved the bustling, noisy city as well. When they passed through the gates Eleonora looked around them with wide eyes. The thrum of the crowd made a sort of music in the way the women's skirts swished, men's shoes slapped the cobblestones, horses pulling carriages whinnied, and everywhere voices called out in an odd harmony.

Eleonora grasped the edge of the carriage and used it to lift herself slightly out of her seat for a better view. "It's so big!"

"Delemy is one of the largest cities in Aleece. It's the capital. See there? At the far end you can see the castle," Tilya told her pointing.

"Does that mean the king and queen live there?" Eleonora asked in awe.

Tilya readily explained, "The king does. The queen died quite a long time ago."

"My aunts live there. Well, some of them. Some of them have moved away due to marriages in other kingdoms." Della scrunched up her face. "It seems like a terrible reason to leave the most wonderous place in the world. Just look at the city around us—everything here is so exciting!"

"Your aunts live at court? Mother says ladies of court are very respectable and well brought up and almost always make an advantageous match."

"No silly! Well, yes, but they live in—"

"We'll get out here," Tilya told their driver, her loud voice cutting across Della's. They had reached the thicker crowds of the inner city. She explained to the girls as they climbed out, "We will get through easier on foot than in the carriage.

Tilya took each girl by the hand and led them through the crowd. Eleonora peered at everything with curiosity, though she clung to the nursemaid. Tilya wriggled their way through the crowd before coming to a stop at a large stage having found a spot where the girls could see easily. A troupe was already performing there. Eleonora's eyes were wide as saucers as she watched a man juggle balls, then flaming batons, then actual swords! Della grinned at her and to her surprise Eleonora grinned back.

Several women took over the stage singing and dancing. They wore varying shades of blue and green with scalloped underskirts of foamy lace. The way they swished and flared their skirts as they danced reminded Della of the crashing ocean waves. Della sang along to all the songs she knew and soaked up any new ones she heard, trying to memorize them. They ended with a hauntingly beautiful melody in a language Della didn't understand, but Tilya's hands tightened on theirs.

"That's siren if I ever heard it," she said looking disturbed.

Eleonora also looked uneasy, but Della had found the song beautiful—though in a way that made her shiver.

"Ladies and gentlemen, we have a spectacular sight for you today! Rumored to live in the craggy mountains of the Lycaria, this creature is spoken of only in legends. However, high in such mountains is a small village that claimed it was more than legend, and one of my brave friends here sought it out. Best known by the glowing feathers of its majestic plumage, I give you the firebird!" the man on stage declared.

Eleonora leaned in and whispered to Della, "Surely firebirds aren't real. Do you think they have some other sort of bird like a macaw that's only red, orange, and yellow?"

"Shush. Just watch!" Della breathed out, squeezing her sister's hand with excitement.

Eleonora turned back as another man had walked on stage. He held a blanketed bundled in his arms. Della heard Eleonora gasp as the first man snatched off the blanket with a flourish, revealing an enormous birdcage underneath. Inside hung a perch and upon the perch was a bird that looked similar to a falcon, but with long, trailing tail feathers that curled beneath it. The firebird's feathers truly did glow in various shades of red, orange, and yellow that pulsed with a light reminiscent of Della's own fireplace at home.

Eleonora blinked several times. "It *is* real."

"Most legends became so because they were told by those with experience." Tilya's eyes stayed on the stage as she shared her wisdom with the girls.

Della stared, enraptured by the bird that flickered and pulsed like firelight. "It's beautiful."

Eleonora turned to Della. "I think I would like to own a firebird one day."

"I don't think such a creature should be caged," Della said simply.

"I'd put it in a beautiful menagerie with other birds and such so that it wouldn't be lonely," Eleonora protested.

"I'm sure you mean well, young one, but Della is right. When we try to cage such creatures and tame them into what we wish, they either slowly fade away or fight with all their might to escape."

The two men covered up the firebird again and left as a storyteller took the stage. Della settled in, content to listen.

"Just what is the meaning of this?" a woman screeched from behind them.

Della whirled around and found herself facing Duchess Mariel. Behind her, the storyteller continued their tale, in a somewhat louder voice as if to discourage any further disruptions.

"My lady." Tilya bobbed a small curtsy.

The duchess narrowed her eyes at the display. Servants in Aleece rarely curtsied or bowed except to royalty. Della had overheard the duchess fighting with her father over the supposed disrespect, but her father had compromised only by asking the servants to give small bows or curtsies. Della could see how the small gestures chafed at the woman even more than it irritated the servants to comply with such a request. Though Della suspected their butler might be giving the shallow bows a bit more often than necessary for that very reason.

"Why is my daughter—daughters—out here on the street like the commonfolk? They are ladies, not peasants," Duchess Mariel hissed.

"We came to see the new troupe! We were told they were exceptional, and indeed, they were." Della's stomach quivered when the woman's face twisted.

Eleonora's eyes shone. "Oh yes! Mother, they have a firebird—a real firebird! It actually glows!"

Tilya squeezed both girls' hands.

"Now they're telling a story! Listen!" Della said eager to draw her new m—Duchess Mariel into the magic of the troupe. Her enthusiasm faltered when Tilya squeezed her hand even tighter.

"No, I will not sit here and listen in the street like a heathen! Come now, into the carriage with Duke Caspari." The duchess turned and walked out of the crowd.

A crestfallen Eleonora obediently followed, but Della didn't move until Tilya tugged her along. She trudged through the throng of cheerful city dwellers. She didn't understand why Duchess Mariel was so upset. The troupes weren't common in Tamaria, but surely they weren't something to avoid like pickpockets.

The duchess marched up to Della's father. "I have found our daughters here without permission and am bringing them home with us now."

"Oh, hello girls! Are you enjoying a day out in the city?" Her father asked them with a smile.

"They went out without me knowing and were watching some street performers!"

"Oh! I had heard there was a new troupe in town that was causing some excitement. Were they any good?" Father asked them eagerly.

"They have a firebird, Father! I wonder if the feathers still glow even when they fall out."

"I bet they do. That's what the legends say. A firebird then? Well, that is exciting!"

"Philip! I cannot believe you are fine with the girls going to the city alone and standing in the street like commoners watching strange people do disturbing acts." The duchess looked appalled.

"Mariel, there's no need to be so distressed. The girls are with Tilya, it isn't like they came here bareback on a horse—though that would be a feat in itself...Aleece is a very versatile country. Here anyone can make a life with whatever talent they have and for some that is joining a troupe. The songs and storytelling are harmless. The girls have now seen a real firebird, which is something that even I haven't experienced despite all my travels. I love the enterprising spirit here—I made my wealth with it. I grew up poor, but unlike most surrounding countries, here I was able to build my wealth before I was ever given the title of Duke."

"I understand that your country is different than mine and that you have greatly improved my circumstance by bringing me here," Duchess Mariel said stiffly.

"Mariel, I wasn't trying to imply—I only meant that the performers aren't like the beggars on the streets in other places. They truly have talent and this country is one that rewards them for it. Music and revelry are a part of the culture here," her father spoke gently now.

"I am raising young ladies to become noblewomen in *any* culture. I thought you wanted a woman's touch in your household," Duchess Mariel sniffed.

"Of course I do. All three girls need the guidance only a mother can provide."

The duchess raised her chin. "Well then, let me *be* a mother figure. That means I must know where they are and what they are learning at all times. They can come into the city when I allow it and attend events that I know will enrich them culturally."

"Very well. They won't come into the city again without getting your approval first." Her father's shoulders had stiffened slightly, but he looked at them and asked, "Will you girls?"

"Of course not, Mother," Eleonora agreed.

Della only glared at the ground.

"Della?" Her father prompted.

"I don't see why I can't come to the city proper when I wish to. You've always let me before."

"You can still come into the city. You only have to let your stepmother know beforehand so that it doesn't interfere with any activities she has planned for you. Besides, you don't want to give her another fright like the one she clearly had seeing you girls here today." Her father's cheerful tone sounded forced.

"Alright," Della agreed, but only because she felt she had no other choice.

CHAPTER THREE

Della hurried down the stairs to breakfast, hoping to catch Eleonora before Marien joined them. Della was delighted at the friendship her younger sister had offered in the year they'd spent together, but Eleonora was still painfully shy when anyone else was around. Della raced past her father's study, but paused when she heard voices. The thick, mahogany door was open a crack. She crept toward it quietly and pressed her ear to the opening.

"I really find this all unnecessary. You're doing such a fine job of running the household," Della's father said.

"Thank you, but it really takes all of my time. I have no time to do anything else." Della rolled her eyes at the pout she could hear in her stepmother's voice.

"Well, I suppose I can accept the new housekeeper if it frees up time for you, but I really don't see how I can let Ernst go."

Della's heart began to pound. Ernst had been their butler her entire life. He could be stern if you crossed him, but he had a soft spot for Della and was as much a part of their household as Tilya or her father. She couldn't imagine him not returning.

"He doesn't like me," Duchess Mariel said rigidly.

Father sighed. "He is simply used to how we have always done things here. You just need to give him time—"

"I've given him a year! I am the mistress of this household, yet he acts as if I am only a—a mistress of your bed! He resents anything I do differently than Adella did. He will never accept me."

"We all miss Adella. This household always will. That doesn't mean we haven't also opened our hearts to you," Father said gently.

"He makes me feel as if I don't belong here. I've gone through that once before—I won't live through that again in my own home." This time her voice quavered.

A long pause fell. Della was about to move away when her father spoke again.

"Very well. I shall give him notice and write a recommendation this afternoon. He shall be allowed to stay on until he finds new work." Her father sounded resigned.

Della stumbled the rest of the way down the hall to the dining room with her head spinning. How could Father allow this? The duchess wouldn't take Tilya away from her next, would she? Della slumped into her seat.

"Are you alright?" Eleonora whispered to Della. "You look as though you've seen a ghost."

Marien shushed them, which was just as well since Della didn't know what to say.

Father walked in, taking his place at the head of the table, and Duchess Mariel flounced in soon after looking wickedly delighted, though her face settled into a haughty elegance before Father looked her way.

"I've hired a governess for the girls," Duchess Mariel said conversationally as they began eating.

"But they have Tilya." Her father frowned.

"She is a nursemaid, not a proper governess. With Della she might have managed, but we can hardly expect her to teach all three girls if she is learning as she goes along."

"Tilya is educated as all Aleeceans are. The girls will learn much from her."

"Oh, I didn't mean to imply she was ignorant, only that she hasn't done the extra schooling a governess has. They have so many subjects memorized and are trained on how to help the children best learn. I wouldn't wish to overwhelm Tilya. Between her and the governess all three girls should be able to get a proper education."

"I suppose that makes sense. We aren't sending Tilya away though."

"Of course not," Duchess Mariel said, but her smile was tight and it didn't reach her eyes.

Della pushed the food around on her plate until breakfast was over and she was excused. She tried to focus during the music lessons her stepmother insisted on, but her voice warbled and she sang the wrong lines. She simply couldn't focus. Her father had said they wouldn't send Tilya away. She repeated that over and over to herself, but she couldn't shake the feeling of dread in the pit of her stomach.

Tilya stopped Della in the hall after teatime. "Your father wishes you to see you."

Della had to refrain from running through the manor in her eagerness to reach the stables. Their time together had become far too limited. A morning with her father and the horses was just what she needed.

"Della! How are you, darling?" Her father's face lit up when he caught sight of her entering the stable.

"I'm fine. How are you?" She ran up to hug him.

He scooped her up and twirled her around in a tight hug, holding her close so she wouldn't knock into any of the stalls.

"I'm doing well. I'm sorry we haven't had as much time together since I remarried. I am working more which as you know takes me away and I have a new wife to attend to. I hope you're enjoying your new sisters in my absence," he said.

"Eleonora is lovely."

Her father laughed knowingly. "Marien isn't horrible either, darling. She's just more like her mother—bound and determined to be a proper Tamarian lady. Though our two countries share boarders there isn't much else we have in common."

"We are very different," Della agreed with a shrug.

"You must always remember to treat others with kindness though, no matter how different they may be. How we treat people is a reflection of ourselves, no matter how they treat us. That said, let me know if anything should happen beyond a sisterly spat. I won't stand for cruelty in my house."

"Of course, Father." Della leaned into his side taking comfort in his strength beside her.

"Would you like to see my latest acquisition?" Eagerness shone in his eyes as he held out a hand to her.

"Yes!" Della looked around the stables trying to see anything new. Her father laughed and led her to a stall further down.

"This is Reynart," he said.

Della's eyes widened at the stallion that towered above even her father's head. Broad shoulders and powerful muscles bunched under its sable coat. She held her breath when it snuffled at her curiously, suddenly feeling nervous.

"Is he a Stronghorse?" Della asked in awe.

"He is indeed! I wasn't sure whether I would try to bond with him or try to sell him—they fetch a hefty price you know—but one look at him and I knew I wouldn't sell him."

"So that means you're trying to bond with him?" Della looked over the horse with a new curiosity.

"I already have," her father said in a satisfied tone.

Della turned wide eyes on him. "Would you tell me about the bond?"

"Stronghorses are the only breed to bond with humans. That's what makes them so expensive. Well, that and the fact that they are very hard to catch or even breed. Once bonded they either cannot or will not bond with another, though I like to think it's because they will not. Stronghorses and humans that are bonded can communicate to each other in a way," he said.

"Father, I know all that," she said, laughing to mask her impatience. "I meant will you tell me what it's like to be bonded? Which of the rumors are true? Can you hear them speak words into your mind or is it more like pictures or an impression of something they *might* be trying to convey?"

"Well, Reynart here is mine, but I have started a search for another Stronghorse. I'm thinking a mare this time. I'm hoping to gift it to Mariel and then breed the pair. Only two Stronghorses can produce another Stronghorse. If I bred Reynart with any mare here she would likely give me a larger than average horse, but not a Stronghorse. Then I hope to give you a Stronghorse of your own someday. When you bond with one you will know which of the rumors are true."

A flare of disappointment went through her as she realized he wouldn't tell her what the bond was like. However, it was quickly burned away by the excitement of her having her own Stronghorse one day.

"Now you've become one of the secretive Stronghorse owners that you always complained about," Della teased.

"Perhaps I am," her father laughed. "But it's not something that is easy to explain, and I don't know if the bond varies from person to person either. Besides, I think you would like to find out by experiencing it yourself."

"Alright, I will promise not to pester you about it if you promise that I will have a Stronghorse one day," Della compromised with a grin.

"A savvy negotiator. Very well, I promise I shall do my very best to ensure that you have your own Stronghorse one day," he told her with a matching grin.

"Oh, thank you Father! My very own Stronghorse," Della said dreamily.

"I haven't even gotten you one yet! For now, why don't you ride with me on mine?"

"I'd love to!" Della squealed.

She watched as her father saddled the enormous horse. She would normally help with the straps, but she was wary of the new creature. Instead, she envisioned herself grown up and saddling her own Stronghorse. She hoped she would have a nice mare that was a bit smaller than Reynart or that she would at least grow tall enough to saddle her Stronghorse with ease. The powerful stallion waited still and patient as her father secured the bridle. He led the horse out, Della following just behind her father.

Once outside her father lifted her up onto the tall mount. Della felt a bubble of giddiness as she saw how far down the ground was. She had her own pony and was a skilled rider, but

Stronghorses were known to be unpredictable unless you were bonded to them. Della gripped the saddle horn tightly. Her father swung up behind her and she nestled her back against him as he brought his arms up securely around her to grip the reins. Her father gently tapped his heels against the stallion and they started off into a trot.

"What do you think? It's a bit different than riding Stonecrop, isn't it?" he asked her.

"It definitely is. One day I hope I can bond with and ride one all on my own, but for now I like that I can saddle and mount Stonecrop on my own." Della smiled at the thought of her pony, golden yellow as the flowers she was named after.

"Shall we try out a gallop?" Her father tapped his heels against Reynart's flank.

The horse began racing before Della could respond and the wind would have whisked her words away, so she didn't bother trying to speak. She hadn't noticed her father spur the horse with his boots or the reins and wondered if they had communicated through the bond. She watched the trees surrounding them blur as they sped past. The wind tugged strands of her hair loose and whipped them about her cheeks and eyes, but she didn't dare let go long enough to push them away. Safe in her father's arms, exhilaration rose up from her stomach at the sheer speed they achieved as they flew. They raced around the house in a wide circle once, twice, three times before they began to slow. The Stronghorse wasn't even panting as if that was the pace he was born for.

"That was amazing!" Della cried.

"I'm glad you enjoyed it!" her father said cheerfully. He dismounted and lifted Della down after him. They walked together back to the stables. Her father removed the riding equipment from the Stronghorse.

"Hand me that brush, then you had better get back to the house. I wouldn't want you to be late for your lessons," he told her.

Della handed him the curry brush and chose not to enlighten him about the fact that she was already late. It had been so nice to spend part of her day with him again like she used to. She couldn't wait to do it again.

Two weeks later Della was still daydreaming about riding her very own Stronghorse. Her father was away trading horses, perhaps he would even bring a Stronghorse back for her this very week! She imagined herself galloping along the coast astride a large mare—the color of which changed daily in her mind—the steed would be kicking up sand as the waves lapped the shoreline they flew across. On the beach they could ride uninterrupted by trees or buildings for miles and—

"Della! Did you hear a word I said?" Eleonora asked, pulling Della out of her fantasy.

"Sorry." Della bit her lip and lifted her shoulders apologetically.

"I asked—"

She broke off as the new butler opened the door to the sitting room where they were taking tea. He offered a silver platter holding a solitary letter to the duchess. She took it and he left the room. Eleonora and Della sipped their tea and tried not to look like they were glancing at the duchess out of the corners of their eyes.

The duchess lifted the letter and opened it with a frown. Her eyes widened as they moved across the page, then her face paled. Della's stomach clenched with unease.

"No," Duchess Mariel breathed and fled from the room. Marien rose and went after her mother.

"What do you think that was about?" Della asked Eleonora.

"Perhaps her latest dress order will arrive too late for the next social," Eleonora suggested with a giggle.

"I bet one of the other courtiers wrote to ask what she thought of an upcoming party, but she realized she hadn't been invited yet," Della guessed with a snicker of her own.

"Maybe one of her friends wrote to say they own the very same hat she just bought."

Tilya entered the room and rushed to Della. She flung her arms around the girl and pulled her into a tight embrace.

Della's words were muffled against the woman's dress as she said, "Tilya, you're smothering me."

"Oh, Little Lady, I'm so sorry!" Tilya pulled back. Her cheeks were tearstained. "The news is simply dreadful!"

"What news?" Della asked as her stomach clenched tighter. "Tilya, you aren't being sent away, are you?!"

Tilya's eyes held an unending sadness as she looked into Della's own. Della's heart plummeted. She had seen that expression before on her father's face when he was missing her mother more than usual. It was a look of loss. Hadn't her father said they wouldn't send Tilya away? Then she couldn't be leaving. Della's stomach settled.

"Tilya, did something happen to your family? I'm so sorry." Della gave her nursemaid a tight squeeze.

"No, Della, it's..." Tilya took a heavy breath before continuing. "It's your father. He sighted a wild Stronghorse and went after it. He was severely injured trying to rope it by himself. His traveling companions tried to bring him to a doctor, but he didn't make it to the town."

"What?" Della tried to make sense of the news as the information slowly registered in her mind.

"Oh Della, I'm so sorry," Eleonora said, but her voice sounded far away.

A roaring filled Della's ears. She couldn't breathe. She felt like the time she fell in the ocean and wave after wave pummeled her underwater into the sand. She didn't know if she was gasping or crying or just sitting there.

The next week was a blur. Tilya forced a few bites of food into her at mealtimes or she wouldn't have bothered to eat at all. Della didn't know how she made it through the funeral. Some of her aunts attended, and the King, of course. She didn't remember what anyone said. She didn't remember what she wore. All she knew was the aching sadness that drowned her on dry land.

As weeks passed, she started to notice that the wealth her father had accumulated was dwindling far quicker than it should have. First all their beautiful horses were sold, all except two for the carriage and her father's Stronghorse, Reynart, simply for the prestige of owning him though the duchess could never bond with him. Then the jewels Della's mother had owned disappeared. Della heard whispers of fine china being sold, silver candlesticks gone, and noticed the bare walls where ta-

pestries had once hung. One by one Della saw servants leave
the manor and never return.

Della awoke in the middle of one night to find Tilya packing
a trunk and a carpetbag in her room. Della sat up in bed and
rubbed her eyes.

"Tilya, what on the Great Cliffs are you doing? Go to sleep."
Della rolled back over.

"Don't use such language! It's rough speak that shouldn't
be used by a lady, even if it isn't true cursing," Tilya whispered
the reprimand to her.

"You and father use it," Della muttered.

"I'm a servant and your father was a merchant. Such language is common amongst us, but you, Little Lady, are nobility." Tilya moved another stack of things into the trunk.

"Whatever this is for can wait until morning," Della told
her. She never ordered Tilya to do anything, but the woman
was making her nervous.

"Hush! I mustn't be discovered before I've finished or I fear
you will lose some things that are precious to you."

"Tilya, what are you talking about? You're frightening me,"
Della whimpered.

Tilya stopped working and came over to the bed. She sat
next to Della and wrapped her in a quick but comforting
hug. She released her to continue packing. "Your stepmother
is leaving. Tonight."

"Where is she going?" Della frowned.

"If I overheard correctly, she's going back to Tamaria. That's where she came from you know. She's taking your stepsisters—and you. I don't believe I'll be invited to come with you," Tilya told her with a practical tone.

"No! You can't leave me, Tilya!" Della wailed.

"Hush girl! Let me give you one last bit of protection from her. But you must be *quiet*," Tilya said sternly.

Della nodded silently. She watched Tilya swiftly pack the trunk and the carpet bag.

"There. I'm finished. Listen closely. The trunk is locked. Everything you need for travel is in the carpet bag. You're to use only that during the trip and as long as possible afterward without it becoming suspicious. I've laid out your travel dress. It has a hidden pocket I sewed into it to protect things from thieves. The key to the trunk is in the hidden pocket. Pretend you cannot find it, that you don't know where it is. The trunk has a false bottom. Beneath it are a few precious things I've kept safe from *her* that were your mother's. They rightfully belong to you, and I want you to have them. If you ever make your way back to Aleece I have a few more things I couldn't fit in there that I will save for you." Tilya scooped the girl up in her arms.

Della's eyes widened. "Couldn't you get into trouble for stealing?"

"They're your things, not your stepmother's. Your mother left them to you and I hid them away before she arrived here, just in case. One never knows what a widowed woman will be like. Thank the stars I had the foresight...Even *if* she does know of these things, she has no way of finding them or proving anything has gone missing. I would only find trouble if *you* wanted to turn me in for stealing, Little Lady, and I trust you won't."

"I would never!" Della whispered so fiercely that Tilya chuckled.

"Know this, dear sweet girl—I love you fiercely and always will. Your aunts do too, busy as they are with matters of court. You will always have a home in Aleece should you ever wish to return."

A loud rapping on the door of the adjoining room made them both jump. Someone was knocking on the door to Tilya's room. She squeezed Della and moved silently into her room.

"Tilya! Wake up!" came Duchess Mariel's voice through the door.

"What do you wish of me, your ladyship?" Tilya somehow managed to make her voice sound as sleepy as if she had only just woken up.

"Get Della dressed and ready for travel. Pack a quick bag for her, but don't worry about overpacking. I will send someone for the rest of her things once we are settled."

"Yes, your ladyship." Tilya scowled at the still closed door.

Tilya quickly got Della dressed and braided her hair for travel. She was just tying the hair ribbon when the door burst open.

"That's quite enough time. Isn't she ready yet? Both my girls are already in the carriage." The duchess grinned triumphantly. Her grin dissolved as she noticed the packed trunk and carpet bag. Her mouth pursed into a tight line before she snapped her fingers for a servant to take the luggage to pack on top of the carriage.

"Come, into the carriage with you." Tilya took Della by the hand and led her down the steps, then out onto the cobblestone drive.

"Can't you come with me?" Della pleaded. Wasn't losing father enough? How could she lose Tilya and her country too?

"Oh, sweet girl, I wish I could." Tilya wrapped her up into a fierce hug. She squeezed tighter when Della began to sob. "None of that now, don't you show her she's getting to you. She's one to use your weaknesses against you."

Della choked back her tears and gulped down the lump forming in her throat. She took some shuddering breaths, trying to calm herself.

Tilya wiped Della's eyes with her apron and stepped back. She tilted the girl's chin up with her finger. "Keep your chin up, dear. You're Adella Caspari of Aleece. You were born out of love and are fiercely loved by those you leave behind today. You *will* be alright. You are strong. You can make it through anything."

Della realized that Tilya's red-rimmed eyes were also glistening with tears. Her nursemaid blinked them back. The door to the manor opened behind Tilya and the duchess swept out.

"That's enough now, we have places to be. Into the carriage," Duchess Mariel snapped.

It was the middle of the night, but none of the servants seemed inclined to argue, not even the carriage driver. Tilya swept Della up in one last quick hug, glaring at the duchess as she climbed inside.

"In you go." Tilya handed Della up into the carriage.

Della sat down next to Eleonora, across from the duchess and Marien. Della watched out the carriage window as her home and the rest of her world fell away.

CHAPTER FOUR

TEN YEARS LATER

T he bell above the door tinkled as Della entered the shop. She placed her basket on the counter and waited for the baker to come to the storefront.

"Hello, Barend." Della greeted the red-faced man that came in from the back.

"Good morning, Della! What can I get for you?" Barend wiped the sweat from his brow with his apron.

"This week's bread, please. I found some portobellos for you, and some herbs for Johanna. Hopefully they will get her feeling back up to tending the storefront again." Della swept open the linen covering the basket.

"That's very kind of you to think of her. We are truly so grateful at the thought of a child, what with our age and all, but we weren't expecting that she'd be so sick."

The poor man looked overwhelmed as he sighed. His gaze fell on the fat mushrooms and brightened. Barend examined each one with delight before plopping them into his own basket along with the packet of herbs. He handed over the bread, discounting the cost of the mushrooms in the price he told her.

"Where are you off to today?"

"Just to Francesca's before I'm needed at home," Della replied as she counted out the coins she owed.

"Something new for you?" Barend's tone was hopeful as he eyed Della's worn clothing that fell a few inches too short in the skirt and sleeves.

"Goodness no. It's a new dress for Marien for...hmm, well some tea party or other."

Barend only huffed and rolled his eyes knowingly as he accepted the payment. The whole city found the duchess' obvious attempts to marry off her daughters to wealthy nobles either amusing or ridiculous—or both. Barend was of the opinion that it was ridiculous.

"Take this with you," he said, sliding a small parcel wrapped in brown paper. "For Francesca."

"Alright. Tell Johanna I said hello." Della's mouth curved up in a fond smile as she thought of the woman. The baker and his wife had reminded her of parents long before Johanna's pregnancy, with Barend tending to spoil favorite customers and Johanna strictly correcting anyone she thought was improper, though she clearly did so because she cared. They balanced each other out perfectly and whenever Della saw the two of them together, they glowed with love. It reminded her of Aleece, where love was the reason almost everyone married. Della hoped that she could find a love like that when she returned to her home country in a few years.

"I'll tell her. Goodbye, Della." With that Barend disappeared back to his ovens once more.

Della smiled as she walked towards Francesca's dress shop.

When Della reached the dress shop the store was empty of people, though a few mannequins displayed the latest styles and the walls shelved all manner of fabrics, ribbons, buttons, and hats.

"Franci?" Della glanced at the two other doors in the shop. Her friend was almost always here, but the question was whether Franci could be found upstairs in her apartments or in the back room working away.

"I'm back here," Francesca called, though the sound was somewhat muffled. Her friend's voice was a blend of accents—Tamarian, where she had lived since she was four, and remnants of Lacaian, the island of Lacai being where her family had immigrated from. While Della had clung to her Aleecean accent, Franci had worked hard to drop her accent, though when she was tired or upset it tended to come out stronger. Della liked the way the Lacaian sounded—dropping the 'h' on words that ended with 'th' and replacing 't' sounds with 'd' sounds. It reminded her of drinking a spiced chocolate drink while Franci's generous and compassionate parents asked her about her life and encouraged her to keep going when she felt down. Just like the drink, the words had warmed her from the inside out.

Della moved into the back room and found Franci pulling pins from her mouth and placing them in a dress she was working on. Her black coils were pulled back in a ponytail that fanned out in a half circle, the dark color contrasting beautifully against the red headscarf she wore. Franci looked good in almost every color, though she preferred bold ones that would have made most of her noblewomen customers look washed out.

"Everyone has fallen in love with giant, lacey ruffles! I love the amount I can charge for the lace, but I don't enjoy so much pinning." Franci's brown eyes sparkled with happiness despite the complaint.

"I don't enjoy all these ruffles and lace at all," Della supplied helpfully.

"And that would be useful if only you'd ever let me make you a gown." Franci eyed Della's dismal attire.

"I don't need anything fancy," Della protested. "Besides, I have plenty of other dress orders for you."

Franci rolled her eyes. "Speaking of which, come with me to the front for the latest pompous creation I've had to make for them."

Though Franci didn't enjoy the requests Della's stepfamily gave her—in large part due to their treatment of her, but also because of their sometimes ridiculous requests—Della knew every dress Franci created was a masterpiece despite it all. The girls walked to the other room and Franci pulled a large brown package out from behind the counter.

"This one is for you from Barend." Della handed her the small parcel before tucking the one from Franci into her basket.

Franci opened it and squealed with delight at the two sticky buns, then rolled her eyes as she read the little card attached to the string that had been holding the parcel closed. She bit into one sticky bun grumpily.

"Johanna sending you more motherly advice?" Della snickered.

"Insisting I get married is *not* motherly advice." Franci pushed the other sticky bun toward Della.

"She only thinks she's looking out for you now that your parents are gone," Della pointed out.

"Heaven forbid a twenty-year-old woman be unmarried without parents or any male relative to control her finances," Franci grumbled. "Oh and *you really ought to go by your full given name, Franci sounds like a boy's name, dear*' is at the end of it."

"At least she cares." Della shrugged.

"She's lucky I don't add extra ruffles to her new maternity gowns," Franci muttered, though Della knew she would never do such a thing.

After Franci's parents and brother died, the baker and his wife had looked after her in whatever ways they could even though she had already been sixteen. Johanna was forever trying to make a match with some man or other for her, and Della knew it was only because they worried what might happen if they too were gone. Tamaria was not a place that looked well on unmarried women, and even less so on unmarried women who ran their own businesses, of which there were very few. Franci's parents had let her begin implementing her designs at their shop when she was only twelve and they had crowed loudly about their daughter's skills rather than claim them for their own. By the time her parents and brother had passed, Franci's skills were so coveted she had no problem continuing her work on her own beyond a few unpleasant whispers that quickly died away as those people were cut off from her designs. No one wanted to be banned from her store.

"Well, I'd better get home and start on the afternoon chores." Della licked the last of the sticky treat off her fingers.

"I wish you wouldn't let them order you around so. You're as much a lady as they are—more so by blood." Franci wiped her own hands on a handkerchief.

Blood meant nothing when titles were inherited by marriage. "It's only for a few more years. Also, I'd rather do chores than be auctioned off to the wealthiest noble that will take me like they will be. You know as well as I do that if I left now poor sweet Eleonora would be forced to do all the chores." Eleonora would find it difficult to marry if she disappeared from society to tend to the house, not to mention the callouses and suntanned skin that would ruin her wifely complexion. So, for now, Della had to stay. At least Della could start over in Aleece and build her life as an independent woman. Eleonora was too meek to be a servant, and too sweet for Della to allow her to be treated as one.

"What do you plan to do once your stepsisters are finally married off? I know you can't possibly intend to stay with Duchess DeVoss."

"Well, then I suppose I shall be free to go wherever I please," Della said with a smile. "I'd like to go back to Aleece. I miss it there."

"You don't deserve the life your stepmother forced you into. You should really just ask your aunts to send someone for you. Surely your *grandfather* woul—"

"We have this same argument every time and the points haven't changed. I wrote my aunts every week for a year when I first moved here. If they wanted to speak to me, surely at least *one* of the eleven would have found the time to respond."

Franci pursed her lips having yet to come up with a good counterargument for that point in all the years since Della had confided that she had been born a noblewoman rather than a servant. What Della hadn't mentioned was her fear that her Aleecean family simply no longer cared about her. It still wasn't something she was ready to admit, not even to Franci.

"Besides, my father told me that we are responsible for all the good that we can do. Those who use and abuse others only do so because they were either taught poorly or they don't know how to help themselves any other way. How one treats others is a reflection of one's self. That means I must do whatever good I can, even for those who aren't kind to me," Della finished.

"You still let them take it too far." Franci frowned in disapproval. "Kindness still requires boundaries for those that would—and do—take advantage of such graciousness."

"Well, in a few years' time I shall leave either way. Hopefully Eleonora will be secure in a suitable marriage by that time. She is a noblewoman through and through, and too gentle to pull out of servitude if she is forced into it. I'm already saving what coin I can, even I couldn't stand to stay in that house with them forever," Della assured her friend.

"Hmm," was all Franci said.

Della gave her friend a gentle smile and slid out the door. She had saved some money from selling that which she foraged. Although a normal serving maid would be paid, Della wouldn't have dared to take any from the widow's stipend that the duchess received each month even if the woman didn't spend it all the second she got it. Della's meager coin purse hidden beneath a floorboard in her room would likely have been overflowing after all these years if she didn't constantly take from it to pay for food and other necessities after the duchess had overspent her money on frivolities. Della's steps slowed to a trudge as she got closer to her home that never really felt like home.

CHAPTER FIVE

D ella carried the last breakfast tray carefully up the sweeping staircase. Her stomach grumbled at the delicious scent of freshly cooked eggs, toast, and sliced strawberries. She would eat after she delivered food to her stepmother and stepsisters—if her stepmother was in a good mood. If not, she would have to do chores, only managing to wolf down a few quick bites each time she neared the kitchen. This was likely one of the reasons she remained unfashionably thinner than her sisters. Eleonora poked her head out of her bedroom door.

"I'll take that. Mother's all aflutter this morning. You'd better get to Marien's room." Eleonora, dark hair tousled from sleep, grabbed a cup of water and one plate of food from the tray.

Della's stomach twisted with nerves. Aflutter was Eleonora's way of saying the Duchess DeVoss was on the warpath. Della had long since stopped calling her Duchess Mariel, though calling her the title at all rankled so Della often just avoided calling her anything wherever possible. If her stepmother was in a mood, she would likely take the brunt of it out on Della. Today Della would probably have to dress everyone and scrub the house until they rushed out the door to some tea or other social visit, all to display her stepsisters like the latest chickens at the market. So much for breakfast.

"Della! Get in here this instant! Where is that lazy—" Duchess Devoss cut off her muttering as Della slipped through the door into Marien's room.

"You called for me?"

"We have a very important engagement today. Why didn't you wake Marien? Did you plan to simply leave her breakfast here to grow cold while she slept?" Duchess Devoss snapped.

Della had attempted to wake all three of them at the hourly bell, but Marien was impossible to wake up unless the girl wanted to get up. "I tried—"

"Don't contradict me! Build up the fire in the hearth, we can't catch a cold from this spring air," Duchess Devoss cut her off.

Della set down the tray holding the other two breakfast plates and cups of water, then turned to stoke the embers back into a gentle fire.

"Water for breakfast? Where is the milk? Really, Della, how do you expect us to survive on this peasant fare?" Duchess DeVoss demanded scornfully. Though she tucked in and ate her food as swiftly as possible while still managing to look like a proper lady.

Della pressed her lips together to keep from stating that the duchess had spent their monthly allotment, which left no room for anything beyond the barest of meals filled out with whatever Della had managed to forage. She longed to have a goat again for the fresh milk. Perhaps one day. Della told the truth in the only way the duchess would accept it. "I haven't been to the market today, so I haven't gotten any milk."

"Where are we going today?" Marien asked, unknowingly sparing Della from another sharp query. She yawned and shoved half a piece of jam-slathered toast into her mouth, munching on it lazily.

"Small bites, dear," Duchess DeVoss admonished. "You are a lady and must act the part. The Marquess Van Den-Berg is hosting a picnic near the hunting grounds. The men shall meet there to dine with us women before going off to hunt. I have heard that Earl De Vries will be there."

"Isn't Earl De Vries four-and-thirty?" Eleonora wrinkled her nose as she entered the room.

Eleonora was only seventeen and most of the men Duchess DeVoss had in mind were much older than her. The only requirement the duchess truly had was noblemen who had enough wealth that she could siphon off plenty for herself without her new son-in-law noticing. Della knew her younger sister secretly hoped to marry for love despite her mother's ambitions. Marien only cared for the things a husband would lavish on her, which aligned nicely with her mother's desires thus earning her favor.

"He's *two*-and-thirty and has a very large estate. Rumor has it he is on the hunt for a new bride." Duchess DeVoss' lips curled into a scheming smile.

"New bride? Did he have one before?" Marien asked as she climbed out of bed.

"Some wraith of a thing, always sickly, who died years ago. Apparently, he had married for love," Duchess DeVoss scoffed at the notion, "and has only now come around to the realization that his estate is without an heir."

"Perhaps he's lonely and hoping to find love again after having grieved her for so long," Eleonora suggested, sympathy tinging her tone.

"Did you get my new hair ribbons?" Marien demanded, already bored with the conversation. She sat at the dressing table and began to powder her face.

Della pulled the ribbons from her apron pocket and laid them on the dressing table. She brushed through Marien's brunette locks before twisting it up fashionably.

"Goodness! Can't you ever tend the hearth without getting cinders and soot everywhere?" sneered Marien.

Della glanced into the dressing table mirror and saw a streak of soot across her cheek. She rubbed it away with the back of her hand.

"You're always so dirty. We may as well call you Cinder Della," Marien continued.

"That's a bit of a mouthful," Eleonora tried to discourage her older sister. Marien had once called Della "Sootstain" for three months before she grew bored with the nickname.

"Hmmm." Marien tapped her chin. "Cinderella! That flows a bit better."

"How clever of you," purred Duchess DeVoss. "Now Marien, I shall point out the Earl to you and you must charm him. Eleonora, continue to gain favor with the women of court, one can never have too many connections. Who knows? Maybe someone will fancy you too. Though I'd prefer to secure Marien's future first, before she grows too old."

"Mother! Nineteen is not an old maid. I'm the perfect marrying age," she insisted, flashing her mother a smile.

"We must hope so," Duchess DeVoss murmured, still looking dissatisfied. "It would be better if you at least had an engagement secured at this age."

Della placed the last pin in Marien's hair before helping her into a dress. The gowns they insisted on had so many flounces, lace, and bows that Della was sure it would have looked terrible if Francesca hadn't been the one to make it. Over the next half hour Della dressed the trio while the duchess multitasked by instructing her girls on how best to charm the people at court and snapping at Della for anything she deemed annoying or done wrong. Then Della was sent to scrub the enormous entrance hall floor. Marien managed to march across the cleaned portion of the floor with soot on the soles of her boots as the three left.

"Cinderella," Marien sneered in a whisper as she marched past. She dragged one foot to create a long smear of filth and tossed a balled handkerchief at Della. It burst open in her face, coating her in soot.

Della contemplated throwing the brush she was scrubbing with at the girl, but she knew it wouldn't be worth the wrath of the duchess. Instead, she scrubbed her face clean on her apron. Marien's gloating grin was cut off when Eleonora closed the door.

"Spiteful sprite," Della muttered under her breath as the wheels of the hired carriage across the cobblestone drive sounded their departure.

Once finished with the hall, Della extinguished all the fireplaces, ate a quick meal, and escaped the dismal house. She marched through several fields and paths until she found her favorite meadow. She walked among the wildflowers up a large hill. It had a lovely view and Della could barely make out the colorful clumps of the people of court far away in the distance. They looked like ants weaving around each other. Though she knew she had hours, it was reassuring that she would be able to see when people began to leave so she could be home before her stepfamily returned. A hired servant shirking their duties might have felt guilty, but she didn't feel that way. She knew she had as much right to enjoy her day as her stepfamily did, but it wasn't worth the extra chores she would be given if they caught her taking even half a day off.

Della laid down on the soft grass and soaked up the sunlight. Despite what the duchess had said that morning, the afternoons were quite warm and summer was almost here. Lying down with the sun on her face was one luxury Tamaria offered her. She would never have laid on the ground at her home in Aleece lest she risk getting trampled by horses. The only places open enough from the trees for such intense sunlight were the pastures or the beach, which came with the caveat of sand in uncomfortable places. Della knew Marien and her stepmother sneered at her lightly tanned skin, but her calloused hands already set her apart from the other nobility. She would never be mistaken as one of them so she might as well enjoy the sunshine as much as she liked. She also thought her father would have happily sunbathed with her when he was home had they lived in Tamaria together.

Della had almost dozed off when a frantic whinny sent her bolting upright. Her eyes scanned the meadow and easily spotted the enormous chestnut horse racing wildly as the rider clung to it frantically. The man yanked roughly on the reins in an attempt to slow the horse, but the animal only reared up, tossing the rider onto the ground. As it neared, she began to wonder if it could possibly be a Stronghorse.

Awe struck Della as it reminded her of the wild stallions her father used to purchase and train. She raced down the hill as the horse sped towards her, stopping partway up the steep hill to give her added height as the horse raced closer. Della launched herself into the air and caught the saddle horn in her left hand and the far side of the saddle in her right. Her arms screamed in protest at the sudden lurch, but the daily household chores had given her muscles that helped her hold on. She scrambled her feet against the saddle, managing to get one leg up and over, sliding herself into the seat properly. She threw her arms around the horse's neck to keep her grip. For a moment she simply breathed calmly into the horse's neck. A grin broke out across her face as she felt the wind whipping her hair wildly. It felt like she was flying.

She laced one hand into the horse's mane and reached for the dangling reins with her other hand. She inched her body up and out of the saddle to extend her reach. The reins swung wildly, brushing her fingertips more than once before she caught them. They had fallen forward over the horse's head when it tossed its rider and she now held both sides of reins on one side of the bridle—useless unless she wanted to agitate the beast further by yanking them in circles. Della slipped back into the saddle and worked the knot in the end quickly. Splitting the reins she slid one side around the horse's neck so she could use them properly. She pulled back, gently increasing the pressure, and held her breath. The sheer size and power of the horse confirmed Della's suspicions that this was indeed a Stronghorse. Della now had to try to coax it to a halt while both not initiating a bond or being thrown, the trickiest part of training a Stronghorse. She had never been allowed on an untrained Stronghorse and wasn't sure what it was that initiated the bond. From the way it had tossed its rider, it was either not bonded yet or stolen. The steed finally slowed to a walk. Della whispered sweet nothings to it and stroked its neck as they picked their way back toward the rider.

The man was dressed in a riding outfit made from the finest red material with golden embroidery. He stomped toward them. The Stronghorse halted and seemed reluctant to go any closer to the man so Della slid down, keeping hold of the reins. She rubbed the horse's neck as it snuffled her hair. Patting its neck she made her way to its front leg, tugging gently. The horse tamely let her pull its leg up for her to inspect its hoof. She was on the third hoof when the man reached them.

"What in the skies do you think you are doing?!"

"Catching a runaway horse," Della replied mildly. "You're welcome."

"He's a wild beast! You're lucky he got tired from all that running or you could have been thrown!"

He made to snatch the reins from her, but she dodged him with ease. The Stronghorse shifted anxiously and Della patted its neck again.

"*He* is a *she* and you're making her nervous," Della responded cooly.

"He's my—" He paused and blinked. "Did you say it's a girl?"

"Yes, she's a girl, and she's clearly been tamed and trained based on the way she let me pull her to a stop so easily. She has a rock stuck under her shoe, which any *decent* rider would have known to look for when facing such behavior from a horse," Della scolded.

"I...didn't realize." He had the decency to look chagrined.

"Is this even your horse? You look too rich to be a horse thief." Della eyed him suspiciously. She shifted her body in front of the Stronghorse.

"It is. Well, that is to say, it's my father's horse. A new one. We just got him—*her*." He shook his head. "Everyone knows Stronghorses are a force of their own so I can't say a pebble under her horseshoe was the first thought that came to my mind when I was holding on for my life."

Della looked him over and realized he couldn't be much older than her. The wild ride had tousled the dark hair now ruffling in the gentle breeze. His dark eyebrows were furrowed in a puzzled expression above warm brown eyes that were taking her in as well. He was handsome, she realized with surprise—not at the fact that the boy was handsome, but that she had noticed such a thing.

"Well, you shouldn't be riding any horse, let alone a Stronghorse, until you are both comfortable with each other." Della sighed and handed him the reins with some reluctance. It seemed unfair that someone with so little knowledge of the creatures got to own such aone.

He grimaced. "Well... Thank you. For catching the horse."

"She is magnificent. Besides, it was exciting. I haven't ridden a horse in a long time. I suppose I haven't ridden any horse in a long time—certainly not a Stronghorse," Della admitted ruefully.

"Really? But you leapt on without any fear and controlled it so well."

"My father used to train and trade horses. Perhaps it is in my blood, or perhaps it's because I was taught from a young age not to fear horses, but rather seek to respect them," Della told him.

"Who is your father? Perhaps I know him." He sounded eager and it made Della nervous.

"He was Aleecean and passed on several years ago." Della looked away and swallowed the sudden lump in her throat.

"Ah. I'm sorry for your loss." He paused at the awkward turn the conversation had taken. "I hear your accent now. It's not as thick as the dignitary who had visited here last, but it's there."

Even though she knew her accent had faded some, it still stung Della to hear someone say so. It was like she was losing the parts of her that she longed for most. The part of her that her father had known, the part of her that had been happy more often than anxious.

"A dignitary? Then you're from court?" Della realized she must sound stupid. His riding outfit was clearly expensive and fashionable. *Of course* he was from court.

He raised his eyebrows at her.

"You must be, to have such a fine horse," she amended. Her cheeks felt hot.

"You haven't been at court, have you? But if you're Aleecean and not visiting our court, then why are you here?" He looked her over curiously.

Della became painfully aware of how she must look with her dirty, too small outfit and wind wild hair. What a ridiculous contrast she must be to his pristine and rich attire. For the first time in a long time, she wished she had allowed Franci to make her something new to wear. But that was impractical. A new gown would only be ruined after a week of her chores. Not to mention the three gowns she had let Franci make her when she was thirteen. The finest had been claimed by Marien, hanging in her wardrobe before Della even had a chance to wear it. Another had formed a mysterious stain overnight of what looked to be the wine she wasn't old enough to drink. Della had found the last's half-charred remains in one of the fireplaces. She had been given extra chores for her supposed clumsiness ruining the two gowns. Della never told Franci, not wanting to see the hurt and fury on her friend's face. She still felt a twinge of guilt each time she dismissed her friend's offer. Della eyed the man before her and realized she hadn't answered his question.

"Why am I in this meadow? Do you own it? I can leave immediately and never return if you wish." Della felt even more foolish than before. She'd never run into anyone here, but it would be just her luck to run into the person who owned these lands. She had few pleasures in this land with this meadow being one of them, but she was used to giving up the pleasant things in life by now.

"No, I don't own this particular meadow. What I meant was, why are you here in Tamaria?"

"I'm... a maid in a house here." It was true and Duchess DeVoss would be furious if she told this man she was her daughter. Her stepmother had kept her away from court, insisting the way Della dressed and acted would bring shame upon them all. Only Franci, Barend, and Johanna knew she was related to the DeVoss family. The woman had even shed her newly married name of Caspari with her return to Tamaria Besides, dressed as Della was, who would believe she was the daughter of a duchess? Her stepmother would only deny it if asked.

"But why would an Aleecean be a maid here in Tamaria?" His eyebrows furrowed in confusion.

"I lost my family in Aleece so I came here." Again it was true, more or less.

"Well, I'm Roric." He extended his hand.

"I'm Della." She held out her own hand to shake his.

"My lady." Instead of shaking her hand he brought it to his lips and kissed it before giving her a shallow bow. She wasn't sure if she should curtsy or not and ended up giving him an awkward bob. He grinned and grabbed the saddle to swing himself up.

"Wait! What are you doing? You can't ride her with a rock in her shoe!" Della cried.

He moved away sheepishly. "Sorry. I forgot."

"You should remove it and walk her back."

"I haven't ever removed a rock from a horse's hoof before." He eyed the intimidating Stronghorse doubtfully.

She stared at him incredulously. The wealthy in Aleece knew how to take care of their horses. Did Tamarians ride out with a stablehand at all times?

"Do you have a knife?" she asked him holding out her hand.

He pulled a jeweled dagger from his belt, turned it so he was holding the blade, and held it out to her. She took the blade and walked around the Stronghorse. She bent its leg upward and examined the hoof again.. The Stronghorse stood there as docile as could be while she gently worked the rock out from under the horseshoe. Roric watched, his eyes widening the slightest bit in surprised amazement.

"There, she'll be much more comfortable now." Della handed back the knife. "You must see that your grooms attend to that foot. It will likely need a poultice to keep away infection and help it heal."

"Will you walk with me? Just for a bit. I have quite a long walk back." He sounded hopeful.

Della hesitated. "I can for a little while. Then I must get back."

They walked in silence for a moment. It wasn't quite awkward, but it wasn't exactly comfortable either.

"If you're from court, why aren't you at the hunt?" Della asked.

"Well, I thought I'd impress all the other men by riding this new Stronghorse at the hunt. However, I lost control of it almost immediately and it was all I could do to nudge it away from the hunt towards these fields and meadows so I didn't make a complete fool of myself in front of everyone at court."

His sheepish honesty surprised Della. She admired the way he had admitted his foolish plan without trying to place the blame on anyone else. If it had been Marien, she would have blamed Della or the horse.

"Don't worry, you only made a fool of yourself in front of one person, and I won't tell. Probably." Della grinned at him. He surprised her by grinning back.

"I shall simply have to hope for the best then," he said brightly.

"Will you be missed from the hunt?"

"Probably by my family, but everyone else is usually more concerned with my older brother. Besides, there's a rather unpleasant duchess trying to thrust her daughter on any man who walks by." Roric wrinkled his nose.

"The Duchess DeVoss?" Della questioned, though she was certain she knew.

"You know of her? Yes. She shouldn't even be at court really, but she weaseled her way in by becoming a duchess somehow in Aleece. I suppose she ran out of money because she came back here rather quickly to get the widow's stipend from the crown. Many people in court feel she shouldn't have been granted the stipend, but when it was created it stated which titles would be given the stipend which include duchesses. It was intended to ensure the wellbeing of the king's relatives and friends, but she found a ridiculous loophole. Who would have thought someone would go to another *kingdom* to gain a title only to return? Sometimes I wonder if her poor husband actually died or simply ran away from such an odious wife."

"Don't say that! He would have never! He was the kindest man," Della defended her father.

"Oh. *Oh!* You're Aleecean! Duchess DeVoss went to Aleece to marry before coming here. You're her maid and came with her when she returned," Roric exclaimed.

Della nodded grimly.

"But why do you stay with such a woman? I can't imagine she's very pleasant to work for and surely you can find employment elsewhere," he said.

"She's not all that pleasant, but Eleonora—her youngest daughter—is kind. Besides, I had no parents and I really didn't know what else to do. I plan to return to Aleece once the girls are married though." Della didn't know why she was telling him her plans. He was a stranger that she would never see again after today.

"I suppose you approve of the duchess trying to marry off her daughters to anyone of wealth?" Roric sounded as if she had disappointed him.

"It's not that I approve, rather I understand that they don't have any better options. In Aleece women can work the same as men though most choose different professions than their male counterparts, but here women are meant to run a household. It doesn't create wealth to live on, especially not for people like the duchess. She was forced to come back and receive the widow's stipend to survive. I'm not surprised that she is using her opportunities at court to try to secure enough money for her daughters for their entire lives. It's so that they might never have to feel the desperation and humiliation she has surely felt. It may not be pleasant, but I believe her to be doing the best she can with what she has been trained all her life to do, and perhaps what any desperate mother might do." Della blinked in surprise. How odd to find herself defending the duchess of all people. Roric looked surprised too. And thoughtful.

"I suppose I never thought of that. Men have always done the work and women have always managed the household. It keeps things running smoothly. Though that's part of why the king before the current king created the widow's stipend. Things like war and illness can leave a widow destitute. There's no other stipend like it in any other country I've heard of!" Roric sounded overly proud of his country's accomplishment.

"It is a solution." Della bit her lip. She didn't know how to tactfully point out that it only helped titled members of the court to live a comfortable life after such a loss. "I think it could be better though."

Roric frowned. "What do you mean?"

"Well, the idea is a good one, especially in a country like Tamaria where women can't do much more than hard labor such as scullery work to make a living. That would be much too hard on an older widow so the stipend saves them from that. However, the stipend only extends to the nobility. It saves the women of court from living like a commoner would."

"Exactly. It's protective. It prevents women that aren't left with a great fortune from falling below their station."

"Yes, but it is usually the commoners who march into battle on the frontlines. They are the first to fall, less protected than the nobility given horses and ranks such as general. Those common men face certain death out of loyalty and their family is not repaid for it." Della's stomach flipped at being so bold. He could have a servant like her punished for saying such things and the duchess would happily carry it out.

Roric considered her thoughtfully. "You have taken one of my country's greatest accomplishments and put it in the light of classism. I don't know whether to hate you or thank you for it."

Della's legs shook. "All hatred comes from a place of fear or pain. I've insulted your country by pointing out a flaw in something good that has been done here. I hope you know that I don't do so to be cruel, I do so because it pains me as well. It is something I would change to be better if I could. You are a nobleman. Perhaps you even know the crown prince. You might be able to influence him towards such change once he is king."

"An interesting idea. Do you approach all the noblemen you meet in hopes of influencing the future king?" He gave her a teasing smile.

"I only approach their runaway horses, and those only ask me for apples or carrots, not my thoughts on politics." Della grinned back.

"Then I feel honored that you deigned to share such thoughts with me despite my lack of hooves." Roric gave her mock bow, still with that easy smile on his face.

They reached the edge of the woods and came to a collective halt.

"Well, I had better let you get back to the hunt and picnic. I'm sure there are plenty of noblewomen hoping for the attention of an eligible lord like yourself."

Della had meant it teasingly, but the grimace on Roric's face made her think she'd hit a more potent truth instead.

"I can't hurry back too fast. I need to walk this Stronghorse to the stables first." He seemed to brighten at the excuse to stay away longer.

"Oh yes, please don't ride her just yet. Tell your stable hands to keep an eye on that hoof. It's not a deep cut, but all the same, it's better to watch out for any chance of infection." Della stroked the beautiful Stronghorse's neck one more time. The horse snuffled at her hair.

"She seems to like you," Roric commented.

"You only need to gain her trust. Try brushing her down yourself and giving her treats. Horses love apples. Perhaps your father can give her a name too," Della advised.

"A name. Yes, I suppose she will need a name," Roric said thoughtfully.

"Well, I truly must get back. There's much to be done before the duchess returns."

"I hope I haven't kept you too long. I wouldn't want to cause you any trouble. I can only imagine the sort of unpleasantness that woman must cause for her servants." Roric made a face that was half a wince.

"I'll be fine. I always manage," Della assured him.

"Before you go, there's something on your face." He handed her a handkerchief.

Della's eyes widened with horror and she scrubbed at her cheeks. The white cloth came away streaked with gray. Soot from the cinders she had cleaned earlier that day, or from Marien's parting gift. She'd had that on her face the whole time? Della wished the ground beneath her would swallow her up.

Della hastily stuffed the handkerchief back in his hand. "Well, goodbye."

"Goodbye...Della."

When she glanced over her shoulder, she saw he was still watching her. He smiled and led the Stronghorse down a different path.

CHAPTER SIX

Despite what Della had told him, the second he was out of view she took off at a run. She was just finishing her chores for the day when Duchess DeVoss and her daughters arrived home. She swept the last of the cinders from the sitting room fireplace into a pail.

"It's so *awful*," moaned Marien. She flopped herself down dramatically across the chaise.

Eleonora took a seat in a large chair near the window. "It's not like he was a likely match anyway."

"Anyone is a possible match until they're engaged," Marien snapped, glaring at her sister.

"Anyone is a possible match until they are *married*. Plenty of engagements don't end in marriage," Duchess DeVoss corrected, entering the room after them.

Marien sat up. "Plus, a second prince is fairly likely to marry a duchess if he selects from nobility."

Eleonora's voice was almost a whisper when she said, "The daughter of a duchess."

It had always seemed wildly unfair to Della that a boy would inherit his father's title, but a girl would only be allotted a title to match her husband. She supposed in one way women had a better opportunity to improve their station, but those with higher titles seemed to only want to marry others with higher titles so their chances were still slim.

Marien smoothed her skirts. "The crown prince was of course betrothed to some princess or other as a toddler, but the second had a chance of marrying someone from court until now."

"Nothing is set in stone yet. Besides, there's always the third prince," Duchess DeVoss soothed her oldest daughter.

"But less of a chance of becoming queen!"

Della barely held back a snort at the thought of Marien as a queen. She was spiteful and greedy, not the traits one would hope for in a queen. She was pretty, but her temperament and vanity made Della doubtful she'd snare a prince anyway. Though it was possible a prince who cared only about beauty and title would want Marien as their wife.

Marien wasn't finished. "Besides, no one knows much about the youngest prince. He avoids all the gatherings that he can, and even when he attends, he keeps among his friends and his cousin, the future duke. If only Lord Faust was a prince. He's quite striking with those ice blue eyes and aquiline nose."

Della had seen Lord Faust riding through town a few times and he always looked rather haughty. Perhaps he would make the perfect match for Marien. Her stepsister was right about the prince as well, Della had never even glimpsed him. He didn't leave the castle grounds as far as she knew, and she rarely heard any gossip about him either.

"A duchess to a princess would still be a social elevation, even if it didn't lead to becoming queen," Eleonora pointed out.

Marien considered that. She settled back into her chair with a satisfied expression, nodding as a sly smile spread across her lips.

"Della, bring our tea!" Duchess DeVoss snapped her fingers even though Della was already leaving the room to do so.

Della resisted the urge to roll her eyes, and instead bobbed a small curtsy. She enjoyed the brief moments away while she waited for the kettle to boil and gathered the tea things onto a serving tray. She found her thoughts drifting to the nobleman Roric. She had little experience with nobles as they had quickly learned to decline the attempts of the duchess to entertain them in her own home and she had been far too young to be interested in them when they had come by. Della was grateful that courtesy still required the nobility invite the duchess and her daughters to the largest parties—parties that gave Della a respite from her family as she was not permitted to attend. So it had been a new experience for Della to speak with a nobleman close to her age. He'd been rather less snobby than she had expected, if a bit inexperienced and naive about his own family's horse. His easy grin had surprised her most of all, including the way it made her want to smile back.

The sharp whistle of the kettle called her from her thoughts and she poured the water into the teapot quickly. Her family was still discussing the second prince's engagement when she reentered the sitting room.

"—at least one good thing to come of the Royal engagement," Marien was saying.

She seemed to have perked up quite a bit. Della set the tea tray on the table and handed out teacups and saucers.

"You'll have to go into town to get a new gown for me of course, Della," Marien said.

"A new gown! But whatever for? I brought your new one only a few weeks ago!" Della couldn't keep the words from bursting out.

"Don't talk back!" snapped Duchess DeVoss.

"I need a ballgown for the ball. I can't very well go in a regular dress you dunce!"

"Yes, you must also take my red ball gown to be updated and the yellow—no, the peach one of Eleonora's. Of course, Marien will need a new one in order to best catch someone's eye. I shall write down the specifications for the dressmaker." The duchess took a sip of her tea.

"Of course, Duchess DeVoss," Della said with a small curtsy that was more of a bob.

She turned to go and tripped over Marien's foot that hadn't been there a moment ago. She crashed into the bucket of ashes as she hit the ground hard, choking on the cloud of dust now around her.

"How clumsy of you, *Cinderella*," sneered Marien.

"Clean that up immediately!" The duchess coughed before storming from the room. Marien flounced after her, shooting Della a gleeful grin.

"Are you alright?" Eleonora asked softly. She came over and observed the mess.

Della scrambled to her feet and brushed herself off. "I'm okay," Della coughed out although inside she was fuming. She snatched up the broom and swept the floor so hard the soot flew back up into the air. She sighed and took a calming breath before sweeping more carefully.

"She shouldn't have done that." Eleonora bent as if to help though she held no broom or rag.

"Wait! Please don't help. It'll be so difficult to wash out of your dress. Mine has been ruined for ages, but I'd rather not waste yours." Della reached out a hand to stop Eleonora, but paused when she realized her hand was just as sooty as the floor.

Eleonora paused, clearly torn between wanting to help and not wanting to make more work for Della. She bit her lip.

"I have it in hand, truly," Della assured her.

"Alright," she said after a moment. But Eleonora still picked up the tea things and took the tray down to the kitchen. Della brushed herself off, swept the floor, and rolled up the rug to be beaten clean outside. This time she made sure to take the pail of ashes with her when she left the room.

She took the rug outside and hung it on the wash line. She whacked it hard with the carpet beater. Over and over again she smacked out her anger as tears of frustration stole down her cheeks. When ash no longer puffed up from the rug she slipped from the yard.

The spring air was warming up nicely this year, but Della still shivered as she entered the cool woods on the far end of their property. As she walked, she kept an eye out for mushrooms as usual, but didn't spot any. She followed the small creek's familiar path upstream until the sound of rushing water grew into a crashing sound. She came around the trees into the small clearing made by a large pool of water. On the far end was a small waterfall cascading from the miniature cliff that she had scaled many times with ease. The pool was deep enough to swim in and on summer days the water was actually quite warm. Today, however, it would still be cold.

Della slipped off her shoes and felt the mossy grass beneath her toes like a natural carpet. She undid the braid her hair was in and stripped down to her undergarments. Della shook her clothes out, shaking off as much ash as she could, beating the cloth against a rock for a few minutes for good measure before laying it down. She stepped into the water and sucked in a breath as cold bit into her skin. It wasn't warm enough to be enjoyable, but it was still refreshing to know it was cleansing her. She waded in until she could easily duck her head under. She came up gasping for air with teeth chattering, but she swam around the pool of water a bit hoping the movement would warm her up or at least pull the rest of the ash from her skin. She had no soap, but swam to the small waterfall and let it pound the ashes from her hair a while before kicking back to the center of the pool.

She preferred this sort of bath. If she drew well water and heated it at home the others were sure to insist they get the warm bath, and likely she'd have to work to heat three baths leaving her too tired for her own. Eleonora would never demand a warm bath on the same day as her stepmother and Marien, but the duchess would insist on it. Or they'd keep Della busy with demands until the water was cold anyway, her efforts to have a warm bath wasted. She had found the pool of water some years back and used it for her baths except in the winter months.

Della floated along on her back and a memory surfaced. Bittersweet, she smiled and felt like crying as she recalled the summer her father had taught her to swim. She had been around five and though she could float and paddle along he had said it was time she learned to really swim. He taught her how to move her arms and kick her feet to create powerful strokes. He had helped her overcome her fear of swimming beneath the surface by playing games of slipping under the smooth surface, gliding along unseen under the water, and popping up to surprise each other from a new angle.

A wave of desperate loneliness swept over Della. She missed her father so much it ached. She waded out of the water and laid on a large rock in an attempt to dry herself off somewhat. The gray stone was slightly warmer than the ground and air as if it held a memory of the day's sun. It felt comforting.

Della sighed as she thought about how angry Duchess De-Voss and Marien would be when they learned she hadn't gone straight to order their ball gowns and adjustments. She hadn't even brought the rest of the laundry to do. She felt a biting annoyance at her position as a servant. When she was eight, she hadn't known what else to do besides come with them to this strange country—she hadn't even considered she might have a choice in staying. It had all happened so fast and she had been too young to argue. She had also still imagined she could win her stepmother's favor, and thereby her love, if she pleased the woman enough. Years of serving as her maidservant had shattered those childish hopes. She also hadn't known how to argue about doing chores, hadn't even fought back when all of it tumbled onto her young shoulders. By eighteen it had solidified into habit, a habit that she felt oddly comfortable with when the alternative was trying to bat her eyes at men she wasn't the least bit interested in.

Still, she was finally growing restless enough to consider her other options. She would leave, like she had told Franci. She would return to her aunts in Aleece, if they would have her, or make her own way in her home country somehow. It was an industrial place, if she remembered correctly. Della would take her place as her own woman like she had been born, not the servant they had turned her into. She could do it. She was already here, ignoring maid duties and enjoying time to herself, after all.

"I have just as much right to take a swim out here as they have to attend parties," Della said out loud. She knew it was true, but she still cringed at the thought of her stepmother's wrath if the woman found out what Della was doing.

Della pulled herself up and tied her damp hair up in a bun so it wouldn't pick up any residual ash from her clothes. She gathered up her things and dressed. She would do all the laundry tomorrow before she went into town. At least she would get to see Franci. Her dearest friend kept her sane through everything she endured. Perhaps after Eleonora was married, Della would accept Franci's offer to work in her dress shop for a few years to earn enough money to buy passage home. The few coins Della saved from selling what she foraged were often depleted so she wouldn't be able to save up enough for a stagecoach on that alone. It certainly wasn't safe to simply purchase a horse and travel alone through the Deep Woods that separated Tamaria and Aleece. Though how could she let Franci pay her to help in the shop if she was living with her and sharing her food? Franci had offered, of course, but it still wasn't fair to her. Della would have to keep track of all the expenses she incurred and send payment back to Franci after she was secure in a job in Aleece. It was the least she could do, considering all that her friend had done for her.

Della's gut twinged with unease as she headed home, but she walked with determination. It felt good to have a plan.

CHAPTER SEVEN

The next morning Della wanted to go straight to Francesca's dress shop, but instead she hurried through the washing so it would dry while she was gone. Then she plated breakfast for the household.

Marien took a bite of one of the pastries that Della had made the evening before and made a face. "It's cold."

"It's supposed to be. I made them last night so I could have an early start going to town to request your new gown. Francesca will likely be flooded with orders for new gowns with the impending ball. If she can't get one done for you in time, I believe I recall a new ballgown made up for you only a few months ago that would be wonderful for such an event," Della told her.

"You're behaving ungratefully, girl," Duchess DeVoss berated Della as she set down her breakfast. "Don't forget your place."

Della bit back a retort about where her *place* truly should be and simply bobbed a quick nod.

"I have been charitable to you. I didn't *have* to bring you with us. You live here off of my money, which I can spend on whatever I see fit—such as a new gown for Marien, which she *needs*. You are not a necessity girl, and you remain here only due to my charity. Keep that in mind," Duchess DeVoss sneered before eating another bite.

Della wanted to point out that it was the king's money, not her stepmother's. Instead, she pictured the duchess trying to cook and clean. The amusing image quickly faded into Eleonora taking on the role and Della reminded herself that she would only need to endure a little longer for her dear younger sister.

The duchess delicately patted her lips with her napkin. "Really, I don't know what you could have thought was more important to get done than this. You should have gone to the dress shop straight away yesterday after hearing about the ball. It will be an important night for Marien."

"I shall do my best to help Marien, but I do need to have time for other things too," Della couldn't help saying. Had her stepmother expected her to walk through town covered in the soot that Marien had all but dumped on Della?

"I suppose you want to dress up and attend gatherings in hopes of marrying up?" Duchess DeVoss scoffed at her. Then her eyes gleamed as she appraised Della thoughtfully.

"Not particularly," Della said quickly. She had no desire to take a more active role in her stepmother's schemes to marry off her girls to the highest bidder.

"I doubt anyone would have you, anyway. What do you need time for? You wish to attend the ball?" she mocked.

Della started to say she didn't have any desire to be around courtiers. Then Roric popped into her mind. He had been dressed like a lord's son and her heart sped up thinking about the chance to see him again.

"Perhaps." Della surprised both the duchess and herself with the admission.

"Well, well, do we ever have high ambitions? And what would you wear? Those rags?" Duchess DeVoss laughed cruelly.

Della glanced down at her shabby attire. Her clothes were clean, but forever stained with the dirt and grime she was always scrubbing away when doing her chores. The hem of her skirt hung several inches above her ankles, revealing scuffed and worn boots. Her shirt was fraying at the ends of the too-short sleeves and her apron had a smattering of mismatched patches to stop the holes from turning it into shreds. Della's cheeks flamed with anger at how every penny went to them when she was the one who worked so hard just to make ends meet to keep decent meals on the table with the rate the duchess spent her allotment of coins. She could afford a new dress for her stepdaughter if she wished it. The duchess, however, mistook Della's red cheeks for embarrassment.

"That's what I thought," she said smugly. "Take the two dresses for myself and Eleonora to be altered, and don't forget to order a new one for Marien."

Della gathered the two dresses Duchess DeVoss had selected from the chair they'd been draped on. Her stepmother handed her a small pouch of coins.

"There's a little more in there than usual, so it should be enough for the three gowns. Don't even *think* about spending any of this on yourself," she snapped before dropping it into Della's waiting palm.

Della turned to the door and rolled her eyes as she walked away. What was in the pouch wouldn't even cover the cost of the alterations and a new dress—it never did. Della hesitated on the stairs, then went up to her attic room and packed one other item into a sack with the dresses before leaving the house.

Della made her way outside to the henhouse in the yard. She looked fondly over her little flock. When they had arrived in Tamaria, she'd spent the last few personal coins she had saved away on two hens and a rooster. The duchess had been furious that Della kept a few meager coins from her greedy grasp, but she stopped complaining when she was served daily eggs and the occasional chicken for dinner. Della had nurtured her two hens into a larger flock, occasionally trading or buying a new rooster to keep the brood going. Della sighed as she selected a few hens and placed them into a crate. Della took the chickens and a basket brimming with eggs to the morning market where they all sold quickly. They wouldn't have chicken for dinner anytime soon, but the extra coins might at least lessen the insult of how little Duchess DeVoss believed one of Franci's designs should cost her. Though it probably wouldn't. Della slipped the extra money into the small pouch anyway.

She finally made her way to Francesca's shop. Della barely heard the bell as she entered and was glad she had left the now empty crate outside. The shop was packed full of women looking at fabrics and gossiping while they waited for their turn to be measured and place their orders. Della heard snatches of conversation as she wove through the crowd looking for Franci.

"It's so exciting, isn't it?"

"—was thinking I'd wear blue or maybe—"

"—the most handsome of the three princes!"

Della found Franci kneeling near the back pinning the hem of a young woman standing on a small platform.

"Hello, Franci!" Della greeted her.

"Della!" Franci cried happily around a mouthful of pins.

The mother of the young woman shot Della a glare for interrupting.

"I only wanted to let you know I was here. Don't worry, I'm happy to wait," Della said mostly for the benefit of the girl and her mother.

"I'm sure you are," Franci chuckled knowingly as she finished pinning the hem.

Della gave Franci a cheery wave and walked back to the front. Della slipped behind the counter to assist those who were only picking up orders or buying hair ribbons as she often did when she stopped by and Franci was busy. Franci left parcels neatly labeled with names and prices behind the counter, so it was easy for Della to help.

"Hello there, Della!" Barend called cheerily.

"Barend! Whatever are you doing here?" Della held back a laugh at the sight of the large, red-faced baker in the dress shop. She noticed his face looked somewhat less flushed away from the heat of his ovens.

"Johanna ordered two nighties for the baby. The midwife won't let her leave the bed, so I'm here to pick it up for her."

"Is she alright?" Della asked as she sifted through the packages.

"She had some—er, what do you call them...contractions! Early, too early. So they told her she has to rest and stay in bed to try to keep the baby from being born too early." Barend scratched his short beard nervously.

"I can't imagine Johanna likes that very much."

"She's going crazy sitting there in bed all day. She's trying to keep busy by knitting and making a quilt for the baby, but she still seems stir crazy while I'm running the bakery away from her all day. To be honest, I miss having her run things up front just as much as she does," he admitted. "Neither of us are too thrilled that I have to close everything up to run errands and go back to her at mealtimes. She isn't supposed to leave the bed even to cook."

"It's lucky she married a man that can bake then. Though as she is a woman who gets things done, I'm sure staying in bed all day and night must be very frustrating for her. I'll try to stop by for a visit if I have some time," Della said looking through the wrapped parcels under the counter.

"Would you? That would be so nice for her!" Barend looked relieved.

Della found the package at last. It was bigger than two nighties would be, which is why she had missed it on the first pass. She smiled when she saw the note attached.

Don't let them pay a cent more than what I wrote on here and don't let them give anything back. I've included an easy pattern and some cut pieces for Johanna to try her hand at making baby clothes as well.

Of course Franci would have heard about Johanna being stuck in bed. Franci was in the midst of the merchants and shops here in town, and her customers liked to gossip too. Della slipped off the note Franci had written for her. She must have known Della would be here today after the announcement of the ball.

"I found it!" Della told Barend the price and gave him his change before handing over the package.

"But that's too much," Barend protested. "Surely two baby nighties can't be that big of a parcel and I haven't paid enough for that much."

"There's some unfinished pieces with instructions for Johanna to try while she's laid up in bed."

He opened his mouth to object again, but Della cut him off. "There's a line behind you, I don't have time to argue. Besides, you'd better get back to the bakery before a customer comes and your wife decides to get out of bed to assist."

Barend hurried out of the shop at that. Della spent the next several hours selling hats and collecting payment for already packaged orders. Her stepmother would assume she was waiting her turn in line to place the order or that she was running other errands while in town. At long last the crowd died down and the final customer had left as the evening sun hung low in the sky.

Franci appeared beside her behind the counter. "Thank you for your help, Della."

"I haven't anything better to do while I wait. Besides, it means you finish faster so I can talk with you." Della shrugged and smiled.

"You know, if you wanted to come work in the shop starting tomorrow you could. It would really help me out. You see how busy it is," Franci said.

"Thanks, Franci, but we've been over this. Eleonora needs me," Della told her.

"I just want you to know you have an option besides being a maid, which is far below you, as you know." Franci shot her a pointed look, lips pulling into a tight line.

"Thank you. Sincerely. For now, will you please tell me what magic you can work with the dresses and coin I brought?" She gave her friend an apologetic look as she handed everything over.

Franci groaned. "I should refuse that woman service for how little she pays. Don't think I don't know that most of these things are paid for with the coins you earn at the market."

"I know it's still not enough, but I'll do what I can to repay you. It will have to be paid in installments as usual, but I will," Della promised.

"With a steep discount, thanks to our friendship. Though I don't see why *she* should be rewarded by it." Franci crossed her arms.

"Because you know she would only make my life unbearable otherwise. Besides, it gives me plenty of excuses to come into town and see you!" Della hugged her friend.

Franci sighed, eyeing the fabric Della had plopped on the counter. "Well, what is it I'm given to work with?"

"This is Eleonora's dress, and this one belongs to the duchess. Those two need to be altered to the latest style as much as possible. Marien needs a new dress—in the latest fashion, of course. Here are their measurements and instructions." Della handed over the paper from the duchess.

"Really now? Just how much did she send you with?" Franci huffed in exasperation.

Della lifted the bag of coins and handed it to her friend.

"I should sew the duchess' dress back together on the barest of threads so it falls apart in front of the whole court!" Franci grumbled.

"But you wouldn't, for my sake and your own reputation."

"She would deserve it though," Franci muttered. "What's that?"

Della startled when Franci pointed to some fabric poking out from underneath the other dresses. She had forgotten that she had brought it.

"Oh, it's nothing—"

Franci snatched at the fabric and pulled. She held the dress up and began examining it. "Who does this gown belong to, Della?"

"No one. Well, it was my mother's. I thought—but no, it was foolish," Della mumbled as she tried to grab it back.

Franci simply held one hand out to stop Della while she looked over the dress. It was the lightest shade of lilac, almost white. The gown was fitted down through the hips before it flared out. It had long sleeves and a modest top. Lace flowers overlaid the gown.

"It's pretty, but nothing like the fashion here."

"I know. It's Aleecean and, like I said, it was a foolish idea." Della stared at her feet, too embarrassed to meet her friend's eye.

"I can do it, but I can't make it the same as the fashions here if I want to do the dress any justice. A larger skirt, yes. The sleeves could be shortened, but they look so lovely I'd leave them. I wouldn't add any lace ruffles either... Alright, I'll do it!" Franci declared.

Della tried to protest, but gave up. She *had* been the one to bring the gown in the first place. A tiny spark of hope lit at the thought of attending the ball.

"I've always wanted to dress you for a party! Come here, let me take your measurements again." Franci was all enthusiasm as she looped her paper tape around Della's body again and again.

The girls fell into an easy pattern of chatter and laughter while Franci sorted out what to do with the dresses. Della gave input only on what Duchess DeVoss would expect and allow for the new gowns. Franci adjusted her sketches accordingly. A little while later Della began the walk home, enjoying the last few rays of the setting sun with a spring in her step.

CHAPTER EIGHT

Four weeks before the ball, the duchess and her daughters received a social invitation. It came as a surprise as most of the courtiers were holding smaller gatherings with their close inner circles as they prepared for the upcoming event.

"Well now, it seems that Duchess Faust values our company," Duchess DeVoss purred as she scanned the invitation Della had brought to her in the sitting room.

Della blinked. Duke Faust was the king's brother. Her family had never received an invitation from the highest of society members. Why would they have received one now? Could Marien have actually caught the eye of their son? Or perhaps he also had a scheming mother who wished to see him wed to one of equal standing.

"It isn't another picnic, is it? It's getting too hot for that in a party dress," Marien complained.

Eleonora was playing the piano beautifully and seemed not to care about the invitation at all. She hadn't glanced up once.

"No, my dears." Duchess DeVoss' lips curled up in a devious grin. "It's an invitation to afternoon tea."

Marien sighed in relief. "Oh wonderful! That should be refreshing."

"I hope there will be macarons. I love macarons." Eleonora sighed with longing, probably daydreaming of the pastry, as she finally looked up. Macarons were not something Della bothered to make with the meager ingredients they had on hand.

"As we haven't worn tea dresses in a while, I don't think those will need any alterations so long as we wear different jewelry." The duchess' eyes narrowed as she calculated how best to appear affluent before the other nobility.

Marien grinned with greedy anticipation. "When is the tea?"

"Tomorrow. Hmm. Well, I suppose people might be pressed for time, so invitations were late going out." Duchess DeVoss pursed her lips.

"Or Duchess Faust realized it was the only day she could host it with all that is going on," Eleonora offered over her shoulder as she started playing a soft tune.

Della thought it was more likely that Duchess Faust had decided on a whim to invite them. Most likely someone else had canceled. The slight of a last-minute invitation would be one that Duchess DeVoss would have to endure however, if she wished to seize the chance to put her daughters on display like an afternoon spread of tea and biscuits.

Della and Duchess DeVoss were both relieved when the three left for the tea party—the duchess reassured of her social standing and Della simply happy to have some time away from being ordered about. Days to herself were a luxury. Della happily helped them out to the carriage and waved them away, only feeling a slight twinge of regret at the cost of the hired driver. It couldn't be helped, she told herself and set her mind to enjoying several hours alone.

She decided to make some tea and had just added the steeped teapot and a few meager biscuits onto the tea tray when she heard a loud knock at the door. Surprised, as they rarely had visitors and Francesca would surely be busy with all the dress orders for the ball, Della went to answer the door. The brilliant sunlight momentarily blinded her as a man pushed past her and shut the door behind him.

"Excuse you! Who do you think you are, barging in here?!" Della demanded. Fear rose within her and she glanced around for anything that could be used as a weapon.

"Della, it's me. Roric."

Her hand flew to her chest. "Oh. You gave me a fright! What on the Great Cliffs are you doing?"

"Sorry. It's just that I don't want anyone to recognize me coming here." He nervously ran a hand through his hair.

Realization hit Della. "You don't want them to gossip about you coming to court one of Duchess DeVoss' daughters."

"Something like that. Everyone at court is a terrible gossip, especially the widows," Roric agreed.

"Well, how did you get here? I think they'll notice a carriage sitting out there."

"Actually, I rode my Stronghorse here. I put her away in your stable for now. I took your advice. I know how to take care of her almost as well as a stable hand now," he told her proudly.

"I thought the Stronghorse was your father's." Della raised an eyebrow.

"Yes, he purchased her for himself, but after my...ride with her, Father saw what I didn't even realize myself at the time," Roric said sheepishly.

"You bonded with her!" Della gasped.

"Yes. My father wasn't exactly happy that I had bonded with his Stronghorse before he even had a chance to go down to the stables to meet her, but he agreed that nothing could be done about it at that point, so he gave her to me," He rubbed the back of his neck. "I also gave her a name. Actually, it's more like she told me her name is Noa."

"That's quite amazing." Della bit back a stab of jealousy that this man had bonded with a Stronghorse. She silently promised herself she would have her own Stronghorse one day. Remembering her manners she asked, "Would you like some tea?"

"I'd love some." Roric grinned.

"Wait here." Della walked off to the kitchen.

She added another cup and saucer to the tray, removed her apron and kerchief, patting her hair. Della picked up the tray and turned to take it upstairs. She was so startled she nearly dropped it when she saw Roric leaning in the doorway. He swept a curious gaze around the room.

"What are you doing in here? I told you to wait by the door," she gasped out.

"So, you make the tea too?" he asked, ignoring her questions.

"I do everything. It's only the four of us here, so I do it all. Except when they go out in the carriage—then it's a hired one since in Tamaria a woman cannot drive a carriage, servant or not. It's rather ridiculous as it was one of the few things I was skilled at when I first came here." She went over to him, trying to edge him out of the small kitchen. He merely side-stepped her and walked around the room.

"I haven't been in a kitchen since I was a boy stealing pastries from the cooks." He picked up a rolling pin and examined it. "The head cook used to swat at me with one of these, but I don't think she ever intended to hit me. She did once and her face went so white I thought she was turning into a ghost before my eyes. I never told on her though and no one noticed the extra bruise on a scrappy young boy who often got into mischief or fell out of trees. But she stopped letting me into the kitchen after that."

"The poor woman was probably frightened she would lose her livelihood. If you had told, she likely would have been punished along with never being able to work as a cook again. If she had any children, they might have starved to death." Della set down the tray to snatch the rolling pin away from him.

"That's a bit morbid, don't you think?" Roric's brows rose in surprise.

"It's reality. You wouldn't understand that fear as a courtier. Anyone with money is protected and can do what they like to those who have to earn a living in Tamaria." Della crossed her arms.

"There are rules to being a courtier too. Courtiers can't simply do whatever they like," he said with a frown.

"But you have more choices than those without. You could decide tomorrow to become a merchant, but Franci couldn't up and decide to become a courtier. Not that she would want to." Della almost laughed at the image. Franci would enjoy it for the gossip, but she got enough of that from those who frequented her shop and a courtier's life would likely bore her.

"Who's Franci?" Roric cocked his head to the side and gave her a curious half smile.

"The best dressmaker in the city and probably the world," Della told him emphatically.

"Does she design your clothes?" He raised his eyebrows.

Della blushed. She was abruptly and painfully reminded of her dingy attire. She may need to buy a new blouse and skirt.

"Of course not! She designs the things the women of court wear mostly," Della snapped, though she straightened her skirt as if that could improve its condition.

"Well, I'm afraid I don't bother much with fashion or dressmakers, but I shall take you at your word that she is the best." His smile offered a truce, one Della found she was eager to accept.

"Shall we go upstairs?" Della picked up the tray once more.

"Yes, but..." Roric stepped close to her.

"But what? The tea is getting co—" Della broke off as he reached out a hand and brushed her cheek with his thumb.

"You have some soot, right there," he told her as he swept his thumb gently across her skin. He chuckled. "Oh dear, I think I've made it worse."

Della felt heat creep into her cheeks. She rubbed her cheek roughly against her shoulder as she turned away from him with the tray still in her hands. Her heart pounded and her stomach was still flipping from his touch.

"The sitting room is this way." Della marched out of the room without checking to see if he would follow.

She heard his footsteps behind her as she ascended the stairs. His closeness sent a delicious shiver down her spine. *She was alone with an attractive nobleman.* She would have laughed if someone had told her she'd ever be in such a situation. Roric moved to her side as they walked down the hallway. She reached for the door to the sitting room, but he opened it first and gestured for her to enter with a slight bow and a grin.

The room was decorated with maroon curtains, settees, and chairs. The heavy furniture was made from dark wood and cushioned. A large clock sat on the mantle. Della set the tea tray on the table and sat down on one of the settees. Roric took the seat opposite her.

Della set out the saucers and cups, then poured the tea. "So why have you come here?"

"Oh. Um, well I'd think that was rather obvious." He looked far too interested in his tea as he brought it to his lips.

"Well, you didn't want to be seen here and you also came while the duchess was away. You didn't ask for her or either of my s—her daughters."

"I know. I may have asked a favor to ensure I would be able to come when they were gone," he said.

"Roric, don't tell me you are a rake coming here when you knew I'd be alone!" She feigned shock.

"Skies no! I would never—I hope you know I didn't come here to—" he sputtered, and she laughed at him. "Ah. You're teasing me."

"You don't seem the type. You weren't overly familiar or flirtatious with me when we met. Though you did come to me now..." She winked.

"I would never. I honestly didn't think that you would be alone. Has the duchess no other servants?"

"I am the only one."

Roric's brows drew together with concern. "I hope I didn't frighten you by coming in. I didn't mean to put you in a compromising position."

"No one would worry about a maidservant's reputation." At her words Roric frowned, but Della waved a hand and changed the subject. "Isn't there a tea party you're missing today?"

"Oh, the men don't go to those. Besides, I am enjoying tea right now." Roric pointedly drank more tea from his cup.

"I'm not sure how long those tea parties last. The duchess is rarely invited to those," Della warned.

"I know. I might have arranged for them to be invited so I could come see you. It seemed more likely to have a successful outcome than aimlessly letting my horse run wild through fields and meadows until I bumped into you again."

"You—you wanted to see *me*?" Della felt a blush bloom across her cheeks.

"I hope that's alright." He looked unsure for the first time since she'd met him.

"Oh, it is. It's just...Well in Aleece such a thing wouldn't be unheard of, but in Tamaria your rules around titles are so formal. You are born into them and keep them all your life. Some marry into them, but it seems to only ever be a slight step up or down. I never hear tales of a courtier looking for a maid."

"Aleece is an interesting country. It's a wonder they can keep track of their own nobility and royalty. The future king is married to one of I think ten daughters the previous king had." Roric shook his head.

"He actually had twelve daughters. The first three, if there are as many as three children, will usually keep their title for the entirety of their lives. If they wish to abdicate in order to follow a different path, they must have a younger sibling willing to take on the title. That way, the royal line is assured with sufficient heirs. That particular king did have some of his daughters forsake their titles in order to pursue other paths.

One became a duchess instead of a princess in order to marry the man she loved below her station for example, so it's not as though they throw away titles for no reason. I think it's a lovely system that allows people to be truly happy by giving them the freedom of choice." Della sipped her tea.

"I can see value in allowing royalty to choose a different life than the one they were born into when there are enough heirs to provide security to the throne." He nodded slowly. "Though it's very different and a bit hard to wrap my head around."

"I suppose with only three princes, such a thing would be moot here." Della shrugged and changed the subject. "Would you tell me what the bond is like? To your Strong-horse I mean."

"It's...difficult to explain." His lips tilted to one side as he thought.

"Is it true they can talk to you?" If he didn't know how to explain it, perhaps she could ask enough questions to form an answer for herself. She wanted to finally *know*.

"It's less talking and more...that I can understand her, what she wants and needs. I can't translate her whinnies into words, though."

"I didn't expect you to." Della rolled her eyes with a laugh. "How is it that you can understand her?"

"I'm told it's different for everyone, though it may be that there are not enough people bonded to them at one time in a geographical area to get an accurate report. There are rumors of what may or may not be true. For me, it's like seeing images in my mind, but they come with feelings—her feelings. It's like I can see her perspective on certain things," Roric explained.

"That's very interesting," Della said genuinely. It was nice to finally have an answer to a question that had plagued her all her life. One that she should have found out with her own Stronghorse and her father by her side, learning what her particular bond was like. Sadness splashed through her and she paused before she shook it off. "Well, I had better clean this up and start on the chores or I'll never get it all done in time."

"Let me help you." Roric picked up the tray that Della was piling the tea things on.

Della looked at him skeptically and burst out in laughter.

"What?"

"Have you ever done a chore in your life, *my Lord*?" Della raised an eyebrow.

"I've done weaponry practice, which felt like a chore." Roric shrugged with a grin.

She laughed as they exited the room. "I don't think it's quite the same."

"I'm carrying this tray just fine for you, aren't I? Besides, I would like to get to know you better. You intrigue me. I didn't come all this way just for tea, pleasant as it was."

Della felt a blush on her cheeks again. She hoped he didn't think she was an idiot with how often her face had turned pink since he'd arrived.

"Well, alright." She gave in, knowing she hadn't fought very hard to take the tray back. It was only that it felt so nice to have someone help her for a change. She imagined it was what it might feel like to be treated like an actual lady.

When they reached the kitchen, she handed him a towel. "I'll wash the dishes and you can dry them and put them away."

"Wouldn't it be better for you to put them away, since I don't know where anything goes?"

"I don't trust you will wash them properly and I don't want to pay the price for it. I'll direct you to the right cabinets." She placed the tray on the counter.

"I can't disagree with such a sound argument." He followed her out the kitchen door to the well near the house.

"I can draw up the water for you at least. Wielding weapons requires strength training, and I skipped that to come here." Roric took the bucket out of her hands and attached it to the rope. He dropped it down into the well with a splash, then began pulling it back up.

Della couldn't help noticing how his shirt sleeves tightened around the muscular bulges of his arm as he worked. She looked away quickly when he turned back to her with the now full bucket, pretending to be more interested in a wildflower growing nearby. Roric followed her gaze and saw the buttercup. He plucked it from the ground, offering it to her.

"A beautiful flower for a beautiful lady." Roric bowed with a flourish.

"Why thank you, sir." Della swept an elegant curtsey. She accepted the flower, bringing it briefly to her nose before tucking it behind an ear.

Della reached for the bucket of water, but Roric maneuvered, holding it away from her.

"I can carry it," he said.

"Thank you." Her chest warmed at his kindness.

They walked back to the kitchen. He poured the water into the small tub she directed him to as she rubbed soap on a rag. She washed each dish, then handed it in turn to Roric for him to dry and put away. She noticed he took great care of the fragile tea dishes in his large hands as he toweled them off.

"Alright, now I must take care of the animals," Della told him as she dried her hands.

"Animals?" Roric looked startled.

"Yes. Perhaps you would like to go. I'm afraid I must get this done before the duchess gets back. I hope you enjoyed the tea."

"I could help you with the animals," Roric offered.

Della eyed him doubtfully.

He folded his arms across his chest and raised an eyebrow. "I take care of my own horse now."

"Alright, if you wish. Come with me." She led him out of the side kitchen door into the yard. They walked to the small chicken coop and she opened one side of the roof to reveal two rows of nests on each side. Most were empty save for a few eggs, but two hens were nestled comfortably in their roosts.

"I usually spread these kitchen scraps out to entice them to leave the henhouse if there are any chickens still in there," Della explained as she shook a pail and scattered its contents on the ground nearby.

Roric peered into the henhouse. "There's still one in there."

"That'll be Griseldis. Watch out, she *will* peck you, courtier or not. Do you want me to get the eggs out?" Della grinned at him.

Realizing he was being tested, Roric shook his head. "No, I can manage."

"Alright, hand them to me when you've got them." Della tied up the corners of her apron to turn it into a large pouch.

Roric pulled out the first few eggs without any trouble. When he got to the ones near Griseldis, he drew back his hand quickly and shook it out.

"She attacked me!" Roric cupped one hand against his chest with indignation.

"She pecked you. I did warn you. Did it actually hurt or did it just surprise you?" Della tried to get a look at his hand, but Roric just turned back to the henhouse with irritated determination.

His hand darted in and out quickly to retrieve one final egg. He proudly handed it to Della. "There you are."

"There's at least one more in there." Della suppressed a giggle as she told him.

Roric frowned. "I made sure. All the nests are empty."

The corners of Della's lips twitched as she held back a grin. "Griseldis is always sitting on one or two."

He looked back at the henhouse, then at Della. He groaned. "You can't be serious."

"It's easy, you simply have to be fast. You don't even have to get her to leave. You just slide your hand under her and grab the egg. You do have to be quick though. I can do it so you don't injure your delicate hand further." A teasing smile accompanied Della's offer.

"No, no, I'll finish the job I started," Roric glowered at Griseldis, eyeing the chicken apprehensively. He waved his hands at her in a half-hearted shooing motion, but she didn't budge. He thrust in his hand and the hen squawked, flapping her wings at him. Roric drew back, but held up his hand that clutched a large brown egg. He grinned triumphantly as a disgruntled Griseldis hopped out and stalked away.

"Well done, sir. You can fetch eggs from a henhouse! I'm sure that will be a useful skill to add to your list of accomplishments. Skilled in fighting, gentlemanly manners, and collecting chicken eggs. You'll be the catch of the season," Della declared. She batted her eyelashes at him.

"You forgot dish dryer," he said with mock offense.

"Oh, what a tragic mistake to forget such an important skill." Della pressed a hand to her heart.

"How many of these beasts do you have?" Roric peered around her at the small flock pecking the ground as he handed her the egg.

"As of now, only five hens and one rooster. They wander around the yard eating bugs during the day, and only Griselda is grumpy." Della turned to see where he was looking. "Oh dear."

"What?" demanded Roric.

"Well, that's the flock's rooster, Eggbert."

The large, rust red chicken strode toward them.

"You named your rooster *Eggbert*?" Roric's mouth hung open. He snapped it shut, shaking his head in disbelief.

"It seemed fitting and a bit humorous, but it does make him sound friendlier than he tends to be." Della bit her lip and shrugged, her face flushing.

The enormous red rooster reached them and puffed up his chest. His head cocked back and forth jerkily as he sized up Roric.

"What do I do?" Roric whispered through his teeth uncomfortably.

"Hold your ground. You need to show him you are in charge."

"I don't think it's working." Roric edged away slowly as the rooster spread his wings and flapped at him.

"No, don't—!" Della started, but it was too late.

Roric darted to the side and Eggbert launched himself into the air after him. It was a whirlwind of flapping wings, extended talons, and squawks from both of them. Della watched helplessly as Roric ran with the aggressive rooster chasing after him. She hurried to the kitchen door as fast as she could without breaking the eggs clutched delicately in her apron.

"Over here, Roric! Hurry!"

Roric zigzagged to change directions and sprinted to the open door. He outpaced the rooster as he ran and when he sailed through the door, Della shut it tight behind him. She winced at the thud and angry screeches that followed. She peeked out the window and saw the bird stomping away looking furious, but ultimately unhurt.

Della turned to Roric. "Are you alright?"

He leaned against the table, panting. His shirt looked a bit wrinkled, one sleeve torn, and the top button had popped open. His hair was askew, there was a small scratch on his face, and his hands also held a few cuts.

"I'll be alright. I think my pride is the only thing truly wounded." He flashed her a chagrined smile.

"Ah yes, the brave warrior defeated by a chicken." Della laughed. "You look like a mess."

"It was an enormously oversized rooster that I am now convinced is part cockatrice," Roric corrected while attempting to smooth his shirt. He ran a hand through his hair, settling it somewhat.

Della placed the eggs gently in their basket before opening a cabinet and taking out a jar. She dipped a rag into the dregs of the water bucket and crossed the room to him.

"Definitely part cockatrice," she agreed.

He smiled at her. She reached up and gently wiped at the cuts. She opened the jar and spread the salve across the small scratch on his cheek. He caught her hand in his and held it there against his cheek for a moment. Her breath caught and she met his eyes. She was suddenly aware of how close together they were standing. She stepped back a half step and he let her hand fall.

"Let me finish seeing to those scratches for you. I don't know how dangerous they are when they come from a cockatrice," she said. But he only offered a weak smile at her joke.

Della focused her eyes only on his hand as she applied the salve. She felt a pressure in the room that hadn't been there before and a shyness that made her unable to meet his eyes. She had the strangest feeling that she'd like to take a step closer to him to see if that strange pressure would ease or contract into something more, but the thought frightened her. When she turned his hand over to examine his palm, her fingers brushed against some unexpected callouses that pulled her out of her reverie.

"It appears you work with your hands more than I expected from a nobleman," Della said with surprise.

He smiled. "Those are from years of swinging a sword."

"If only you'd had a sword a few minutes ago."

"You would be having chicken for dinner." He winked.

"There, I think we've patched you up." Della was relieved that putting the jar of salve away gave her an excuse to turn away from him for a moment. She didn't understand her feelings for him. She had never met a man that made her breath catch the way he did. Her heart was pounding as if she were frightened, but she wasn't scared just...oddly nervous. Perhaps she was on edge waiting for her stepmother to return. That must be it. She discarded the used rag and turned back to him.

"Thank you," Roric said sincerely. His face turned slightly regretful. "I think I should be going."

"Oh, but of course." Disappointment settled on her like a mantle, but she didn't know why. It was best that he go before the duchess returned. She brushed the feeling off as she walked with him toward the door.

Roric paused at the front door. Della looked at him quietly waiting, though for what she didn't know.

After a moment Roric said, "It's not that I don't want to stay, it's only that I will be missed if I stay away too long."

"I understand." Della laid a hand on his arm. A strange thrill rose up from her stomach, and back down to her toes at the contact. She pulled her hand back, but when it left his arm Roric caught it and brought it to his lips in a brief kiss.

"Until I see you again, my lady." He gave her a gentle smile, but there was an intensity burning in his eyes that heated her to the core.

"I look forward to it," Della told him and she meant it with every fiber of her being.

He let go of her hand, opened the door, and walked to the stables. She closed the door most of the way and watched for a bit. Roric led his horse out a few minutes later. She couldn't hold back a soft smile as she realized he had to have spent the time re-saddling and bridling his horse, which meant he had taken the time to make her comfortable in the stable, despite knowing he wouldn't stay long. Della didn't know if that kind of care for a horse was common among the lords of Tamaria, but she doubted it. A tendril of tenderness unfurled in her heart for him.

Roric swung up on the large Stronghorse with practiced ease. He must have indeed been spending time working with her, though that was unsurprising. Being bonded with a Stronghorse was sought after, especially amongst the nobility. Della again felt a small pang of jealousy and an ache of longing for such a bond. *One day.*

Della let out a small squeak when Roric suddenly looked back and caught her eye. He waved and she blew out a breath as she waved back, hoping he hadn't heard her. She couldn't tell if his shoulders shook with quiet laughter or merely from the Stronghorse's brisk trot as he rode away.

Della shut the door and leaned against it. She closed her eyes and stayed there for a long moment as she breathed, not daring to even try to sort out her feelings.

CHAPTER NINE

Della walked down the hall past her stepfamily's rooms carrying a basket of clothes to be ironed. A smile tugged at her lips as she imagined Roric trying to help her with the ironing. He'd likely burn his fingers and need more salve. She shook her head as she held in a laugh. Eleonora poked her head out of her bedroom door.

"Della, come in here."

"I'm in the middle of—"

Eleonora grabbed Della's arm and pulled her into her room with a grin. Eleonora closed her door and took the basket out of her hands, depositing it on the floor. She pushed Della toward the dressing table and forced her down onto the small, cushioned stool. "You're always busy. When was the last time you took a proper break? Mother and Marien are still sleeping, they'll never know. Besides, it's been ages since we've been able to spend any time together."

Della opened her mouth to protest that she didn't have time, but Eleonora's eager face made her shut her mouth. She sighed in defeat, but did it with a smile. Eleonora squealed happily and then clamped a hand over her mouth to prevent any further noise from waking the others.

"I'm going to do your hair!" Eleonora picked up her horse-hair brush and started pulling it through a lock of Della's hair that she held in one hand.

Della winced internally, knowing that her hair was going to become a poofy mess. She would simply have to braid it back later. Of course it had been the one day she'd left her waves down, bound back only by her headscarf. She had thought the curls looked particularly nice and had wanted to enjoy them rather than pinning her hair back. This was a sacrifice she was willing to make for Eleonora, who was treating Della like a sister rather than a servant. Eleonora might not be able to stand up to her mother, but she didn't participate in the cruelty that Marien found pleasure in.

"Do you miss Aleece?" Eleonora startled Della with the sudden question.

"Very much."

Eleonora pulled the brush through the same clump of hair for a few more strokes. "I do too."

Della met her sister's eyes in the mirror.

Eleonora smiled ruefully. "You're surprised."

"I just never thought you would miss a place you only lived in for almost a year and a half." Della looked at her sister again, but Eleonora's attention was focused on the brush.

"I thought Aleece was the most wonderful place I had ever experienced. We lived in a very small town before that, near the border. Well, the border into the woods. Then we went to Aleece and suddenly there was so much color and sound and magic. People embraced magical creatures, seeking them out rather than chasing them away. People sang and danced and did all manner of shows in the streets for anyone to watch, not just the wealthy. Most of all, I thought it was terribly romantic that the country idolized marrying for love rather than station."

How had Della not known Eleonora had loved all the same things about Aleece that she did? Della smiled. "I miss all those things too. Is that why you hope to marry for love?"

Eleonora dropped the brush, her mouth agape. "How did you—I—I mean—Is it that obvious?"

"I don't think anyone else has noticed." Della turned her shoulders to face Eleonora.

Eleonora bent down to retrieve the brush. She straightened and bit her lip. "Mother would be furious."

"I don't think she is aware," Della said again to ease her sister's nerves.

"It's really not fair that she would be so upset about it. After all, she married for love once. Of course, we did end up destitute, but..." Eleonora sighed. She stared at the frizzy disaster that was now one side of Della's hair. "Oh dear, I've made a mess of this."

Della took the brush out of her hands and replaced it with a wide comb. "Try this instead."

Eleonora accepted the comb and Della turned around. Della was definitely going to have to braid back her hair after this, but she knew how busy hands could make it easier for one to talk when they are nervous. At least the comb would keep her wavy hair from becoming a complete poofy mess.

Eleonora's eyes unfocused, as if she were far away when she spoke again. "My mother was the daughter of a baron. Her parents' marriage was arranged and no love ever grew there. My mother craved more. She was kept isolated on their grounds, but a boy saw her once. He left her flowers and trinkets. She found excuses to go to the fence and speak with him. She even snuck off to spend time with him. Had anyone found out, her reputation would have been ruined. She didn't care though, she was young and reckless—made that way by love."

"So they got married?" Della knew her two stepsisters were proof they had wed.

"No. He asked my grandfather for her hand, but of course my grandfather refused. He turned his nose up at the common boy who had to labor for a living. He arranged for her to marry a nobleman instead. So, my mother ran away. She and my father were wed in another town and by the time my grandfather found them, it was too late." Eleonora's voice turned sad. "He disowned her."

"That's awful." Della couldn't imagine being so furious that someone had found love. Would the duchess disown Eleonora if she fell in love with anyone besides a nobleman? Would she repeat history? "How can she possibly be so set on you two marrying for wealth when she chose love herself?"

Eleonora knew immediately who she was talking about. "It ended badly. A plague hit the area. First, Father's work suffered because so many were ill. We couldn't afford much, but that made things even more difficult for us. Then the farmers fell sick, and the crops suffered with no one to tend to them. Food became scarce. Then Father fell ill. Mother said he had been skipping meals just to ensure the rest of us ate and his strength failed him. Marien and I also became ill. I remember being hot and cold and aching down to my bones."

Eleonora paused and met Della's gaze. Her eyes held a sorrow that Della had never seen there before.

"Mother was desperate. She abandoned her pride and made her way back to her family. Her father wouldn't even let her into the house. She begged him for the money to pay for a physician. He told her that she had brought this upon herself, then sent her away. Marien and I never met him. I was told he succumbed to the illness himself sometime later."

Della bit back the urge to say she was lucky to be rid of him. "Eleonora, I'm so sorry. That's horrible."

"When my father didn't recover—" Eleonora's voice broke. She picked up the comb and pulled it through Della's hair again. "We were left destitute. My mother did what she could, but she had been trained as a noblewoman and her few years with my father hadn't given her any skills to make a living. Your father found her, found us. He saved us. My mother is harsh, but she is doing what she can to prevent us from ever starving again."

There was a tightness in her throat that Della tried to swallow away. "No one ever told me how bad it was for you. I knew you had grown up in a small village from what you had told me, and the way you all adjusted to life in the Delemy, but I hadn't realized you were barely surviving."

Eleonora nodded. "My mother thought the widow's stipend would be the best option with three young girls, so she returned here, but Tamaria is where choosing love cost her everything."

"Not everything. She gained *you*. And Marien." Della squeezed Eleonora's hand.

Eleonora gave her a soft smile. "Yes, I suppose that's true. I will forever be grateful for my time in Aleece, though. It gave me hope that I can someday have a love like my parents had."

Della's heart ached for Eleonora. As the youngest sister, she was spared from an arranged marriage while the duchess focused on Marien, but Della knew that if a wealthy enough man showed any interest in the beautiful Eleonora, the girl would be packed off faster than a Stronghorse could run. Della *had* to help her sister. She would be extra attentive when doing her hair and dressing her. If Eleonora could find love before Marien found a match, then she would have a chance at a loving marriage. It would also conveniently free Della from her stepmother's claws sooner, but she brushed that thought aside with a twinge of guilt. She was going to help Eleonora because she cared for her younger sister, not because it helped herself.

"Eleonora, I believe that you *can* have true love."

She started. "You do? But how? Mother wants me to marry for wealth."

"Well, no one said you had to marry a commoner to fall in love. If you and a nobleman fell in love, he'd likely be wealthy enough that the duchess couldn't argue against the match." A grin spread across Della's face.

Her sister tilted her head, considering. "I think you may actually be right!"

"I know that you're shy, but you must try to get to know each of the men while the duchess is busy with Marien. Avoid anyone you already know you don't like. See if there's anyone you're drawn to and if they might have an interest in you as well."

Eleonora nodded, a soft smile lighting up her face. "Oh Della, you've given me such hope!" She threw her arms around Della and squeezed with surprising strength.

"Can't. Breathe," Della coughed out, the words muffled against Eleonora's shoulder.

"Oops." Eleonora released her, still grinning.

A bell rang from the other room and Della jumped to her feet.

"I had better go."

"Della? Thank you."

Della smiled. "You don't have to thank me. Just live the life you've dreamed of, a life full of love."

CHAPTER TEN

The next day they all went into town for Marien's dress fitting. While Della usually liked going to Franci's, it was never a good idea to go there with her stepfamily. Franci would get even more irritated at the way they treated Della and stick Marien with pins "accidentally" in her vindictive frustration. So Della came with them into town, but would take care of other errands rather than accompanying them while they shopped. Della's first stop was the jewelry shop.

She greeted the store owner and walked up to the displays of jewelry. She wandered down the aisles, not really hoping to purchase anything, but keeping an eye out for anything that might match Marien's new dress as well as watching for what was most discounted, even if that meant it was most likely pawned. Della always felt a twinge of remorse when she bought a cheaper piece, knowing the previous owner had likely been desperate and might be hoping to purchase it again in the future when their fortunes improved.

Della passed by a pearl necklace, but something about it bothered her so she went back to examine it more closely.

"Did you come by this recently?" she asked the shop owner, Gregor.

"I acquired it since you were last in," Gregor replied smoothly. He never gave any clues to his buyers and his discretion only improved his business. Della knew he made a fair bit of the jewelry as well and was quite skilled at it. His was the first stop most made when shopping for or selling jewelry for both those reasons.

"Something about it caught my eye... The clasp. It's an ornate S clasp in Aleecean style rather than the rectangular clasps typically found in Tamaria." Della frowned as she realized what had stood out to her.

Gregor gave the briefest pause of surprise before recovering. "Courtiers from other countries do visit from time to time."

"Courtiers that have money to travel here, but then need to sell their jewelry?" Della's lips tightened into a thin line. She thought of the small jewelry box up in her attic room. It was a small box that held very little, but it did have one Aleecean pearl necklace left to her by her mother.

"You know I never share information about my sellers. Perhaps they have a monetary need, perhaps they simply no longer liked the item. It's better for business that I do not even ask why they sell such things," Gregor hedged. "For having left at such a young age, you certainly know specific details about Aleecean jewelry."

"I had a few pieces from my mother. I looked at them when I missed her, which was often enough to recognize the differences once I began buying the Tamarian pieces for the duchess and her daughters."

"Such a lamentable tale to have befallen one so young." Gregor turned away to hide the distress flickering in his eyes. He picked up a ring and began to polish it.

Della felt a sudden rush to leave the jewelry store. "Well, I must go and get on with my errands." She made her way to the door. Her mind whirled as she tried not to think too hard about where that necklace could have come from.

"A good day to you." Gregor gave her a courteous nod, but there was something in his eyes that might have been pity.

Della felt the crushing need to breathe fresh air. The busy streets felt too crowded, as if they were pressing in on her, stealing the very breath from her lungs. She wove through the throng with a panic rising in her as though she might suffocate. She reached the large wall that surrounded the city and followed it to the massive gate that permitted people in and out of the city. It was teeming with all the inhabitants and visitors today, and Della was waiting impatiently in the long queue when she spotted a familiar guard on one side. Her friend, Anton. She waved at him and he smiled as he waved back at her before gesturing to her come over.

"Leaving the city today?" Anton asked her cheerfully when she reached him.

"I wanted to get away from the bustle of everything for a moment. I feel a bit overwhelmed and a walk outside the walls would do me some good."

"Ah, yes, there's so much activity with the impending ball. The crowds are thicker with visitors too. There have been quite a few from other cities and even countries coming to prepare and attend the festivities. I'll let you through the side door if you're quick about it." He winked.

"I would greatly appreciate that." Della's gratitude shone in her eyes.

Anton led her a few feet to the reinforced wooden door in the wall. He unlocked it and opened it just wide enough for her to slip through.

"Here you are, m'lady."

Della had tried to discourage the title until she realized that Anton called every woman and girl that no matter their station. It was a small show of kindness and respect that Tamaria could certainly use.

"Thank you, Anton," she said warmly.

"And Della..."

"Yes?"

"Er, I—well... I mean to say... Do be careful," Anton finished briskly, though his words didn't explain why his ears had turned red.

"I always am," Della assured him.

Della suspected he meant to ask to call on her sometime, but he always lost his nerve. Truth be told, she hoped he never did find it where she was concerned. She was fond enough of him, but she had never developed feelings of desire for anything beyond a mild friendship with him.

The door shut behind her and Della found herself in the dark inner hallway of the wall. Though the walls were thick, many held a thin hallway inside that allowed troops to mobilize against threats more easily. She felt along the opposite wall for the spot to push that would unlatch the hidden stone door to reach the outside. The door swung open and she slipped out into the sunlight. She would have to cross the drawbridge through the main gate to reenter the city as the outer door could only be opened from within, but by then she anticipated feeling much less stifled.

Della moved away from the hidden door quickly to prevent suspicion should anyone see her. She didn't think the guards often used these doors themselves and she didn't want to get Anton into trouble as she doubted he was supposed to be letting ladies through the small passageway.

Della's chest eased and she began to relax as she gulped in the fresh air the countryside provided. She walked around the wall to the side of the city, taking a lightly worn path rather than the main road everyone else was traveling on. She wasn't alone though—she could see a wagon of some sort up ahead. When she reached the wagon, she saw it was a small vardo, the type of wagon one usually saw with a caravan as they were fully enclosed and often held beds within for long-term travel. This one had shuttered shelves built into the outsides to display wares and was so small there was probably just barely enough room inside to cram a small bed.

"Hello," Della called cheerfully when she noticed the man sitting on a large rock near the wagon. His neatly combed white hair was plentiful on his head and brushed his shoulders. He was covered in wrinkles, but sat with a straightness that belied his age. He looked up warily at her call and slowly stood up.

"M'lady." He gave her a small, creaking bow. He had the strange accent of one who has traveled all their life and picked up odd pieces of dialect here and there.

Della curtsied back. "Oh please, there's no need to stand on my account. I'm only out for a walk to escape the bustle of the city and the duchess for a bit. Besides, I'm hardly a lady."

"Ah, a servant for a duchess? A fortunate household to end up in." The merchant settled back down on his rock.

"I suppose that would depend on the demeanor of the particular duchess." Della gave him a wry smile.

"Ah, very true," he said with a chuckle. The laughter fell from his face a moment later. "It seems a general attitude of disdain permeates Tamaria of late."

"Have people been unkind? There is usually an air of forced politeness at the very least here in the Fellsantra, but with the upcoming ball the city has been put in quite a frenzy."

"Yes, and every coin is evidently being used to prepare for the ball with not one that can be spared elsewhere." The man sighed and then his stomach grumbled loudly, as if to prove his point.

"Well, I don't have any spare coin myself, unfortunately. However, I do have a sandwich and apple that will go to waste, as all these ball preparations have quite put me off my lunch. Would you accept it as a trade? Perhaps there's some small trifle among your wares you wouldn't mind parting with in exchange." Della pulled the offered food out of her basket.

While her stepmother and stepsisters would dine at one of the tearooms in town, Della was never afforded such a luxury. She was happy to part with her lunch, however, as she knew where her next meal would be coming from. The man debated for a moment so she let the wrapping on the sandwich fall open. The man couldn't resist licking his lips as he eyed the meal.

"Yes... I might just have something," he said slowly, nodding.

"Alright then." Della pushed the food into his hands before he could argue.

He sank his teeth quickly into the sandwich and settled back on his rock. Della sat down in the grass and leaned back on her elbows with her face tipped up to the sun. It felt deliciously warm on her skin.

"Your accent. You're not from Tamaria, are you?" the man asked before starting in on the apple, having already devoured the sandwich. Della wished she had more to give him, but her own rations were slim as it was.

"I'm Aleecean, but after my parents died I found myself here. I plan to travel back in the next few years though, if I can save up the money. I miss my country. Everything is so stiff and formal here. It's almost like girls only have dresses and marriage to look forward to, and in many instances both are uncomfortable," Della told him honestly. She was rewarded by his barking laugh.

"That's a way of putting it! Yes. I am planning to head toward Aleece myself. It's such a beautiful country full of kind people. Full of possibilities too. I almost settled down there as a young man, but a tragic accident lost my closest friend and I found a need to keep moving on. I might have made something else of myself if I had stayed, but the everyday reminders were too painful at the time." He shook his head ruefully.

"I'm sorry about your friend." Della laid her hand on the man's arm. He looked surprised at her touch.

"I believe you actually mean those words." He cocked his head to consider her.

Della blinked. "Why would I say it if I didn't mean them?"

"You would be surprised by the many ways people can seek to deceive." He fed the apple core to his horse. "Well, I'd better show you what you can have."

He stood up and pulled a key from his pocket. He opened the shutters on the wagon, revealing all sorts of baubles. Glass figurines, wooden animals, and tin soldiers sparkled in the light. The man harrumphed, closed the shutters back up, and motioned her around to the other side of the wagon, where he opened those shutters as well. Like the first side, there were rows of shelves holding an assortment of trinkets.

"Let's see, let's see..." he mumbled to himself as he scanned the shelves.

Della admired the many items while she waited patiently for him to select whichever item he felt was worth the meal. It would surely be one of the small ones and she had a bit of fun trying to decide what it would be. Perhaps the wooden horse? Or maybe that wooden spinning top?

With a snap, the man closed the shutters again. He locked them back up and promptly shut himself inside his wagon. Della walked over to the peddler's horse to wait. It was the beautiful pale golden color of wheat.

"Aren't you a beauty? Do you think he's coming back?" Della whispered to the horse as she slid her palm down its nose, across its muscled cheeks.

The horse only shifted closer to Della.

"Well, I suppose that's that," Della said with a laugh to the merchant's horse. She stroked its neck for another moment while it snuffled her, looking for treats. "I'm sorry, I'm all out of apples."

Della picked up her basket and started back toward the city.

"Just where are you going?" The merchant demanded from behind her. She whirled around in surprise.

"Oh, my apologies! I thought—" Della broke off, her cheeks filling with the ruddy color of embarrassment.

"I have a good idea of what you thought," he grunted. "However, I take my bargains very seriously. I was only looking for the perfect thing to give you in return."

"Of course you were," Della replied smoothly as she stepped back toward him.

The merchant held a small bundle in his hands that she moved closer to see. He pulled back the fabric to reveal a sparkling pair of shoes. They had low heels, as were the fashion, and soft, white fur on the soles. They sparkled beautifully, almost like—

"Is that glass?" Della asked in awe.

The merchant nodded eagerly. "They're the finest glass slippers in all the land!"

"I think they're the *only* glass slippers I'd find in all the land," Della said with a laugh.

"Try them on." He held them out to her.

"Are you sure?" Della tried to keep the skepticism out of her voice, but it leaked in.

"You'll find they're sturdier than you think. They're dwarvish made. Try them on!"

He shooed her excitedly toward the rock so she sighed and sat down upon it. She knelt to unlace her shoes, and he placed the glass slippers before her on the ground. Della slid one foot at a time into the shoes. They seemed to fit her feet perfectly. Tentatively she stood up, keeping one hand braced against the rock as she put more and more weight on the shoes. She fully expected to feel them crack and shatter beneath her feet, but to her surprise they held. The fur covering the soles felt luxurious and she was again taken aback at how glass shoes could feel as comfortable—perhaps even more so—than her own shoes.

"Take a few steps. Go on," the merchant encouraged.

Della took a few hesitant steps and grew bolder. She walked and twirled, testing the astonishing shoes.

"These are truly a wonder! Thank you for showing them to me," she exclaimed with a delighted laugh as she sat down to take them off. She put her own shoes back on and held the glass slippers out to the peddler.

"Oh no. Those are yours now. It's our trade." He gave her a toothy grin.

"I couldn't possibly accept these! They must be worth a fortune, not just an apple and a sandwich," Della protested.

"They are worth the meal and the kindness you have shown me. I'm a stranger—you owe me nothing and yet you were kind. Such compassion is rare and deserves to be rewarded. Seeing your delight in them was a true merchant's pleasure as well. Besides, you'd be surprised how hard it is to sell glass shoes." He winked, but Della had the feeling he'd never tried to sell the glass slippers before.

"You're too kind." The bell tower tolling the hour startled her. "I'm terribly sorry, but I really must go! I wish you the best in your travels!"

Della carefully wrapped up the glass slippers and hid them in the bottom of her basket.

"I truly wish you the best too, fair maiden." The peddler smiled sincerely. He put his fist over his heart and lowered his head in a brief bow.

Della waved and hurried back to town to find her stepmother and stepsisters. She accompanied them home and went to her room to check her jewelry box. There was no pearl necklace inside.

Her heart wrenched and tears slipped down her cheeks as she sat on her bed holding the small wooden box. She had lost her mother, her father, Tilya, and the rest of the household staff that she had grown up with. She had lost her manor, her friends, and her country. Now even her jewelry was being ripped away.

Della berated herself for taking the box out of its hiding place in the false bottom of her trunk. No one had bothered to climb the stairs to the attic in years and she had grown lax. She hid the jewelry box, with the few remaining items it contained, away in her trunk. She could only hope that her stepmother wouldn't go looking for it now that she knew that Della had it.

CHAPTER ELEVEN

I t was unbearably hot the day after the dress fitting. Della's arms ached as she alternated fanning the duchess and her stepsisters in the sitting room.

"If you should encounter the king and queen, you must show them your deepest, most graceful curtsy. You must never speak first, instead wait to see if they wish to engage in conversation with you," Duchess DeVoss droned on.

"Then how is Marien supposed to convince the prince to court her?" Eleonora asked without interest. She looked wilted in her overstuffed chair. She fanned her face with her hand when her mother wasn't looking.

"You may speak first to the princes, though it is much better if they begin the conversation. However, we wouldn't want to insult the King and Queen, who are of higher importance than the princes and therefore cannot be spoken to first. Speaking first to a prince would be considered bold, but speaking first to the king or queen would be an insult. Now, what is the most important thing you must remember?"

"To make a good impression?" Eleonora suggested half-heartedly.

"About the king and queen?" Duchess DeVoss prompted impatiently.

"That you must never turn your back to them," Marien supplied lazily from where she was lounging on a chaise. She shot a smug smile at her sister.

"What? We have to wander around trying to face them all night?" Eleonora asked incredulously.

Della snorted despite herself and reflexively lifted a hand to cover her nose and mouth.

"Was something funny?" Duchess DeVoss demanded, swiveling her head to glare at Della.

"No, sorry. I was stifling a cough. It came out a bit more unladylike than I thought," Della said quickly.

"You're so uncouth. And fan me faster! It's stifling in here," Duchess DeVoss snapped. "Eleonora, of course you wouldn't wander around backwards. That's only if you're presented to them or were conversing with them. If you should be so lucky as to experience that, then you may either walk backwards, or sideways away from them. Sideways is more ladylike and therefore preferable."

"We don't have to do that with the princes though, only the reigning monarchs."

"Very good, Marien."

"Imagine if the third prince fell in love with me and introduced me to his parents! What a way to meet the king and queen!" Marien squealed.

It seemed a rather unlikely way to meet the king and queen to Della.

"That would be ideal," Duchess DeVoss purred. "You must work hard to please him. I shall do my best to maneuver you around the court to be near him. Eleonora, you must help distract any girls who are trying to get near so that your sister may talk to him alone."

"How am I supposed to do that?" Eleonora shot up straight in her chair, staring at her mother with her mouth open.

"Close your mouth." Duchess DeVoss frowned at her.

"You look like a fish," Marien snickered.

Eleonora snapped her mouth shut with a click.

"Really, Eleonora, you go to all these social events with us and haven't made any friends? You're always chattering away with those girls. Surely you can engage them in conversation, lead them away to the refreshment table, or stun them with some bit of gossip that they simply must stay with you to hear." Duchess DeVoss waved a hand in the air.

"I shall try." Eleonora sounded miserable at the prospect.

"You don't have to waste the opportunity either—use the time to get closer to anyone who might introduce you to an eligible gentleman," Duchess DeVoss instructed.

Eleonora slumped back into her chair.

"I think that's enough tutelage for today. It's far too hot to continue. Della, go make us some chilled tea."

Della, arms aching from fanning them, happily left for the kitchen, though she knew she'd soon be boiling like the kettle from the fire in that small room. She found respite in the long time it took for the tea to cool before bringing it to her stepfamily. The rest of the day passed in a blur of heat and chores.

The next morning Della stood in her room tying her apron over her clothes in preparation for the day. She had just grabbed her headscarf when she heard wagon wheels. She peeked out her minuscule window and saw Barend making his weekly delivery of bread to the widows, who didn't come into town often. He had offered to do so for Della, of course, but she enjoyed the extra trips into the busier part of the city.

Della opened the window and called down to him. "Barend! Barend!"

He looked around, and she waved to him when he glanced up. He halted his horse, so she dashed down the three flights of stairs and raced outside.

"Hello there, Della!" he said while she caught her breath.

"Hello Barend. Are you very busy today?"

"Just the usual amount. I always have time for a friend though." He smiled.

"Would you mind terribly if I rode back with you into town? I want to take something to Franci and I don't think I can manage to carry it the whole walk."

"Of course! It will take me half an hour to make my rounds and then I'll be back," Barend said.

Della thanked him and rushed back inside. She made cold sandwiches and poured precious milk she had bought at the market for her family's breakfast, leaving the trays outside their rooms. It would anger them, but she hoped the bit of rare milk might mollify them a bit. She rushed back upstairs to her room. She took out her other day outfit, her riding habit, stockings, and an extra pair of shoes from her small trunk, laying them on her bed to put away later. Della looked at what still lay inside—at the top was her small jewelry box and the glass shoes. For a moment she fingered the few lovely gowns of her mother's that lay beneath. She closed the lid and lugged it as quietly as she could so she wouldn't wake the sleeping women.

Barend was waiting for her when she came out.

"Finally planning to leave this place, are you? It's about time." Barend lifted the trunk into the wagon bed.

"No, I left all my essentials out. This is just...extra things I don't want to go missing," Della said without meeting his eye.

Barend gave an annoyed grunt as he handed her up onto the seat in front and Della knew the sound wasn't directed at her. The seat sagged slightly when he pulled himself up next to her. He flicked the reins and they began the trek into the part of town where most of the shops were.

"You're going to Francesca's?" Barend asked.

"Yes, but you don't have to go out of your way to drop me there. The ride into the center of town is enough. I should be able to carry my trunk from there."

He said nothing, but steered the horse toward the west road rather than his bakery in the east.

"You're out early this morning," Della commented.

"I know I usually do my deliveries in the evening, but I already have to work all day in the bakery, I can't leave Johanna to take care of the baby all evening too. I got up extra early to bake today and am doing my deliveries now that that's done so I can spend time with my family in the evening instead."

"How are Johanna and the baby doing?"

Barend's face lit up. "They're both doing well. Johanna doesn't want to stay in bed now that she's had the babe, but the midwife insists and so do I. For a few weeks, at least while she recovers. The baby is plumping right up like a fatted calf too! Charlotte Fournier. Though we're calling her Lotte like Johanna wanted."

"That's a beautiful name."

They fell into a comfortable silence as they rode. The early morning light illuminated the early risers who moved about quietly as they started on the day's chores. Della loved the rare times she got to see the center of the city awakening slowly. Widow's Court was on the edge of the Tamrian capital, Fellsantra, and usually didn't start to show the small signs of life until the afternoon. It was built to be a serene place for widows to live out the rest of their days in blissful peace, but it only made Della ache for the noisy streets of Aleece where performers abounded singing or playing instruments. She missed being able to see troupes perform whenever she wanted.

"Ho-hoooo," Barend called to the horse as they pulled up to Franci's shop. They stopped obediently.

"Thank you again," Della told him as she climbed out of the wagon.

"Any time you need a ride, don't hesitate to ask." Barend set her trunk down beside her. He tipped his hat and climbed back into his wagon with a grin. With another flick of the reins he was on his way back to the bakery.

Della picked up the trunk and lugged it into Franci's shop. Franci was already with a customer showing swatches of fabric. She looked up at the bell tinkling and met Della's eyes with a smile. Della set the trunk behind the counter and took money from another customer, giving them change and packaging the hat they had purchased, no doubt to go with one of Franci's fine gowns.

"Hello Della! I wasn't expecting to see you here. Does Marien need a new gown? Or perhaps some new hair ribbons?" Franci asked as the early customers left her shop.

"Well…" Della lowered her voice and looked at the floor before continuing. "Do you mind if I leave a trunk of my things in your apartment?"

"Of course not! Does this mean you've finally decided to take me up on my offer to live here? You can take the second bedroom."

"No, it's not that… I just had a few things go missing. It's possible I misplaced them, but the other day in the jewelry shop I saw—" Della broke off as she looked up and saw the fury on Franci's face.

"Those little—"

"Oh, I don't have any proof, so I really shouldn't say such things. But I'd feel better if the things I have left of Mother—the only possessions I care about really—were kept safe here. That way, even if it is me misplacing them, I won't be able to do that."

"*Misplacing*. As if you would misplace anything, especially something so dear to you," Franci muttered with contempt.

"So can I leave these here with you?" Della asked, trying to steer Franci away from her angry thoughts.

"Of course, Della! You or your things are always welcome. Besides, this will make it easier when you do finally agree to move in with me!" Franci grinned.

Franci grabbed one end of the trunk and led the way to the stairs that went to the apartment over the shop. They ignored the door to their right, the larger bedroom that had belonged to Franci's parents, that she had moved into for comfort after their passing. Franci instead opened another door to a small, but cozy bedroom. The bed against one wall was covered with a homemade quilt in every color that Della knew Franci's mother had made from scraps of leftover fabric. A small side table and a chest of drawers were the only other furniture in the room.

"This was my old room, as you know. You can put the chest in here. If you ever decide to stay, this room is yours."

"Thank you." The two girls set the chest at the foot of the bed. "I appreciate always knowing I have a place to go if things get truly awful."

"Of course, Della! You are my dearest friend—my sister in everything but blood. Now, let's go get the petticoats I've finished for your stepfamily's new dresses so that you have a reason to be walking home from the city center." Franci threw an arm around Della's shoulders and ushered her back down to the shop.

CHAPTER TWELVE

D ella was enjoying the day without her stepfamily. They had gone to a social event again today and would be gone until the evening meal. Della had finished her chores quickly. When the duchess was home, she knew how to make herself look busy so that she wasn't given more chores. She had learned that lesson the hard way when she was a girl, having hoped that if she finished quickly enough she would be allowed to play and attend lessons with her stepsisters. Of course, that was back when they could still afford a governess.

She had been just about to prepare a cup of tea and some biscuits in the kitchen when she heard a knock at the door. A frown creased her brow at the interruption, but it dropped away when she realized it was likely another invitation being dropped off. Another day without her stepfamily would be bliss! She opened the door and blinked in surprise.

"Oh, hello!" Della's stomach fluttered at the sight before her.

"Hello, Della." Roric gave her a smile that suggested he knew he had caught her by surprise and also knew that she wouldn't turn him away.

"Um, would you like to come in?" Della opened the door wider.

"Actually, I was hoping you would join me for a ride." Roric gestured behind him.

Della peered past him and saw his Stronghorse and another mounted rider.

"Who is that?" She arched a questioning brow.

"Well, I thought it best to have a friend accompany us in case we are seen to protect your reputation," Roric replied smoothly.

"Oh. That's very thoughtful of you." Della flashed him a sincere smile. No one had ever worried about propriety with her before. It was one of the many differences between being treated like a lady or a servant. The fact that he believed her to be a serving maid, yet still respected her reputation, was touching.

"So, would you like to come for a ride?" Roric prompted.

"Yes, I think I will. Do you mind if I change into a riding outfit first?"

"Of course."

"Would you and your friend like to come in and wait while I ready myself?" Della knew she couldn't leave them in the courtyard or others might see. She quelled a bit as she imagined her stepmother's fury at the rumors such a thing would start. Maybe she should just send them away. Della shook off the thought.

"I think we'll go into the stable and saddle your horse for you," Roric suggested instead.

Della breathed a sigh of relief. She couldn't imagine what the duchess would do if she returned early and found two lords in her parlor. It was unlikely since the duchess often overstayed her welcome at social events—a fact Della had overheard from gossiping servants—but the men staying outside still eased Della's mind. "Very well. I'll be down shortly."

Della closed the door and raced up the stairs so fast she was winded. She did have one riding habit. It was a sturdy fabric of a faded brown, but it fit and was much better for riding in than her regular attire. She took the kerchief off her head and instead pinned it up into a simple but elegant chignon. She changed quickly, hopping into her boots on each landing as she hurried back downstairs.

Della indeed found them in the stables. The family's sole remaining horse, Reynart, was bridled and saddled to perfection, to her surprise. Roric looked up from where he had been cinching the saddle.

"You—you have a Stronghorse!" Roric sounded surprised, standing there holding Reynart's reins.

"I thought you'd already been in my stables. Didn't you notice him?" Della asked Roric with a teasing grin.

"I was in a bit of a hurry," Roric said sheepishly. He rubbed the back of his neck with his free hand.

"He was the duke's horse. He is not bonded to anyone here and cannot be bonded to anyone else. Or will not. I'm not truly sure how choosing the bond works. I like to believe Stronghorses are fiercely loyal and thus refuse to bond with another even if sold or their person dies." Della took Reynart's reins and stroked him fondly. She didn't add that he truly couldn't be sold—no buyer would take a Stronghorse that had already been bonded, and the prestige of owning such an expensive creature, bonded or not, was enough to keep the duchess from sending him to the slaughterhouse. The other horses had all been sold, all of her father's work breeding specific bloodlines squandered, spread throughout the continent to various buyers like fallen leaves scattered in the wind.

Roric pulled Della out of her melancholy thoughts. "Della, this is my friend Pieter—"

"Lord Faust!" Della gasped and swept a curtsy. Della would recognize those icy blue eyes and hooked nose anywhere. He looked different with Roric, more relaxed and a smile hinted on his lips, making him look less pompous than the few times she had seen him ride through town. He was a few inches taller than Roric too, adding to the imperious impression he gave off.

"So, you know who I am." The future duke looked amused. Then his eyes narrowed as he looked her up and down, taking her in, and his lips tightened.

"Of course! Though I confess I'm surprised to see you here on such an errand."

"Roric is always roping me into things that might get me into trouble. We are rather close, having grown up together as boys."

"You've gotten me into a few scrapes as well," Roric retorted.

"Just because you get caught doesn't make it my fault." Lord Faust cast him a knowing grin.

"Well, shall we go?" Roric glanced around.

Della shook off the shock of having the future duke with them. Lord Faust was cousin to the princes. Roric certainly associated with the highest of society. If Lord Faust was his friend, he might even know the princes! They had better leave before Duchess DeVoss came home and tried to find a way to utilize the two noblemen on her property. "Yes, let's be on our way."

She had already swung up onto Reynart by the time she realized Roric had moved to help her up. She blushed in embarrassment, but Lord Faust let out an impressed whistle.

"The lady can mount a Stronghorse without help."

"I told you she was interesting." Roric grinned.

Della's heart fluttered. Roric had told his friend about her! He had brought him along on this outing as well. Did that mean Roric hoped for this to develop into a true courtship? Nerves shot through her at the thought of meeting his family.

"This is where the Lady Eleonora resides, isn't it? She isn't home by chance, is she?" Lord Faust sounded almost hopeful as they trotted through the courtyard out onto the street.

Della shook her head. "She's out until the evening."

"Just as planned so this outing could happen." Roric shot Lord Faust a look.

Of course. Roric must have arranged for her stepfamily to be invited out again. They were never gone so often. Gratitude swelled within Della. There was no way the duchess would have let Della ride off with a lord and a future duke! Instead, the two men would likely have been trapped inside with her stepfamily while Della served them all tea. Della shuddered at the thought.

They all three fell silent for a time as Roric nudged his horse into the lead. He rode along the edge of Widow's Court and crossed through a field heading towards the woods. Della wondered if he intended for them to go hunting, but the men had no arrows. Why were they heading into the woods?

"Where are we going?"

"There's a hill not too far from here where we will stop," Roric replied.

They wove through trees until they ended abruptly in a meadow. The entire place was covered in purple flowers. The smell hit her—a nostalgic smell of the bunched blooms her mother would put under Della's pillow when she was anxious. Della blinked back tears at the rare memory and her heart ached for the mother she wished she could remember better. She closed her eyes and breathed in, letting the scent relax her.

"Lavender," Della breathed, opening her eyes again to marvel at the sight. "I've never seen so much of it before!"

The flowers rippled gently in the breeze, reminding Della of the ocean on a calm day. A glorious purple ocean that smelled heavenly instead of briny, though both were tranquil places.

"The view is even better from up there," Roric said from her left.

He had pulled his horse up close to her and her heart leapt into her throat at the nearness. She followed his pointed finger to see a large hill rising above the sea of flowers and arcing almost above the tops of the trees. The three tied off their horses at the edge of the clearing near the base of the hill. They climbed up the wide mound leisurely. It had a gentle slope and took up most of one end of the clearing. Lavender grew in patches here and there, but hadn't fully overtaken the grass covering the hill.

The hill grew steeper towards the top and Della stumbled over a rock. She went sprawling toward the ground when strong arms caught her. Della looked up into Roric's very near face and thought he must be able to hear her heart with how violently it was thundering in her chest. He stared into her eyes for a long moment. Lord Faust cleared his throat and Roric quickly righted Della, though he took her hand in his as he led her up the rest of the way.

Della gasped in delight when she finally reached the top of the hill. To one side was the ocean of lavender, but on the other side she could see past the trees to the city. Even in the distance, she could easily make out the castle in the west. "It's a beautiful view."

"I like to come here to think sometimes." Roric smiled at her.

"So you do use that brain in there occasionally?" Lord Faust drawled.

Della glanced at him and saw he was laying out a large blanket. She had been so caught up with the meadow and Roric that she hadn't noticed him lugging a large basket up the hill. Della dropped Roric's hand and stepped toward Lord Faust. "Would you like some help?"

"Please." He gestured at the basket.

Della reached in and pulled out three plates, goblets, and silverware. She laid them out on the blanket and began setting out dishes of food with Lord Faust.

It was a rich feast—roasted duck sandwiches, meat pies, berry tarts, fresh fruit, and a sweet tea made specifically to be drunk cold—perfect for a picnic.

"My Lord Duke, do you know you are the talk of the season?" Della teased him before popping a grape into her mouth.

Lord Faust had been watching Roric, but he turned toward her at this. He cocked an eyebrow. "I would think the prince would be the talk of the season."

"Which one? The oldest is married. The second is now engaged, so the ladies only speak of him to lament their lost chance or praise his parents for throwing a ball in his honor so they may attend another lavish party." Della shrugged. She bit into a cherry tart and tried not to look like she was enjoying it too much. It was such a decadent feast that she was unlikely to experience anything like it again anytime soon.

"There's a third prince, you know. One who is quite unengaged." Lord Faust threw her a sly look.

Roric choked on the meat pie he had just bit into.

"Hmm, yes the ladies of the city do seem to share one solitary thought of him," Della said.

Roric only choked harder. He down a goblet of sweetened tea and came up gasping for air.

"What would that be?" Roric's voice was hoarse.

"That he is a lost cause they have all given up on. It seems he has given the impression that he isn't interested in courting any lady now or in the near future," Della replied airily.

"I certainly haven't seen him show favor to any lady of the court now that you mention it. Though I would think the opportunity to become a princess would tempt many ladies into still trying to catch his eye," Lord Faust said.

Della nodded agreeably. "One would think, but it seems he's been rather aloof so the majority have given up. When the point of being a princess is brought up, most tend to say he's only a third son. The second might give one the opportunity to become queen, but the third? Most wouldn't count on it. Though it's rather dark to imagine advancing one's social standing when it requires the demise of one's in-laws, if you ask me."

"When you put it that way, it makes me weary of all women in court." Roric laughed.

"You needn't worry, I haven't heard a single thing about you, Lord Roric. Though I suppose that would be because it's your given name—which is rather familiar of me to call you by, but it's the only name you've given me. Besides, you call me by my given name, after all." Della realized as she talked how little she knew about this man. They had only met three times, but the last time she had let him into her house unaccompanied. A situation that he had clearly not intended, but Della hadn't sent him away. He paid attention to her and saw her as a person rather than a maidservant, which felt wonderful. What's more, he had helped her with her chores! He was a rather unusual lord.

"It is my given name."

"What *is* your surname?" Della's curiosity was piqued. There was no lord she hadn't heard at least a few tidbits of gossip about. What did people who knew Lord Roric well think of him?

"What is *your* surname, maiden?" Lord Faust countered. He eyed her like a hawk assessing a field mouse.

Della clamped her mouth shut. She wasn't ashamed of who she was, but somehow it felt wrong to say her family's name when she had been thrust into such a low position. They probably wouldn't know the Aleecean nobility anyway, but if they did... She didn't want to tarnish her family's name. Shame filled her and she looked down.

"It's alright. I prefer it this way. Let's simply call each other Roric and Della. The lack of formality is refreshing." Roric covered her hand with his and squeezed. She looked up to see him smiling at her. He let go of her hand to pick up a square of sandwich, offering it to her. She took it with a shy smile of her own.

She glanced back at the field of lavender as she chewed and out of the corner of her eye she caught Roric flicking a grape at Lord Faust. The latter caught it, popping it into his mouth jovially. Then, moving so casually she almost missed it, Lord

Faust brushed at the edge of a dish so briskly that it sent a tomato flying back toward Roric, who dodged it effortlessly. A tiny smile played across her lips at their brotherly friendship.

Lord Faust turned his attention back to Della. "Has he told you how he once turned a ball into an indoor picnic?"

"That sounds quite fun." She looked questioningly at Roric.

"His mother certainly didn't think so." Lord Faust snickered.

"It was a dare from my older brother, Freddie. I should have known better as he likes to make mischief, but I was just a boy trying to prove I was as capable as my older brothers." Roric let out a long-suffering sigh.

Della looked at him curiously and motioned for him to continue as she chewed another bite of her sandwich.

"We were supposed to be in bed. Freddie convinced me—quite easily, I was only seven—to sneak down with him to spy on the party. I found the courtiers talking and dancing to be quite boring, and evidently Freddie did too. He dared me to go get him some food. It seemed an easy task to prove my bravery as all I had to do was slip in, get some food, and slip out. The consequences if I were caught were likely a light scolding and being sent back to bed at worst. Or so I thought.

"Getting down to the party was easy. Freddie took me down the servant's stairway and we hung back in the shadows while he pointed out what food he wanted. It all seemed rather easy, though I did find it odd that he wanted a particular melon that hadn't been sliced yet, but sometimes he found joy in chucking such things off high perches and watching it splatter on the ground the way young boys do so I brushed it off.

"My plan was simple—be as quick as possible to limit the likelihood of getting caught. I grabbed a plate and filled it with all the food my brother had specified. All that remained to grab was the melon. I set down the plate and used two hands to yank it towards me, planning to tuck it under one arm and carry the plate back with my other hand. Only I was so focused on being swift that I hadn't noticed that the carefully spaced uncut melons held up a large, tiered platter of food." Roric looked abashed.

"Oh no!" Della both laughed and winced at the mistake young Roric had made.

"Oh, *yes*." Lord Faust grinned in wicked delight.

"As you can imagine, the entire thing came tumbling down with a loud crash launching food across the floor." Roric cringed at the memory.

"It covered a few unfortunate courtiers too," Lord Faust added helpfully.

"When my mother's eyes locked on me, I felt a fear I'd never felt before as I saw the fury in them. Her perfect party was ruined. Fruit had rolled and bounced all over the floor, making it impossible for the dancing to continue, which doesn't bode well for a ball. Thankfully, my oldest brother, Henri, rushed in at that moment clutching an armful of blankets. He flung some out and handed off the rest to intermittent courtiers, declaring it was a surprise picnic he and his brothers had planned for them all. He tugged me out of the room before our mother could reach us and servants flooded in to gather up all the food that had fallen on the floor. We found Freddie back in our room, doubled over in laughter. Henri and I were forced to attend lessons on ball etiquette for an entire week, supervised by our mother. Freddie, as usual, escaped consequence by not being seen, despite having orchestrated the whole thing," Roric finished his tale and looked at her with apprehension in his eyes.

"That was quite kind of your oldest brother, to step in and try to salvage the ball for your mother and to try to help you," Della observed.

"He's always been like that. He takes his duties to the family and beyond very seriously. It's lucky for me that he was clever enough to think of something to save that particular evening. My mother's 'picnic ball' was considered the highlight of the season in the social papers that year and she forgave us when that came out."

"How could she not?" Della said. "Are you very close with your brothers?"

"I would say so. We have our differences, but we have a good time together and when it counts Freddie is truly loyal." Roric smiled, fondness crinkling his eyes.

"That sounds so nice," Della said a bit wistfully.

"Do you have any siblings?" Lord Faust asked her.

"Eleonora has always been a sister to me. I've also found the close kinship of sisterhood in a dear friend in town. We are sisters in all but blood, as we like to say."

"I can understand that." Lord Faust nodded. Della knew he was the only child the Duke and Duchess had, but clearly Roric was as good as a brother to him.

After eating and chatting for a while longer, Della stood up and stretched. "I should be getting back."

"We should as well," Lord Faust agreed, noting the position of the sun.

Roric and Lord Faust gathered up the dishes while Della repacked the food. The boys had tried to help her pack it at first, but stacked things so oddly that not everything could fit in the hamper despite there being significantly less food.

"I think I'd better do this part. You two can fold up the blanket." Della shooed them away.

It went much faster without their attempts to help and she was fastening the hamper'ss lid closed when Roric walked back over to her. He offered her his hand and helped her up. Once standing, she found herself surprisingly close to Roric with only the length of their clasped hands between them. She made to drop his hand and pull back, but he held her hand tighter so she couldn't move away.

"I'll take this blanket back down to the horses," Lord Faust called, rolling his eyes. Della barely heard him over the pounding of her heart.

"I- I had a lovely time." She blushed at her nervous stutter.

"I did too. I'd... Well, I don't think I should, but I'd like to see you again," Roric told her softly.

"It is a strange situation. The duchess would never approve." Della almost winced at the thought of her stepmother's anger. Still, she yearned to be near him.

"My mother most definitely wouldn't approve. Yet I can't seem to stay away," Roric told her.

"Then don't." Della surprised herself with her boldness.

"Be careful what you say. That sounds far too tempting." Roric smiled mischievously and took another step toward her, forcing him to drop their hands as the space between them shrank.

Della couldn't say anything. She could barely breathe. She knew she should step back, should put more space between them. Instead, she took a small step toward him herself. Their noses were almost touching. Her eyes dared him to back away first.

He didn't step back, however. He closed the gap and caught her lips up in his. Her hands flew up against his chest in shock, meaning to push him away, but instead she found herself melting into the kiss. It was as if a fire had ignited inside her blood, the heat of passion burned through her. Her hands crept up behind his neck and his arm found its way around her waist, the other cupping the back of her head. Della's mind swirled with heady confusion and pleasure. Her stomach thrummed as if she'd swallowed butterflies and pure delight flooded through her.

A horse neighed loudly, and they both turned their heads to look, breaking the kiss. Between two of the horses was Lord Faust, his arms crossed as he stared at them. Della's cheeks heated as she withdrew her hands and stepped back to catch her breath. Roric's hands reluctantly fell away from her waist as she put more distance between them. Della picked up the picnic basket and held it like a barrier between them. Roric was frowning as he stared down at the horses.

"Shall we go?" Della prompted.

"Oh, yes. Here, let me take that." Roric lifted the basket out of her arms and offered her his elbow.

Della took his arm, and they made their way down the hill. Once they reached Lord Faust and the horses, Della dropped Roric's arm and moved to untie her own horse.

"You did that on purpose, didn't you?" Roric muttered in a low voice to Lord Faust as the duke secured the basket to his horse's saddle.

"I'm sure I don't know what you mean," Lord Faust said a little too innocently as he swung up onto his horse.

"I'm thoroughly convinced." Roric rolled his eyes. He mounted his own horse, Della having already swung herself up on Reynart.

Della only smiled softly to herself. Even if Lord Faust had somehow bothered the horses into interrupting their kiss, she didn't mind. It was enough to have enjoyed the moment and to know that Roric had liked enough to be mildly annoyed at his friend's meddling.

They rode back through the edge of the woods in relative silence. Della's head was still reeling from the kiss and she couldn't seem to focus enough to bother making conversation. She had never been kissed before. She had always assumed it wouldn't happen until she returned to Aleece and had rebuilt a life for herself there. Somehow the thought of going back to her country wasn't as inviting as it had been before. Not that it mattered, as she still had to help Eleonora find love before Marien married anyway. She had more time in Tamaria and she was starting to actually enjoy it, to look forward to her days here.

Once they reached the field near Widow's Court Della pulled her horse to a stop. "I think it would be best if we part ways here."

"Nonsense, we can escort you home. It's no bother," Roric assured her.

"It's more the gossip that I fear. The way back is filled with townspeople and worse—widows with nothing better to do than watch at the windows so they have something to gossip about with their friends. There is not often much excitement in the streets of Widow's Court, so I worry a young lady with two young men would be the talk of the town very soon."

"We rode out that way together," Roric argued.

"All the more reason not to return together. Especially if the future duke is recognized," Della told him pointedly.

Lord Faust snorted and Roric's face looked strained. Della nudged her horse close to Roric's. Della laid her hand on his arm reassuringly. His eyes met hers with a look that had her stomach thrumming again. She resisted the urge to lean toward him, reminding herself she could fall off her horse.

"I'll be fine. It's daylight and I'm heading into town. The way is safe. I must be home before the duchess returns." Della lifted her hand off his arm.

"Then go safely and swiftly, my lady." Roric caught her hand in his and pressed a kiss to it. She smiled before turning to his friend.

"Lord Faust." Della nodded a polite goodbye that he returned.

She gently kicked Reynart's flank and rode back home. Della thought again of the kiss on the hill above a purple sea of flowers and a shining city. Her stomach did a flip and she grinned. She bent low on Reynart's neck and pressed a kiss there too.

"I had the most wonderful time!" she whispered. She let out a blissful sigh.

When she reached the street their house was on, she saw to her horror a carriage turning onto the cobblestone drive. Panic flooded through her and she pulled Reynart to a stop, trying to decide if she should wait for them to enter the house or ride up now. In the end, her fear paralyzed her and she waited in the distance until the three figures disappeared through the door. Then she hurried Reynart toward the house, swinging off and leading him into the barn. She quickly removed the saddle and bridle.

"I'll come brush you down as soon as I can," she promised him.

Della hurried into the house from the kitchen's back door. The call bell was ringing violently at her. Della rushed into the hall ready to race upstairs, but her stepfamily was still standing in the entranceway.

"Della! There you are! Make us some tea and come help us change into more comfortable—where on earth have *you* been?" Her stepmother's angry voice cracked like a whip when she caught sight of Della.

Della winced and realized too late she was wearing her riding outfit. Though plain, it wasn't shabby, and it seemed to irritate Duchess DeVoss to see her in it. Della wasn't sure if it was the idea of her riding leisurely or that she looked like a respectable young lady in the attire that irritated her stepmother so.

"I took Reynart for a ride. To exercise his muscles."

The slap caught her off guard and sent her reeling to the side, landing on her hands and knees. Della gasped and held her cheek even as her knees throbbed from taking the brunt of her fall.

"Insolent girl! Who told you that you could take the afternoon off? I look after you all this time and *all* I require is you contribute to this household, and this is what you do? You lazy vagrant!" Duchess DeVoss screeched.

Della riled at being called lazy, but bit her tongue. The duchess was in one of the worst moods she had seen her in, and Della didn't particularly want to be slapped again. She clenched her jaw and stood up outside the woman's reach. "I'll go make the tea."

"Wait! Take these first." Duchess DeVoss shoved her hat and wrap into Della's arms.

Marien followed suit and Eleonora did too, with a look of pleading regret in her eyes. Della held back a sigh. They were already going up, but now she'd have to put all these down, then make the tea, then carry the hats and wraps up while the kettle boiled, then come back down again to make the tea tray and bring all that up too. She glared at the stairs.

"You smell of horses, cinder girl. Make sure you don't get that smell on my things," Marien called from the stairs before ascending after her mother with her nose in the air.

Della somehow refrained from banging the tea things on every surface that she set them on as she prepped the tea tray. Her legs protested as she climbed the stairs and put the women's things away in their respective rooms, then went back down to the kitchen. She winced at the pain as she ascended yet again with the now ready tray.

"Today was an absolute waste of our time. The ratio of young ladies to eligible gentlemen was positively depressing," Duchess Devoss lamented as Della brought in the tea.

"Of the men there, there weren't many of decent means." Marien sniffed as if she had been personally affronted.

Della barely kept herself from rolling her eyes. Most of the eligible men had plenty of funds, but Marien and the duchess wanted men who had enough money that they didn't have to worry about any sort of frugality when spending it extravagantly every day.

"Lord Dalman was there, and Lord Kraus," Eleonora mentioned two rather wealthy lords.

"They hardly count with only the title of Lord," Marien huffed.

"Where could they all have run off to?" Duchess DeVoss asked irritably. "Not even the duke's son was there!"

"That was odd. He's almost always at social functions. Even his mother seemed confused to not see him there," Eleonora agreed.

Della had to fight to keep the grin off her face. *She* had spent the afternoon with the future duke while her stepfamily had mourned his absence. Not that she had any interest in Lord Faust, but the irony of the situation still caused a thrill in her stomach. She had enjoyed the afternoon with Roric, who must be the least wealthy lord in Fellsantra to not ever be mentioned by her stepfamily. Della was sure she had heard all the wealthy lord's given names at least once by now. She barely heard her stepfamily's bickering as she tidied the room, lost in reliving the afternoon she'd just had.

"You spoke with his mother? Very well, do keep at it. She seems to like you and it's better for Marien if we are in her good graces. Just imagine the thought of not knowing where your children are, though!" Duchess DeVoss exclaimed. She didn't notice that Eleonora had stiffened at her words.

"The youngest prince wasn't there either," Marien practically wailed.

"He's almost never at such functions, though. The oldest prince wasn't either. I'm sure as princes they're very busy," Eleonora pointed out.

"He's the third prince, how busy can he be?" their mother snapped irritably.

"Well, they are putting on a ball—" Eleonora started to say.

"To be a princess though. Even a third prince would be a decent catch," Marien sighed dreamily talking over Eleonora as if she didn't exist.

"You must look *perfect* for the ball. It might be in honor of Prince Frederick's engagement, but that means the youngest prince is sure to be there. It may be our only chance," Duchess DeVoss said fervently.

"Being married to the youngest prince sounds lovely now that I've thought about it. All the luxuries of being a princess with none of the boring responsibilities," Marien declared as she settled down to lounge on a chaise.

"You make an excellent point, my darling." The duchess curved her lips into a catlike grin.

Della held back a snort—she was in enough trouble as it is without contradicting them today. Honestly, did they really think such a position would hold no responsibilities beyond being waited on and feasting? They probably did, she realized and sighed internally. She wondered what responsibilities would be required for the wife of Lord Roric. Her face flushed at the idea, but where was the harm in a daydream? She hummed dreamily to herself as she left to brush Reynart down and give him some well-deserved oats.

CHAPTER THIRTEEN

D ella enjoyed the long walk to the market. Widow's Court was on the far edge of town away from the bustling noise so many merchants made specific deliveries to the old women who lived there. They had offered to do the same for Della to spare her the long walk, but she had long since dissuaded them so that she could have the excuse to stretch her legs and gain a bit more time to herself. She swung her basket happily as she walked. She had found a large clump of one of the rarer mushrooms. When she had spotted the honeycombed tops in the forest the previous evening, she'd let out a joyful squeal. She could trade them easily in the market as food or to the doctors in the city as medicine, either for a decent price. It wouldn't cover the cost she owed Franci, but it would at least make a small dent in the ever-growing amount she owed her friend.

A carriage rode up next to Della and the footman hopped down, opening the door directly into her path. Della moved to step around, but as she did so the person in the carriage cleared their throat. Della reflexively looked toward the sound and Lord Faust smirked back.

"Do join me." He gestured at the bench across from him. When she hesitated he added, "I don't bite. I also don't pick up random maids on the street, but you can probably guess who sent me."

That was all it took for Della to climb into the carriage. She settled into her seat as they started moving. "Roric sent you to find me?"

"To deliver you to him. Who else?" His tone was bored, but his eyes sharpened. "*Is* there someone else competing for your affections?"

"No, of course not. I just hadn't expected..." Della waved a hand at Lord Faust and the carriage.

"People would talk if I had picked you up from the home of the duchess. This was less conspicuous." Lord Faust straightened his already impeccable sleeve.

"It wasn't simply you stopping to get me now. It's all of this. The meetings, the attention, the effort Roric puts into seeing me. I'm not used to it. I'd never have expected such a thing," Della told him honestly.

"Because you're a maid," Lord Faust said flatly.

"Because I'm not noticed in that way. Certainly not by noblemen," Della corrected.

"Because you're a maid." He said it as if it were the most obvious thing in the world, and the only thing that mattered.

Della's voice was quiet, but firm. "You know nothing of my position."

"Then tell me! I'd love to learn all about you—your name, your position, anything I don't already know, which does seem to be very little." A challenge gleamed in Lord Faust's eyes.

Della looked out the window. Lord Faust settled back in an exaggerated nonchalance with his hands behind his head and one foot resting on the opposite knee.

She frowned at him. "You dislike me."

"I dislike deception, and we don't even know your sur-name. I care for Th—Roric. I can see a thousand ways this can go wrong and ruin him." Lord Faust sat up straight.

"Everything I have told him, told you, is the truth, and so is this—I would never do anything to hurt him." Della looked Lord Faust in the eye.

"Then why do you let this charade go on? You must know you can never be with him. A maid with someone in his position? He knows it is impossible too, but you continue to smile at him, charming him, being oh so alluring until he can't stay away. If you truly cared for him, you would end it."

"You say he has lost his senses because of me, is powerless to stop seeing me, as if I am controlling him. Yet I do not know where he lives. I do not even know his surname! I couldn't seek him out if I wanted to. If he is so charmed by me, wouldn't he have told me how I might find him if I wished? Yes, I do wish it because he has been kind to me and I enjoy his company." Della swallowed. Why hadn't he told her where he lived? Perhaps it was be an oversight on his part as in Tamaria a man went to a woman to court her, the woman did not go to the gentleman's home without an invitation. Such a thing was considered scandalous here, though it made Della want to roll her eyes. "I was also raised to believe titles matter less than love. If he wishes to seek me out and I wish to see him, then why should I send him away?"

"Because this will only end in tragedy." Lord Faust sat back, resigned.

"It doesn't have to be that way."

"It is the way things are. You are not in Aleece any longer. A serving maid cannot marry higher than a merchant. If this comes out, *you* will be ruined. Put an end to it before it goes that far."

Della wanted to shake the future duke. "You came with Roric the last time. You came to get me today. *You* seem to be the one most able to stop him out of the three of us. If you oppose this so much, why don't you?"

"I cannot command him, only counsel him. He knows my view on this, yet he continues this dalliance. So, I help only to prevent him from any blunders that might cause a scandal for him." Lord Faust rubbed the bridge of his nose wearily.

"I would never do anything to tarnish his reputation."

"Being seen so familiar with a servant would be enough." Lord Faust's eyes swept over her from head to toe, condemning her with that rapid evaluation.

"He must think it's worth it," Della countered, her heart swelling at the thought. Lord Faust thought this was impossible, had told Roric as much, yet he continued to see her. He must want something more, he had to believe it was possible for them to be together.

Lord Faust only stared at her gravely. Then he blinked and grabbed a package that Della hadn't noticed on the seat next to him. He tossed it into her lap. "Courtesy of Roric. You are to change into that when we arrive."

Della opened the package and found a powder blue riding outfit complete with one of the riding hats that were so in fashion among the ladies of Fellsantra. Underneath lay a pair of gleaming brown riding boots. A note lay on top of the outfit.

I thought this color would bring out your eyes exquisitely.

"It's too much." Della looked up at Lord Faust.

"You tell *him* that. Before you do though, consider how dressing like a proper lady may help fend off some forms of gossip." He pressed his lips together in a tight, displeased line as if it pained him to aid their time together.

"Did he pick this, or did you?"

"He wanted to get you a gift. I might have steered him toward something that would be useful as well." Lord Faust shrugged.

Della frowned and they didn't speak for the rest of the ride. When the carriage at last halted, Lord Faust opened the door and hopped out.

"You'll need to change in here." He snapped the door shut on her.

Della glowered at the command in his voice and the rudeness of shutting the door on her face. She found she could stand inside the carriage—it was nothing like the cramped hired carriages her stepfamily paid for. She made sure the curtains were closed tightly before she stripped down to her underthings. The muslin riding habit was soft and cool against her skin as she pulled it on. Della luxuriated in the fabric she hadn't worn since she was a little girl. Even her worn brown riding habit was made of cambric, still soft, but made for cooler months when the wind created by riding would chill her. Della noted small stars embroidered on the bodice and hem in silver thread.

Dressed, Della removed the kerchief from around her head. She rolled the fabric and used it to tie her waves back into a low ponytail before pinning the hat atop her head with the provided hat pins. She neatly folded her shirt, skirt, and apron before placing them in her basket on the bench. Hoping she hadn't taken an awkwardly long time while getting ready, Della opened the carriage door and stepped out.

Chapter Fourteen

Joy and grief warred within Della at the all too familiar sight before her. They had come to a horse trader's home. Two of the three fenced rings held horses of various colors and sizes. The trader's large house sat in the distance. He likely sold the bulk of the courtier's horses to have a home that size. Memories cascaded through Della's mind—large, calloused hands showing her child sized ones how to brush a horse, lead it with a rope, and the promise that had hung between them to let her ride a wild horse and learn to train it when she was older. A larger promise of her very own Stronghorse. That one stung the most.

"Ah, here the lady is now!" Roric said warmly, coming up to help her down from the carriage.

The horse trader inclined his head to her in an overly polite nod, his expression showing he didn't think a woman should have any part of horse trading. Della raised her chin and looked him over imperiously. He was a lanky man, dark hair streaked with gray, with a pointed nose and chin. He was taller than Della, but the same height as Roric, and the latter would likely grow a few more inches in the next couple of years. The trader's eyes narrowed at her appraisal.

"Della, this is Cheval. He's a favored horse trader among my family. Cheval, this is the Lady Della, who has a love of horses," Roric introduced them.

"Perhaps the lady would like to look over the mares. I have some quite gentle ones." Cheval's eyes gleamed at the potential sale.

"Perhaps his lordship here could use a nice, gentle mare. Although he seems to have improved his riding since we first met." Della gave Roric a teasing grin.

Cheval choked.

"Lady Della can certainly handle herself on any horse, including stallions and Stronghorses." Roric smiled at her.

Della's heart warmed at his praise.

"My *Lord*, is the rumor true that you have acquired a new Stronghorse?" Cheval changed the subject, sounding somewhat disappointed about the lord's new acquisition.

"Yes, though that was more of a happy accident than anything else. My father bought it from across the seas. I happened to be the one that bonded with it. They are notoriously hard to obtain, as you well know, so do not think your services are no longer appreciated or needed. It was simply part of an ongoing search," Roric replied.

"Of course." Cheval bowed low, though Della wasn't sure the man actually felt any humility.

"Which brings us to why we are here. Why don't you show us what prized horses you have for sale?" Roric smoothed over the man's disappointment with the balm of a potential purchase.

"Right this way, S—My Lord." Cheval shot a sideways glance at Della. "Perhaps the lady would like to take refreshments in the house with my wife and daughters?"

"She will be examining the horses with us," Roric told him firmly.

"As you wish. Right this way." Cheval led them over to a corral that held several horses.

Despite the ornery trader, Della drank in the sight of the beautiful creatures. It had been a long time since she had seen so many horses together in one place. The familiar sounds of stomping hooves and soft whinnies washed over her.

"That gray stallion over there is a fine specimen from the mountains of Lycaria. Those horses are excellent at climbing stone cliffs and are exceptionally surefooted." The trader indicated one horse.

Della looked over the steed while he talked. The horse's coat was a mix of soft and darker gray hairs that must blend in well on the Lycarian mountains. The country of Lycaria was known for its craggy peaks that housed more than Strong-horses. The horse's legs were longer, but somewhat thinner than the other horses around it, with small hooves. Perfect for scaling steep ridges. Della glanced at Roric, who looked intrigued as he assessed the horse.

Della let her expertise roll off her tongue, a rare occurrence for her in this country, and one that she relished. "Lycarian horses are indeed great at scaling mountains and cliffs. Some Aleeceans are partial to them if they like to navigate down the Great Cliffs to the beach below. However, a Lycarian horse is not very practical for someone in Tamaria, where there are no rocky cliffs, only grassy hillsides. They are also not suited to carrying heavier passengers like soldiers in full armor because of their thinner legs. They can't be used as pack or cart horses for this reason as well, and thus aren't very useful for travel. They are better for places with more stone than grass."

The trader frowned at her words.

"The lady speaks true, I have no need for such a horse. Though if there were any stony mountains nearby you can be assured I would purchase one in a heartbeat. If only for the adventure of climbing such a difficult path that would otherwise be impossible." Roric's gaze moved past the Lycarian horse.

"Perhaps you would prefer a horse in the Stronghorse family. This horse has Stronghorse blood, which can increase the likelihood of a Stronghorse offspring when mated with one that also has the blood, or perhaps a pureblood like your own." Cheval grasped the halter of a large black horse. The horse was indeed larger than the others around it, though not as tall as a true Stronghorse.

Della shook her head. "There has never been a Stronghorse born from anything besides a pair of Stronghorses."

The trader glowered at Della for countering him yet again, but he quickly forced a smile. Della gave him an easy, soft smile back.

"Perhaps not yet, but the potential is there," the trader said tightly.

"With respect, sir, it is highly improbable. There are so many traders and breeders who have dedicated time trying to produce Stronghorses in order to make their fortunes. There have been only horses with half blood or less, but never any true Stronghorses produced from anything besides a pair of true, pureblood Stronghorses. Only a true Stronghorse has the bond. Without the bond, all that one has is a horse that is larger and perhaps somewhat more intelligent than its peers, but a horse with Stronghorse blood is not worth the price when you are essentially still getting just a horse." Della kept her tone courteous, but the trader's face was turning red with anger.

"One simply cannot undervalue the bloodline of a horse, whether or not it has the bond." Cheval clenched his fists in irritation.

"I could tell you that I have the blood of royalty, yet without the title it does me no good in Tamaria. I cannot own my own land here or hold a place in court. A Stronghorse without the bond is like a person without a title—their bloodline alone isn't enough." Della's heart quickened at her honesty regarding her background, but the men around her dismissed it as a mere example rather than a pearl of truth.

"The lady makes an interesting case." Lord Faust surprised Della with his comment. She shot him a startled glance, to which he only shrugged.

"You don't happen to have any leads on a Stronghorse, do you?" Roric sounded only slightly hopeful.

"I'm afraid not Your H—" he coughed. "—Lordship. They are very difficult to find and even more difficult to catch. I only know of one breeder who has a pair they keep and even they have only produced three Stronghorses in the decade they have had them." Cheval shook his head.

"True purebreds can produce regular horses?" Lord Faust looked incredulous.

"No, it's only that they do not procreate every year. When one is trying to produce a pureblood, they must only breed the Stronghorse with another pureblood, so there is less chance of a foal. They also don't seem to reproduce as often from what the reports around the world say." Cheval shrugged.

"Perhaps it is a form of self-preservation. Horses can live up to thirty years, yet Stronghorses have been noted to live closer to forty or so. Couple that with the fact that they are more durable than other horses, so experience fewer injuries, which helps guarantee more of them survive for longer. If they produced offspring every breeding season, then surely they would overpopulate their areas and begin to deplete their food sources," Della mused.

"That's a very interesting theory. I shall have to inquire about it further." Roric was contemplative.

"Well, I don't know about all that, only that they are a scarce breed that everyone desires." The trader folded his arms.

"It's a shame. A Stronghorse would make a wonderful gift for my brother. He could use some cheering up."

Della wondered what had Roric's brother feeling down. Her mind whirled through remedies to recommend if he was ill. Though if a horse would cheer him up, then he was likely fit enough to ride. Perhaps a quarrel with a friend or a falling out with a woman he was courting. Whatever it was, it was sweet of Roric to look for ways to lift his brother's spirits. Her heart warmed at his kindness.

"Freddie doesn't need to cheer up, he needs to grow up," Lord Faust muttered.

"I believe growing up is what got him into this woebegone situation in the first place." Roric laughed. He looked back at the trader. "Do let me know if you get any leads on one."

"You shall be the very first to hear of it," Cheval promised.

"Do you see any horses you like?" Roric turned to Della.

The trader eyed her again, his expression warring between dislike and the shrewd eagerness of a potential sale.

"Though there are some fair horses here, I would hate to bring a new one home and make Reynart jealous," Della replied. There was no way Duchess DeVoss wouldn't notice a new horse in their stables even if she could afford one. She didn't think Roric was offering to purchase one for her, but she couldn't be sure, so it was better to dissuade him of the notion just in case. With their finances as they were, Della couldn't possibly explain a new horse away. She would either be blamed for stealing the money or stealing the horse, and if Della even tried to explain about Lord Roric...Well, Della didn't think the duchess would take kindly to that either.

"Reynart, did you say? Is that your father's name?" Cheval squinted his eyes.

"No, he's a horse." Della laughed.

"I thought it sounded familiar, but perhaps not." Cheval shrugged it off.

Della's stomach dropped. Had Cheval known her father? Many horse traders knew each other, or at least knew of the others. From what Della knew, her father had been quite renowned, but she wasn't sure how far that extended beyond Aleece. She had never inquired after his name in Tamaria, as she didn't want to get any questions asked of her in return. The duchess had only allowed Della to leave the house a year after they had moved here on the condition that Della never reveal who she was. Della had been so desperate to get outside that she had agreed, though she later confided in Franci about her lineage despite the command.

"It is a Stronghorse. Surely there are so few that you've heard of them all." Lord Faust looked meaningfully at Cheval, but the trader only shook his head.

"It wasn't one that I sold. Perhaps I heard of it in passing. That is fairly common when it comes to that breed. You ride a Stronghorse?" Cheval appraised her jealously.

"It is the family Stronghorse, not mine. He was bonded long ago."

"Ah." He nodded as if that made much more sense to him than her riding such a powerful steed. She felt a flash of irritation.

Roric gestured to a large black stallion. "I would like to ride that one."

"I will ready him immediately." Cheval led the steed out of his corral to the empty one which Della knew was kept empty so buyers could ride potential purchases. The trader grabbed a saddle blanket, saddle, and bridle that had been hanging on the fence of the corral and worked to saddle the horse with surprising speed.

"Do you think you will purchase him?" Della looked up at Roric. Standing so close their height difference made her tip her head back to see his face.

"I don't know. I shall ride him and find out."

They walked over to the corral where Cheval prepared the horse.

"He is ready for you." Cheval bowed low and held open the gate.

Roric took Della's hand and pulled her into the corral with him.

"What are you doing?" Della didn't resist him though, admittedly because she was enjoying the feel of her hand in his, even through the gloves. It was the intimacy of it—no one else touched her like this.

"I want your opinion. You know far more than I do about horses."

Della opened her mouth, but all that came out was a squeak when Roric lifted her up by her waist onto the stallion. Her face flushed at Cheval's concerned look. He likely thought she had shrieked out of fear rather than surprise.

"I would be happy to fetch a sidesaddle for the lady if you wish her to ride." Cheval started to turn toward his large stable.

"I don't think we'd fit comfortably on such a saddle." Roric's tone was cheerful as he swung up behind her.

"I'm not sure we fit comfortably now." Della went rigid at the closeness of their bodies, trying to shift away from Roric, but there was no room.

"Are you uncomfortable, my lady?" Roric's voice was soft and laced with concern, but her stomach fluttered at hearing it in her ear, making it hard to focus on what he was asking.

"I—it's only that—well!" Della looked helplessly at Lord Faust, who shot her a withering stare. She lifted her chin. "Actually, I am comfortable, as impractical as this is."

Roric chuckled softly in her ear. "Good. I'm quite enjoying this, but would dismount immediately if you were not as well."

Roric settled a hand on the saddle horn and the other wrapped around her waist. He gently tugged her back and she relaxed against his chest. It felt warm and safe sitting here between his arms. Della picked up the reins for him.

"Go on, then," Roric encouraged.

"Do you mean for me to lead?"

"Of course. I know that you are a skilled horsewoman. It's time to remove Cheval's doubts as well. The man is becoming unbearable. Had I known how he would treat you, I wouldn't have brought you here. As I've never brought a lady here before, I had no grounds to suspect such a thing. As he hasn't been outright disrespectful, I cannot put him in his place, but *you* can, which is honestly better. I've seen you ride. Show him that you can handle the largest stallion he has."

Della's heart swelled with Roric's kindness. He had provided her with a way to fight this battle for respect. It was clear

Cheval would never have let her ride this stallion had she asked. She tapped the horse with her heels and they started off at a trot as Della let the horse adjust to the two riders.

"Do you think this horse really has the blood of a Stronghorse?" Roric's breath tickled her ear at his question.

"Probably. It is larger than average. We could test the theory."

"Test it how?"

Della only grinned and spurred the horse into a gallop. They circled the corral twice before she steered the stallion into a straight line.

"Della! If it rears—"

"Scared of the challenge, my lord? I might be too, had I had your first Stronghorse experience." Della grinned.

"I was only frightened for you should we be tossed off," Roric growled in her ear.

"It wouldn't be the first time I've been tossed off a horse. You're not the only one who has stolen a horse from their father. Anyway, I would think you might cushion the fall as you're sitting behind me. However, if you wish me to stop us, I will oblige." Della eyed the shortening distance between them and the fence.

"You are full of wonder and mystery."

"If you would like me to stop us, I must turn the horse now," Della prompted.

"Roric!" Lord Faust's yell sounded horrified.

Cheval's face contorted in panic. "Lady, you must turn the horse!"

Roric's breath was warm on her ear. "I trust you."

"As I'm trusting this horse and the word of the trader, but I don't know either very well." Della kept the steed on course despite her words. It *should* be powerful enough from the muscles and stature that she had sized up. If she was wrong... Well, she wouldn't doubt herself now.

Roric's arm tightened around Della's waist as the horse leapt. Della grinned and Roric let out a whoop. The horse sailed over the tall corral fence—a feat that a regular horse would not have been able to accomplish—and landed at a gallop racing past the two watching men. She gave the horse its head and it raced along the expanse of grass. The wind tugged at her bound hair and a thrill rose in her stomach. She wished they could ride forever, with Roric's muscled body against her back. Just the wind and a horse, and Roric—that would be enough for her to be happy for the rest of her days. Della tightened the reins enough to be back in full control, leading it into a galloping circle. They went around the pastures and the manor before Della slowed the horse back to a trot.

She let out a delighted laugh. "I think it's definitely part Stronghorse."

"Stop here," Roric said when they were halfway back to the pastures.

"Why?" Had she frightened him with the jump? Or was he angry she had let the horse keep going afterward? Her stomach tightened as she pulled the horse to a halt. Della could see the two men they had left behind racing towards them.

"Because—" Roric dismounted and swept her down after him. "—we only have a few moments where the horse will block us from view and I want to do this."

Roric pulled her into a kiss that was wild, rushed, and passionate. Della felt as if she was bursting into flames from the heat and desire of it. He broke it off and stepped away as footsteps reached them from the other side of the horse.

"What do you think you were doing?!" Lord Faust demanded when he rounded the horse. Della flinched from the fury in his eyes. She got the feeling that he would flay her alive if he could.

"You could have been hurt!" Cheval looked Roric over.

"We were just having a bit of fun." Roric placed his arm around her waist and drew her to him protectively. "You did say the stallion was part Stronghorse after all."

Cheval gaped and Lord Faust narrowed his eyes at his friend.

"No one was hurt, and I have made up my mind. I will purchase this stallion for Freddie. It's a fine steed, and he will certainly enjoy leaping over fences with it."

Cheval brightened. He led the horse back to the solitary corral and left to get the papers for the steed. Della pictured a man a few years older than Roric leaping over fences and bushes with the horse. She found she was happy to see the horse find a home with someone who would truly appreciate it. She hoped Freddie knew how to take care of horses, or that Roric taught him at least.

"You cannot be so reckless! Your mother would have my head if you got hurt."

"Pieter, calm down. I've gotten plenty bruised up before and the blame always fell squarely on my own head."

Lord Faust looked furious, but didn't respond to his friend. Instead, he shot a glare at Della.

Cheval chose that moment to reappear. "Shall I bring the horse and papers up to you after I've brushed him down?"

Roric nodded. "That would be perfect."

"Would you show me that dappled horse over there?" An irritable Lord Faust asked the trader.

"Of course, my lord." Cheval walked with him to the far end of the corral.

Della reached up to pet the nose of a sand-colored horse. The horse leaned into her touch, shifting to stand closer. Della stroked its cheek up to its neck and down its flank. The horse snuffled her hair appreciatively.

"You truly love the creatures, don't you?" Roric moved so close to her side that their arms brushed.

"I spent the happiest years of my life around them. I grew up in a place not too different from this, though instead of the many fields there were acres of trees. Each tree had to be painstakingly removed in order to add each pasture or corral." Della was still stroking the horse, trying to distract herself from the way her stomach quivered at his nearness.

"Do you miss Aleece greatly?"

"I miss it with all my heart. It's not that I haven't found any happiness here, I have some very dear friends, it's just that my country always held so much magic and wonder. The geography and culture create such a different environment. Even the fact that people marry for love more than caring about what wealth or status they can gain from matrimony. Including the royals wherever possible. There's a sort of magic in that. My parents were very happy together. In some ways, the great sorrow I sometimes saw in my father's eyes after my mother's death was a testament to how much joy their union had held. I want something like that. I want to live in a place where I can have that." Della blushed at telling him such a thing. Would he think she was trying to be forward? She hadn't meant it like that, hadn't meant to spill the dream she kept so tightly inside like a secret.

"It's a pity that the Deep Woods make it so dangerous to go back and forth. Trade routes and society would benefit from being closer. Perhaps Tamaria would have become more relaxed about intermixing between social classes by now. Though I must admit that I never thought about it much before I met you." Roric cleared his throat. "It must have been hard to lose your family and your country so young."

Della nodded. "Sometimes I wonder if it truly was as magical as I remember, or if it was because I was viewing it with the marveling eyes of a child. I'll find out someday."

"Does that mean you are planning to return to Aleece eventually?" Roric regarded her.

"I always planned to. Though that was before...It would be difficult to leave now. I would miss Franci and Barend and Johanna. And the stars. There are too many trees to see the stars the way you can here. Sometimes I go out at night just to lie on the ground and look up at them stretching on and on as far as the eye can see. I could see some from my home in Aleece, of course, since we had cleared the trees, but there was always a border of treetops hedging them in."

"My tutors told me that the trees grew so thickly in Aleece that even the capital extends into the forest."

"It's true. Sometimes I miss them. When I first came here it all felt too open. It frightened me a little, can you imagine that?" Della laughed at her younger self. The laugh died away quickly as she thought about how that fear had made her willing to stay inside as the duchess had ordered. How she had fallen from nobility to servant without realizing it was happening.

Della gave him a shy smile. How had he seen into her soul like that? He had seen and understood instead of laughing at her. He truly had a kind heart.

"I suppose that trees would give you a place to hide or something to climb if you were in danger, whereas the grassy plains here don't offer the same protection." Roric gave her a kind smile. "When I was little, I was afraid of thunderstorms. Well, the lightning in them I suppose."

"You were?" Della's heart melted at the thought of a young Roric huddled beneath his blankets when lightning clapped.

"Yes. For a time, I had a cantankerous nursemaid who told me a story about the storms. She said they only came when little boys had done something bad, the thunder yelling chastisements so loud our mortal ears couldn't hear them. The lightning struck any who did not confess and beg forgiveness for whatever grievance they had committed. I'm embarrassed to say I admitted far too many of my misdeeds during stormy weather out of fear of being fried to a crisp." Roric's face reddened.

"I can't decide if that nursemaid was clever or just cruel."

"She was both. She left us a few years later and I was never more relieved." Roric shook his head. "I never told anyone that story. Only my brothers knew, since they had also confessed to her under the same duress." He cocked his head. "Something about you makes me confess my flaws."

"Perhaps as a lord you've never truly known if people accept your flaws or keep close to you due to your position." Della was suddenly grateful she knew there were people who loved her no matter her social standing.

"You don't know how right you are," he said softly.

Roric fell into a thoughtful silence. He reached up and stroked the same sandy horse. His chest rested against Della's shoulder and as he ran his hand down the horse his fingers slid over hers. She looked at him over her shoulder to find his face only inches from hers. He met her gaze, then his eyes dropped to her lips. Her breath grew shallow. Was he going to kiss her again?

"Well, we should go!" Lord Faust said loudly from a few feet behind them.

Della jumped and Roric whipped around to face him. Cheval was standing nearby looking particularly agitated.

"Impeccable timing as always, Pieter," Roric said dryly.

"I do enjoy a well-timed entrance," Lord Faust grinned.

"You and I define well-timed differently."

"I should be getting back anyway," Della stepped away from the horses.

"Let us go then." Roric walked her back to the carriage.

Roric helped Della up, then climbed in himself. He glanced at the two seats and settled himself on the same one as Della. The back of their hands brushed. Lord Faust frowned when he entered the carriage and found the lone empty seat. The footman shut the door as he sat down, and the carriage began moving a few moments later.

"Thank you for coming today."

"Thank you for bringing me. I loved seeing the horses." Della smiled at him.

"I loved seeing you."

Della blushed. Lord Faust snorted. Roric glared at him and Lord Faust rolled his eyes before turning to stare intently out the window.

"Ignore Pieter. He's fallen for a girl with a rather repugnant mother and he's too cowardly to pursue her with such an obstacle. Shows of affection only rankle him at the moment." Roric winked.

"Well, it can be difficult if the mother of your beloved is unpleasant and living in the same city, and you marry into that. I can understand his hesitation to pursue her."

"I suggested he simply wed the girl, sweep her away to his manor, and be done with it." Roric grinned.

"That would put me in the unfortunate situation of having the obligation to invite her mother to every social event. I'm not sure who would hate me more—society or myself." Lord Faust scowled.

"That is a perplexing problem. I suppose you shall have to decide whether you like the girl more than you hate her mother, or if it's the other way around." Della wasn't sure what she would do in such a situation, but that seemed the most obvious thing to consider. Della wondered for a moment if Lord Faust might be speaking of Eleonora. He *had* asked if she was home the day they went out riding, and Duchess DeVoss was quite odious. She made a mental note to ask Eleonora how she felt about the future duke. Perhaps her stepsister's chance at love was closer than they had realized.

"I haven't made up my mind about it yet," Lord Faust grumbled.

"He's lying. He won't entertain any other girl. He just hasn't admitted his feelings to himself yet," Roric whispered loudly to her.

Lord Faust crossed his arms and sulked in his seat, pointedly ignoring Roric's comment.

"Well, I do hope she wins him over soon. Or that she doesn't fall for another gentleman while he is coming to terms with the situation," Della pretended to whisper back.

Lord Faust shot up straight in his seat, looking alarmed.

"What is it, Pieter?" Roric raised his eyebrows, fighting a grin.

"Nothing. Absolutely nothing," Lord Faust said sourly.

CHAPTER FIFTEEN

Della stepped out of the carriage on an unoccupied side street in town. She took a few steps and realized she was still wearing the soft, powder blue riding habit. Della kept her head down and hurried to Franci's shop.

"Can I help—Della?" Franci's jaw dropped as she recognized her.

"Can I use the back room to change?" Della moved before her friend could answer.

"Where did you get that? You let someone else dress you?" Franci sounded both shocked and hurt as she followed Della back.

"Someone gave it to me to look more presentable to go see some horses." Della peeled off the luxurious feeling fabric.

"Your stepmother is trying to buy horses? Surely even she knows she can't afford that. Reynart I can understand, but the upkeep of another pair of horses..." Franci shook her head.

"No, she wasn't the one buying them. It was...a friend who knows I love horses and invited me. He found a nice horse for his brother, and it was nice for me to be in such an environment again. It reminded me of home." Della pulled on her usual dingy skirt.

"*He?* Just exactly who is this man, Della?" Franci crossed her arms.

"He's a lord. I think." Della used the laces on her shirt as an excuse to not look Franci in the eye.

"You *think*? Della, what is going on?" Franci stepped directly in front of Della.

Della looked up and grimaced at her friend's expression.

"I met this man. Well, I caught his runaway Stronghorse. You should see her, she's the most magnificent creature. She's just like the one I always dreamed of having. Of course, he's bonded to her so she would never be mine, but even simply riding her without the bond was exhilarating." Della grinned.

"I didn't ask about his horse!" Franci threw up her hands exasperated.

"Sorry. Well, anyway, I met this man, Roric. That's his given name though. He has visited me a few times. He took me on a picnic on a hill above a sea of lavender. Oh, it was so lovely!" Della smiled at the memory.

"Della. Does this man know who you are?"

"Yes and no. He knows me only as Della and that I'm a serving maid for the duchess. I know him only as Roric." Della's cheeks colored. She knew it sounded absurd, but it was nice to not have any expectations from someone for once. "You haven't heard of a Lord Roric, have you?"

"No, I haven't. Which isn't a comforting thought as I hear all the gossip. I suppose that means I haven't heard any bad rumors about him either, but if he were an eligible bachelor, I would have surely heard about him from *someone* during a dress fitting," Franci cautioned her.

Della's face fell. "I know. It's just that he's been so kind. He seeks me out and genuinely seems to want to—well I don't know if court me is the right way to put it, but it feels strangely nice to be yearned for enough to make such an effort to see me. Oh, and the way it feels when he kisses me—"

"You've kissed him?!" Franci exclaimed.

"Well, yes." Della blushed again. She tied her headscarf back over her hair and busied herself with folding the riding habit.

"Honestly Della, how did you let things get so far without even telling me?" Franci sounded hurt and guilt sliced through Della.

"I'm sorry. The first time I met him I really didn't think I'd see him again. Then he came to the house and—"

"Della! What did the duchess do?" Franci looked aghast.

"Oh, she wasn't home. Franci, he drew the water for me and even helped me with my chores. He treated me like a lady without seeming to mind my duties as a maid." Della sighed dreamily.

"I would caution you not to fall for this man, but it seems I am too late." Franci huffed out a very different kind of sigh.

"Oh Franci, I don't know what to do. I always planned to go back to Aleece after Eleonora married in a year or two, but now I feel like my heart is being tugged in two different directions." Della wrung her hands.

"Why don't you let me see if I can discover anything about a lord with the name Roric. I'll say I heard the name and thought it might be a gentleman coming for the ball. I can pretend I'm hoping he has a wife who needs a ballgown in the latest style."

"I would appreciate that very much!" Della hugged her friend.

"I just want to make sure you aren't being dragged into anything that could ruin you." Franci's words made Della think of Lord Faust's earlier that morning.

"Do you mind if I leave this here with my other things?" Della held up the riding outfit.

"Of course. I'll put it away for you. I'm sure from your full basket that you need to rush to the market before it closes to sell whatever is in there." Franci lifted it out of her hands, examining it with a frown.

"Thank you!" Della picked up her basket.

"Come back as soon as you can! I want to hear more about what *exactly* you and this mysterious lord have been up to," Franci told her.

"I will!" Della hurried from the shop.

Della reached the market only to find it empty save a few merchants taking down the last remaining stalls. The market was made up of fabric stalls that were rented cheaply to those who either didn't have enough wares or money to own an actual shop in the city. Della saw a troupe setting up a small stage in the center.

Della approached the troupe. "Hello. I suppose the market won't be reinstated until the festivities of the ball are over?"

"Yes, they gave us room to perform here until the night of the ball. It's always a pleasure to perform in a city square." The girl who responded had an Aleecean accent. The girl's blonde hair hung in a long braid from the top of her head. She wore a bright red belted tunic and orange leggings in lieu of a dress.

"You're from Aleece!" Della exclaimed excitedly.

"Do I detect a bit of our home country in your voice as well?" The girl grinned.

"Yes. I'm Della."

"I'm Trixie. It's a pleasure to meet you. I didn't know some Aleeceans had immigrated to Tamaria."

"I'm the only one that I know of. Facing the dangers of crossing the Deep Woods is not one that is braved often by those who wish to put down roots somewhere. Well, I'll try to see you perform if I have time before the ball. I miss the street performances." Excitement built up inside Della at the prospect of seeing a troupe perform after all these years. She would have to be strategic to get away with the ball happening so soon, but she was sure it would be worth it.

"We are going to have a practice as soon as we set up if you'd like to stay. It's quite a fun performance, especially if you haven't seen one in a while," Trixie offered.

"Unfortunately, I haven't the time. I have to sell these mushrooms and hurry back." Della held up her basket.

"Are they food or medicinal?" Trixie peered at them curiously.

"They can be used as either, depending on what you do with them. Since the market is gone, I'll take them to the city physicians."

"Do you mind if I come with you? Felix isn't feeling well. I think it's nerves—he isn't fond of traveling so far, but he fell for Jenell and decided to switch troupes and we travel more—but I told him I'd find a tonic from a doctor for him anyway, to make him feel better." Trixie barely took a breath as she talked about people that Della could only assume were other members of her troupe.

"I'm happy to show you the way." Della led her toward the nearest apothecary.

"You must tell me how an Aleecean wound up living in Tamaria. I would guess you came for love, but your accent has somewhat faded which suggests years of time away and you can't be much older than me." Trixie smiled encouragingly at her.

"No, my father married a woman from here. He died when I was a girl and my stepmother brought us back here. I was almost nine at the time, too young to even imagine going back through the Deep Woods alone. Not that I would now either." Della shuddered.

"I wouldn't brave the Deep Woods alone and I've been through it many times. Even being with the troupe it's a bit frightening crossing through, though the vardos offer some protection. Do you ever think about going back to Aleece now that you're older?"

"All the time." Della smiled wistfully.

"Well, why don't you come with us? After the ball we are heading back to Aleece for a time. We're going all the way to the capital!" Trixie skipped as they turned down another street.

"Oh, I wouldn't want to impose on your troupe." Della shifted the basket to her other hand, out of Trixie's way.

"Nonsense! We always have an extra bunk or two open in case we find someone with talent—or a fellow Aleecean! You'd have to help with the chores and gathering food, but other than that it's mostly fun as we tell stories and practice songs and such while we travel. Plus, it would be much cheaper than hiring a carriage to take you across the two countries since you'd pay with labor." Trixie elbowed her and grinned.

"Your offer is very kind, but I'm not sure that I'm ready to leave quite so soon." Della was caught off guard by the offer. It would be the most realistic way for her to return home, but could she? What about Eleonora and now Roric?

"Well, think on it. We will be staying through until the ball. We will perform at the ball, but only at the beginning.

In the later hours they want the attention on those giving speeches for the engaged royalty. Of course, we are always given some food in the kitchens below after our performance, which we heartily enjoy. We will leave soon after midnight, by one o'clock at the latest." Trixie twirled in a whimsical circle.

"That's an odd time to leave. Won't you be tired after your performance?" Surprise burst through Della.

"Yes, but most of us will sleep while we drive out. The vardos have bunks built in, you know. We switch off driving and those who don't perform—like Hannah who sews our costumes—take the first shift since she can sleep until we return. It's much easier to leave in the night than to fight all the other carriages that will be leaving in the morning after the festivities," Trixie explained.

"That's rather efficient." Della was impressed.

"We'll be just outside the gates since they don't like to open them for the vardos at night. They have a side door they agreed to let us through to leave so late. If you decide you want to come with us back to Aleece, then meet me there." Trixie stopped moving around to look Della in the eye.

"I will consider it. Thank you." Della turned them down another street.

Trixie grinned and launched into a tale of how Felix ripped his costume trying to impress Jenell. She bumped into Della when she stopped in front of the apothecary.

"Sorry." Trixie giggled, breaking off her tale.

"That's alright." Della held the door open for them.

"Hello, Della! Let me see what you brought." The wizened physician strode forward.

"Morels." Della pulled them from her basket.

"Good. I ran out of them during the winter and the pesky things are dreadfully hard to find." He looked over the pile, holding up one and turning it around.

"I stumbled across this bunch through pure luck," Della admitted.

"Will this do?" The physician handed her some coins.

"Yes, that's a fair price," Della agreed. She turned to Trixie. "It was lovely meeting you!"

"Don't forget to come the night of the ball," Trixie said.

Della was spared answering by Trixie turning to the physician and listing all the symptoms of everyone in the troupe. Della shook her head with a grin as she hurried out the door and headed home.

CHAPTER SIXTEEN

Two nights later Della awoke to a tapping sound. She rubbed her bleary eyes and squinted in the dark. It was the middle of the night, but she heard that tapping sound again. She slid out of her bed and went to her door, wondering what the duchess could possibly want right now. The last time Della had been woken in the night because of her, Della had been torn away from everything she knew. Had the duchess finally decided to throw her out? But no, Della reasoned as her mind started to awaken, the duchess knew she couldn't possibly do everything that Della did and she certainly couldn't afford to hire on an actual serving maid. Della sighed and opened the door, hoping the woman wasn't in a furious mood.

There was no one there. Della peered into the dim hallway, but as far as she could see in the darkness there was no one there. Surely the duchess wouldn't climb up here without even a candle to light her way. The tapping sounded again, rapidly as if growing frantic. She whirled around and stared at her window. Illuminated by moonlight, a face stared back. Della shrieked.

"Della! It's me. Open the window." Roric's voice was muffled by the glass.

Della shut her door and hurried across the room to the small window. She pushed open the glass.

"What are you doing there?! How did you even climb up?"

"I used the tree down there to climb part of the way up, then this trellis here. It unfortunately has roses on it that are rather prickly." Roric held up one hand that dripped blood from a few small cuts. He maneuvered so he was holding onto the inside of the windowsill and hauled himself up, but he was stopped by the narrowness of the window.

"I think your shoulders are too broad to fit through there. I can barely lean out it myself." Della's heart beat nervously.

"It's just as well. I didn't mean to climb into your bedroom at night—I know I shouldn't be in there at all. I only wanted to wake you and invite you down. My hands are just a bit sore from the thorns and holding on. You took a bit of time to wake up, and I'm not sure how long the trellis will hold my weight." Roric shifted and the wood creaked.

"Well, climb down now and I'll meet you outside."

He withdrew from the window and started climbing down. The trellis groaned and swayed with his weight. Della shut the window, snatched up a handkerchief, and grabbed her cloak before hurrying quietly down the stairs. She crept silently down the hallway that held the three rooms her stepfamily slept in. A loud snoring resounded behind Marien's door and Della bit back an amused smile at the sound. She reached the stairs and hurried down, flinging her cloak around her shoulders. She crossed through the house to the kitchen and out the back door.

Roric leaned against the trunk of the apple tree. As Della stepped toward him, her feet felt the cold, dewy ground and she realized she never put shoes on.

"Della." Roric's voice was tender as he reached for her.

Della instead grasped his injured hand and tied the handkerchief around it. "There. That should help a bit for now. Though your clothes look somewhat worse for wear as well.

Roric glanced down and grimaced. He wore unusually casual garb consisting of a simple white shirt and tight brown breeches that slipped into his black boots. His flowy shirt had a few tears where thorns had snatched at it. His cloak had been pushed behind his shoulders, but the end had a tear on one side and a snag on the other.

"That's what I get for not changing out of my nightshirt in my haste to come see you," he said.

Despite her cloak, Della shivered from the chill night air. Though her nightgown had long sleeves, it was thin with wear and had already been made from a delicate fabric. Her cloak was also worn and rather small, as she had gotten it years ago when she was shorter. It didn't close fully in the front and hung only midway to her calves.

"You're cold!" Roric said with a start. He pulled off his cloak and wrapped it around her. It pooled around her bare feet, warm from the heat of his body. He tugged the front closed, giving her both modesty and protection from the cold.

"Thank you." Della felt enveloped in warmth from the inside out at his kindness.

"I should have thought about the cold before I invited you out here. My apologies." Roric brushed his fingers across her cheek.

Della didn't reply as her breath hitched. He smiled at the sound and gazed into her eyes as he brought his face close to hers.

"I just can't seem to stay away from you," he murmured so close that his breath warmed her lips.

Della took a tiny step forward and closed the gap between their lips. He grinned through the kiss and moved his hands to her hips, tugging her against him under the shadow of the tree. Her lips parted and his tongue slipped in, tasting her. She gasped in surprise and his tongue retreated, but she let herself taste him back. His hands tightened on her waist as he turned her around, pressing her against the trunk of the tree. Della clung to him as he deepened the kiss. One of his hands slid up to her hair and he tangled his fingers in the loose waves, tightening them around the strands to keep her face locked in place. She gripped the front of his shirt and tugged him closer. His body obligingly pressed into hers and she slid her hands around his neck. Della's blood pulsed like hot fire racing through her.

Roric's lips left her mouth to trail kisses across her jaw. She sighed softly as he trailed them down her neck, his hand gently pulling her hair to tilt her head back better exposing her neck. He reached the spot where the two cloaks clasped around her collar and released her, breathing hard. He stepped back a few paces and ran a hand through his hair.

Della's head reeled from the kisses, but she looked at him with concern. "Is something wrong?"

"I got carried away. You are intoxicating. I didn't come here for this, I only wanted to spend time with you. I remembered how you said you liked to look at the stars and I thought we might do so together." Roric looked chagrined.

"I would like that."

"Come." He held out his hand to her again.

Della took it and he led her to the fence where he had tied Noa. He lifted her into the saddle and swung up behind her. Della reveled in the feel of his arms around her as he brought up the reins and led the horse away from the house and all of Widow's Court.

Roric brought her back to the hill above the field of lavender. The flowers were a dusky blue in the night, but their lovely scent was the same. He tied off his mare and pulled a small blanket from the saddlebag. They climbed the steep hill hand in hand. At the top, Roric spread the blanket and they lay down on it. The blanket had just enough room for them to lay with their sides pressed together. Della gazed up at the starry night sky.

"It's so beautiful." Della admired how much closer the stars looked from the hilltop.

"Indeed," Roric said, but when Della turned to look at him, she found that he was gazing at her instead.

Della blushed and hoped the darkness of night covered it. Her heart beat rapidly at his nearness. She drank in the heady scent of lavender as she stared up at the twinkling lights above.

"You know, I think I shall forever be reminded of you whenever I smell lavender."

"It's nice to think that I will be remembered," he said quietly.

"I don't think I could ever forget you." Della rolled onto her side and propped herself up on an elbow, her head resting on her palm.

He rolled to face her as well. "What is it about the stars that fascinate you so?"

"For one thing, they are beautiful. I also admire how brightly they can shine in the darkness. It can't be easy to stand out amongst such bleakness, yet they gleam every night, doing their best to fight against the gloom that tries to devour them. My father used to say the stars were the souls of our lost loved ones. That when you see one shoot across the sky it's because they are trying to come closer to you. He would always tell me to make a wish, that if the soul managed to catch it, then the wish would come true. Perhaps he is up there now, one of the stars that we are looking at tonight." Della sat up and leaned back against her hands. She tilted her head back to stare at the sky.

"That's a lovely sentiment. It must be consoling to those who grieve."

"I've taken much comfort in the thought through the years." Della smiled softly in the darkness.

Roric shifted so his head rested in her lap. Her heart thudded in her chest at this new sort of intimacy. She sat up fully and reached down to run a trembling hand through his hair, still looking at the sky.

"I also like to think there's more to them than what we can see. They're so far away. If I was able to reach into the sky, would they really be so small that I could hold a cluster of them in my hand? Or would they be so large and bright that I'd have to turn away? Do they hold little worlds like the one we live on? Though that thought seems silly as our ground doesn't glow. It's the idea that what we see may not be truly what they are that creates a sort of wonder. There's no way for us to find out as we cannot fly like birds, but I do like to guess at the possibilities." Della stroked his silky hair.

"You, Della, are the most enchanting dreamer I have ever met. Your mind is as beautiful as your features."

She looked at him then and he met her eyes with a smile. He sat up, taking her hand in his.

"I am truly glad I met you." Roric's eyes were full of sincerity. He lifted her hand to his lips and pressed a kiss to it. "I shall have to thank Noa for throwing me off that day."

Della laughed softly. "She is a wonderful steed."

"The very best," Roric agreed.

"Who are you? Truly?"

Roric sighed. "I am a man with too many responsibilities—though if you ask my family, I don't have enough. I am someone who has always longed to forge my own path, yet has never had the courage to step off the path I was told to follow until I met you."

Della examined him. Her question had been about his title, yet he had answered with his soul.

"Who are you, My Lady?"

"I am a wild spirit who was taken from my home and my freedom. I have always longed to be free again, yet I have never had the courage to leave where I was placed."

"What has stopped you from returning to Aleece?"

"Money for one thing. I don't have much of it and passage through the Deep Woods is expensive as most don't wish to brave ogres and other dangerous creatures that lurk in the deep thickets. The other is, I'm ashamed to admit, fear."

Roric laid a comforting hand on top of hers. "You shouldn't be ashamed to be afraid of ogres. I think most people are."

Della laughed. "Oh, it's not fear of the creatures in the Deep Woods that makes me a coward. Wariness of those creatures is well placed. It's a more ridiculous fear. I'm afraid that my family won't want to see me, and I'm afraid to fail at making a life for myself. It's easier to stay with the duchess and accept this life than to move on from it." That, more than helping Eleonora, was the greatest thing holding her here.

"Well, I think you are smart enough and determined enough to forge a life for yourself anywhere you wish to go. As for your family, why would you think they wouldn't want to see you?" Roric squeezed her hand.

"I wrote them many letters when I first came here. I never heard back from any of them." She looked away so he wouldn't see the tears stinging her eyes. Even after all this time, it still hurt to feel so completely abandoned.

Roric wrapped gentle fingers under her chin and turned her face toward him. His thumb brushed at the silver liquid in her eyes. "Oh, Della."

He pulled her into his arms. Della couldn't hold it back any longer. She sobbed against his chest, letting the tears release all the hurt and sorrow she had been holding inside for so long. She had cried with Franci before, but it seemed silly to keep complaining to her friend throughout the years even though the ache had remained. Somehow, here in Roric's arms, she felt safe enough to let it out. It felt cleansing.

Roric stroked her hair as she cried. When she had spent herself and was only sniffling, he spoke again. "Crossing the Deep Woods is difficult, even for couriers. Is it possible your letters were simply not delivered? Accidents do happen."

"I wrote every week for a year." Della sniffed.

He handed her his handkerchief, which she accepted gratefully.

"Do you know which courier you used? Perhaps if you told me their name and the year, I could look into it." Roric stroked her back soothingly.

"I don't know, I wasn't the one—"

"You weren't the one that what?"

Della only shook her head. "I'll look into it. Thank you for the idea."

"Of course."

Roric sounded concerned, but Della's mind was whirling too fast for her to focus on that. She had written every week of that first year. The year that she had been kept inside the house to grieve while her stepfamily attended social events. She had never delivered the letters to the couriers, she had given them to her stepmother. In return, her stepmother had always told her that she had not received any letters from her family. Why would the duchess stop communication with her family? What would it matter if Della had gone back to them? The only answer she could come up with was that they couldn't afford an actual servant with the way the duchess spent money.

Della pulled back, her eyes and face now wiped clean by his handkerchief. She would wash and press it before returning it to him. "Thank you."

Roric tilted his head and smiled. "For what?"

"For listening to me. For staying with me as I cried. For bringing me here both times. For wanting to help me figure out what happened with the letters." For reminding me of my worth, she wanted to say.

"It has been my pleasure. If your greatest desire is to reunite with your family, then I would do all my power to help you do so."

Della's heart warmed. "You're too kind. I think my greatest desire at this moment is just to spend this time here with you."

Roric wrapped an arm around Della and they lay back on the blanket, her head resting on his chest. They stayed that way as the sky slowly began to lighten. When yellow and orange streaks crept into the sky, Della pulled away from him gently and stood up.

"I really must return before the household wakes up." She wished she could stay there forever in Roric's arms, watching the sky change from night to day and back again.

"I should as well," Roric said regretfully.

They walked back down the hill. At the base, Roric plucked several of the long lavender stems. He held the bouquet out to her.

"A parting gift, My Lady."

"Thank you." Della buried her face in them and inhaled deeply. She smiled at Roric.

He lifted her onto the Stronghorse and untied the mount. Della shifted the flowers into the crook of her arm as Roric swung up behind her. Della leaned back against him as he spurred Noa into motion. He took them through the woods so they wouldn't be seen in the growing light. He stopped at the edge of the woods nearest Widow's Court and lifted her down.

"Will this be far enough for you? I can take you closer, but we risk being seen as the day awakens."

"This is fine. The house isn't far. I walk here all the time," Della assured him.

"Alright."

She removed his cloak and gave it back to him. "Thank you. Not only for the cloak, but tonight as well. It was wonderful. Every moment with you has been so wonderful."

Roric pulled her to him in a fierce embrace. He pressed his lips to the top of her head.

"I have enjoyed it all too. Goodbye, Della." Roric released her. His eyes held reluctance, but he didn't reach out for her again.

"Goodbye, Roric." Della turned and walked quickly back to the house, slipping inside past three sleeping women to get ready for the day. She would be tired, but her heart was full.

Chapter Seventeen

"Mother has requested your presence in the sitting room," Eleonora told Della from the kitchen doorway.

Della froze, clutching a half-washed dish from lunch in one hand and a dishrag in the other. With the ball in a few days, no other parties or social gatherings were being held, which had put Duchess DeVoss and Marien in especially foul moods.

"It will only be worse if you make her wait," Eleonora said gently. Worry swirled in her warm brown eyes.

"I'll go now." Della set down the dish and placed a reassuring hand on Eleonora's shoulder as she passed. She was dimly aware of Eleonora heading toward the tub of dirty dishes.

Della felt dread welling up inside her as she knocked on the door of the sitting room. She could only guess at what Duchess DeVoss had found fault with this time. Della knew the duchess couldn't accomplish half of what Della did for them, that they simply wouldn't survive without her. Yet Della was constantly punished for not being enough. Anger rose within her, but she pushed it down as she thought of Eleonora. She only had to make it until Eleonora secured a good match. Eleonora was the only one who had been kind to her in her own home here and Della didn't wish to see her sister forced into a terrible match out of desperation after being forced into Della's current role of serving maid. She wouldn't let that happen.

"Enter," came the imposing voice.

Della walked into the room. Her eyes flickered to the vase on a side table that held the bouquet of lavender Roric had given her. She looked away from it quickly, toward the duchess who stood by the open window on the far end of the room, hair ruffling slightly at the soft breeze that blew in.

"Close the door and light the fire." Duchess DeVoss had a brisk tone, but there was an edge to it that made Della's heart speed up.

"In this summer heat?" Della was incredulous, though she closed the door obediently.

"Don't question me, insolent girl. Light the fire!"

Della went over to the fireplace and settled some logs above the kindling. She breathed life into the fire, then stood up. When she turned around she felt two different heats—the fire behind her already making her sweat and the duchess glaring at her from across the room.

"*Who is he?*" Duchess DeVoss snarled, voice low enough to not be heard beyond the room.

"Who do you mean?" Della's stomach clenched painfully and her heartbeat quickened even more.

"The man you've been traipsing around with! You think you can make a mockery of me? Running around enticing some lord while I'm doing everything in my power to ensure your sisters marry well. You will ruin their good names! How could you jeopardize their reputations?" Duchess DeVoss snapped.

"Are they my sisters or the ladies I serve? You tell me to treat them as my sisters, then force me to be a servant to them.

Which do you want it to be? It cannot be both," Della snapped back.

"Everyone must do their part in this family! You do not have the prowess or skills to ensure financial safety for us through marriage, therefore you must help your sisters to succeed."

"And whose fault is it that I was denied the same education they continued to receive after my father died?" Della knew she shouldn't push the duchess, not when the woman was already furious, but she was tired of being treated as someone who was worthless. As if she'd had any control over how low she had fallen.

"I had to make a decision about what would best serve this family. We couldn't afford a maid *and* a governess. Futures in Tamaria are determined by marriage. Was I supposed to think an uncouth wild child who snuck out to see street performers and rode horses bareback would be easily groomed into a befitting bride? No, I knew, I *knew* you would continue to dishonor this family with the heathenistic things you do. So, I educated them instead. After all, you were likely to run away back to Aleece the first chance you got and then where would I be?" The duchess sniffed.

"You thought an eight-year-old girl would run away into the Deep Woods full of deadly creatures?" Della barked out a harsh laugh.

"Perhaps not right away, but eventually. Do you deny that you are planning it now? Where have your things disappeared to if not?" Her eyes glinted with an icy harshness.

"So you *have* been taking my things. You were the one who sold my mother's pearls to the jeweler, weren't you?" Della seethed.

"We must all contribute in whatever ways we can." The duchess adjusted the expensive lace cuffs on her dress.

"I don't see you selling any of your own jewelry, scouring floors, or even rinsing out a teacup," Della hissed.

"*I* am the only one who can arrange marriages for the three of you. Think of that before you spew more venom towards me, girl." Duchess DeVoss drew herself up like a viper preparing to strike.

Della clamped her mouth shut. The duchess wouldn't, would she? It had to be an empty threat. The duchess herself had said Della wouldn't be deemed a suitable match for any lord of the court. Roric flashed across Della's mind and a small hope flickered within her that perhaps one nobleman thought her worthy.

"Yet it seems you have been trying to secure yourself a match on your own. You've no doubt made a fool of yourself. Who exactly does this 'Lord Roric' think you are?" Duchess DeVoss demanded.

Della's eyes widened in shock and she felt her heart sink. Her stepmother's eyes narrowed.

"How did you...?" Della's blood ran cold.

"Did you think I wouldn't find out? Now tell me immediately! I must know what damage has been done so I may ensure the reputations of your sisters have not been tainted." Fury crackled like lightning in the duchess' eyes.

"He—he doesn't know they're my stepsisters. He wouldn't think to associate them with me in such a familial way. He only knows me to be a servant here." Shame filled Della at the admission.

"Well, he must be one of the poorer barons to both have the title of Lord and fraternize with a servant. I've certainly never heard of him. Unless... Did you give yourself away to him, let him touch you in indecent ways." The duchess sneered at her.

"No! Of course not!" Della felt her face burn at the implication that she had ever done anything more than kiss him. Though even a kiss might be considered scandalous in this country.

"Well, he wrote something about a fire on a hill above a purple ocean or some other nonsense. That sounds so absurd it could only mean something indelicate that shouldn't be written down for all to see!"

That the duchess so easily believed such a thing stung, though Della knew it shouldn't. This woman should have been a mother to her! She should want to assume the best and protect Della from the worst. She should have thought the fire was real or that it was simply what her daughter had felt—Della's head jerked up. She hadn't written this letter, Roric had. It had to be what *he* had felt. *So, he had felt it too.*

"I swear to you, I didn't do anything indecent with him. You said he wrote about that? He wrote a letter to you?" Della's mind reeled at the betrayal that he would think to write to her employer implying she had been indecent. But why mention the purple sea of flowers? Realization rushed through her. "He wrote that to me, didn't he? Where is the letter? It's mine!"

"I am the head of this household and as such it is my duty to ensure everyone in it is behaving properly! Imagine my surprise when I opened the door while you were in town to find a letter addressed to *you*. Naturally, I needed to know why anyone would bother with such an inconsequential member of my household," Duchess DeVoss said sharply.

Della crossed the room until she was only a few feet away from her stepmother.

"*Where is the letter?*" Della demanded in a dangerous tone.

Her stepmother's eyes widened and she took a step back from Della. Then she grinned maliciously. The duchess walked away from Della and over to the fireplace. She lifted a piece of parchment down from the mantle and waved it in the air.

"This letter?" she taunted.

As Della strode back across the room the duchess threw the paper into the fire.

"No!" Della cried, racing forward even though she knew it would be too late. She fell to her knees with that heat blasting her face, watching the flames desperately as if the longing in her heart alone would preserve the note. The fire had already curled most of the parchment into blackness and smoke. In the middle, an unmarked seal of wax hissed as it melted and began to evaporate. She stared at the ruined letter as it burned, the blob of wax a rare purple color that seemed to be an ode to all she and Roric felt when they were together.

"Oh dear, it slipped," Duchess DeVoss mocked as the page turned to ash. "I'm sparing you, really, from the harsh truth inside that letter. You should be grateful. It seems even that lord found you to be lacking and had written to break things off. He likely found a suitable match and knew it was time to dispose of his insignificant plaything."

Della shook her head as if that could shake out the cruel words, but her heart seized with a quiet fear that penetrated to her very bones. She thought back to his words the last night she had seen him and something in them rang of a goodbye that she had failed to notice before. Was he truly done with her? She had never given Roric a reason to believe she was anything more than the cinder girl Marien was so fond of calling her.

Could it really be all that he saw? Or was his affection for her because he was able to see her more clearly, to see what lay beneath the cinders? She didn't know.

"Do put out the fire. You should have known igniting such flames would only bring discomfort on a day so hot. Clean out the cinders too. I wouldn't want the soot to blow around from the breeze."

With that, the duchess swept out of the room. Della sank to her knees before the fire. A salty drop hit her hand, and she wasn't sure if it was sweat or a tear until more fell down in a tiny stream. When the tears dried up they left her numb.

Eventually Della stood and mechanically put out the fire. She went about her day and as she worked she began to think. She hadn't seen Roric recently, but he had written to her. Perhaps that meant he couldn't come to see her or maybe he had written to ask her to meet him. A part of her whispered that her stepmother may have been telling the truth and Roric felt that Della wasn't worth the efforts he exerted to see her. With the letter burned she would never know. But why then had he mentioned the place they had shared? They hadn't lit a fire, so the fire he had mentioned had to be the heat of the passion they had shared. Why would he write about that if he didn't wish to see her again? Duchess DeVoss would certainly do anything to keep Della away from a lord of this court, including lying to Della.

In the kitchen once more, Della roughly plopped down the bread dough she was making onto the table in frustration. She kneaded it forcefully as she mulled things over in her mind. Roric had always come to her, so she didn't know where he lived. She didn't know his title or his last name to discover his residence either. She could see only two options. The first was to ask around and see if anyone recognized the name. The second was to attend the ball and hope she could find him there. Both were distressingly slim chances that she could discover him, but as it was all she could do, Della was determined to try. Since Franci had already offered to ask after Roric, she decided she would start by seeing what her friend had discovered.

The next day Della visited Franci under the guise of checking if her stepfamily's dresses were ready. Franci was handing a customer their change when Della walked in.

"Hello, Della!" Franci grinned at her.

"Hello Franci. Do you have time to talk?" Della asked her.

"With you? Always," Franci told her. She walked her customer out the door and locked it, drawing the shades to signal she was closed for the time being. Franci often did this when she had too many orders she needed to fill before accepting new customers. With the ball so close it wouldn't be unusual at all.

"Have you discovered anything about Lord Roric?"

"I haven't. It's very odd." Franci frowned.

"I need to find him." Della sighed.

Franci arched an eyebrow at her as they walked into the back room and sat down in the chairs Franci kept there for when she was sewing. Franci picked up a dress and began to attach the sleeve that was pinned to it.

"Della, you are worrying me. Has something happened with this man?" Franci glanced at her friend over the stitches she was making.

Della sighed again. "Apparently, he wrote me a letter. Which the duchess received instead of me. You can imagine how that went."

"I'm impressed you escaped the house after such an incident." Franci reassessed her as if looking for signs of injury.

"I've only been allowed out to retrieve their dresses for the ball," Della groaned.

"Which I have finished," Franci assured her.

"But what do I do about the letter? The duchess said he wrote to break things off, but I have no way to know if that was true since she burned the letter. I have to ask him about it. How can I possibly find him?" Della dropped her heads into her hands in frustration.

"I will keep trying to ask about him. If that doesn't work, you can find him at the ball."

"I've thought of that, but what if he isn't there?" Della didn't know what she would do if she went to the ball and he wasn't even there or she couldn't find him in the crowd.

"If he's a lord living in the Fellsantra he will be there. And you're in luck. I've finished your dress. Try it on to make sure it fits!" Franci tossed aside the gown she was sewing.

Della obliged her friend. Franci helped her undress and redress in the ballgown. Della stared at herself in the enormous mirror that was kept here for dress fittings. The pale purple gown had been altered to be more current, yet it was still something wholly different. The Aleecean trumpet style skirt from decades ago now had a wide lilac overskirt attached at the waist. A removable lilac capelet had been added to cover her shoulders and give a mock ruffle, as was the fashion here in Tamaria. The long sleeves were still Aleecean, as most women here wore short, puffed sleeves or delicate loops across their upper arms instead.

"I look..." Della was at a loss for words. She almost said she looked like her mother, but there was her father's nose, his chin, and a smattering of faint freckles that the life of a servant had given her. These features were familiar to her, and yet when put into a proper ballgown...All she knew is she had never looked quite like this before. Seeing herself like this had her standing up straighter.

Franci looked into the mirror over Della's shoulder. "You look lovely. Like the courtier that you were born to be."

"It's beautiful! The capelet, the skirt, it's all so lovely. It's both Aleecean and Tamarian, and somehow something else entirely," Della breathed.

"Like you are," Franci said with a satisfied smile.

Della whirled to face her friend. "You are truly remarkable, Franci."

"I know." Franci had an amused glint in her eyes. "But I am not the only one who is."

"Franci," was all Della could choke out as emotions closed her throat.

"Go to the ball. Find your lord and let him bring you out of the darkness you have dwelt in for so long and into the light at last." Franci embraced her.

"Even in the darkness of night there is the light of stars," Della softly echoed the words her father had spoken long ago.

"Dazzle your lord under the starlight of an evening walk then. Just make sure he gets a good look at you in the candles and torchlight as well, to fully appreciate my handiwork. That is—to help him see who you truly are." Franci winked.

Della took one last look in the mirror before she shed the dress, feeling the loss as it left her body as though she were stepping out of another life, the one she might have lived. She shook her head to clear the thought, then donned her servant attire and returned to Widow's Court with four packaged dresses. Della made sure to enter through the kitchen and stow her own dress away before bringing up her stepfamily's new gowns along with the lunch tray. She would take it up to her room after they were all asleep, and perhaps try it on once more.

CHAPTER EIGHTEEN

The day of the ball was a true test of Della's patience. Duchess DeVoss had run her ragged scrubbing the entrance hall, grand staircase, and the front steps. She had to tidy all Marien's room three times as Marien pulled the room apart getting ready, then insisted Della clean it as she couldn't find this item or that one. Della's arms ached as she tugged at the laces on Marien's dress.

"Don't I look fetching?" Marien purred at herself in the mirror.

"You do look lovely in this gown," Della admitted as she finished tying the back.

The bright blue looked beautiful with Marien's complexion. Della had done the girl's hair in a small bun atop the back of her head with chocolate brown curls spilling out of it down her neck. Marien and Eleonora had slept in curl cloths that were only taken out a few hours before the ball in order to preserve the curls as long as possible.

"You're so lucky you have natural curls," Eleonora had sighed when Della painstakingly removed each piece of cloth from her head.

Marien held up two different blue earrings to her ears. One was a silver and sapphire set that dangled down in a teardrop shape. The other was made of blue topaz crafted to look like large flowers.

"Oh, the teardrop ones are lovely. You should wear those," Eleonora said entering Marien's room.

"You look nice. Not as beautiful as me, but perhaps a baron will take a fancy to you." That was as close as Marien got to complimenting her little sister.

Eleonora beamed and twirled in her peach ballgown. Franci had updated it beautifully and it hung off Eleonora's shoulders with a ruffly flounce that provided both a womanly style and the modesty expected for her age. The gown tugged in to show her waist before flaring out in more ruffles that Franci had somehow managed to make look tasteful. She wore small pearl earrings and a single strand of pearls around her neck.

"You do look wonderful," Della murmured to Eleonora quietly.

"Thank you! Oh, I do hope so." Eleonora blushed and patted her hair anxiously as she looked in the mirror.

Della raised her eyebrows, but didn't ask who her little sister might be hoping would admire her newly updated gown. She wouldn't ask about Lord Faust in front of Marien.

"For sky's sake, do wear the other earrings. You want to make a good impression, don't you? Hurry up, I'm going to see if the carriage is here. I'll be waiting downstairs," Duchess DeVoss called from the doorway.

Marien paused with one sapphire earring in her ear and quickly changed it out for the other pair. Della handed both girls their wraps.

"Do you need any further assistance?"

Eleonora smiled. "No, I think you can go."

"Yes, yes, you can leave." Marien waved a dismissive hand without looking at Della.

Della left the room and rushed up the stairs to her attic room. If she was lucky the hired carriage wouldn't have arrived yet and Marien would fuss with her appearance for a few more minutes longer. Della hurried to get into the dress Franci had altered for her. She was grateful that Aleecean gowns were often made to be easy to put on without assistance as most women didn't have a lady's maid except for royalty. Della removed her kerchief and checked her hair that she had done up in pretty loops and curls early that morning. She wove a matching pale purple ribbon through it as she fixed a few spots.

Della rushed down the stairs and saw Marien's room was now empty. She raced to reach the top of the grand staircase without even checking Eleonora's room. She saw the duchess and her stepsisters opening the front door to leave.

"Wait! Please wait a moment for me!" Della cried as she lifted her skirts and rushed down the stairs. Her heart pounded with the exertion and fear as she faced her stepmother.

"Della?" Eleonora's voice was laced with surprise.

"What do *you* think you're doing?!" Marien cried.

"I've finished all my chores. I have something to wear. I promise I won't go near the princes—I wouldn't even want to. You can let me out of the carriage before the castle and I'll arrive on my own and stay far away from you all. I won't embarrass you or cause any trouble. Please, just let me go with you." Della held her breath. She didn't know what she would do if the duchess merely swept out the door and left her behind. The woman looked her over carefully. Della's heart pounded in her chest, but she held her chin up.

"Did you leave the girls to fend for themselves to give yourself time to get ready?" Her stepmother's lip curled.

"Of course not!"

"We told her she could leave us. She only got ready after we were done," Eleonora insisted fervently.

"I didn't ask you, Eleonora. Let me see if you are actually suitable looking." The duchess circled around Della. "Where did you get this dress?"

"It was my mother's." Della closed her eyes for a moment, throwing a wish up to the stars—to her father and mother.

"I'm sure your little dressmaker friend had a hand in this too. Though it's not quite the latest fashion, I suppose it will do."

Della wondered if the woman only gave in to avoid offending Franci. The dresses she provided them with were invaluable at court and too important to lose. Della sent up a silent thank you to her friend for being so skilled and unafraid of cutting off the nobles who slighted her. Then she sent another thank you to her parents among the stars.

"But mother—!" Marien cut off her protest when the duchess raised her palm to silence her.

"Very well, let's go." Duchess DeVoss gestured for Della to go ahead.

Della couldn't believe her luck. She held back a grin lest she goad her stepmother into changing her mind.

"You look lovely," Eleonora whispered.

"Thank you!" Della whispered back with a smile the duchess couldn't see from her position still behind her.

Della took two steps forward and heard a loud rip. The heart wrenching sound echoed around the entrance hall. Della looked back to see the duchess lifting her foot off the back of her dress a smirk slipping across her face.

"Oh, *Della*," Eleonora mourned.

"Tsk, tsk. They made dresses so *delicate* back in your mother's day." Duchess DeVoss fingered the capelet and then tore it off. She grasped the sleeve just below the shoulder and yanked down, splitting the seam.

"Is that one of my hair ribbons?" Marien cried. She was on Della in an instant, tearing at her with vicious glee and sending hairpins flying.

"It isn't! It's not! It's my own!" Della fell to her knees trying to fend her off, but it was too late. Her hair was a wreck.

"Well now. I could never allow you to go like that. You look like such a mess! What would people say?" Duchess DeVoss sneered. "Come along girls!"

The duchess swept out the door to the waiting carriage outside. Marien threw one last wicked grin before flouncing after her.

"Enjoy your evening by the fireplaces, *Cinderella*," Marien jeered over her shoulder.

Eleonora knelt next to Della on the floor, pulling her into her arms. Della felt herself shaking and realized she was crying.

"I'm so sorry, Della." Eleonora stroked her hair while Della sobbed. "You looked so beautiful. I think she became jealous and frightened. I think that was the first time Marien saw you as competition since we moved here. It doesn't excuse what they did—"

"Eleonora! Get out here now!" Duchess DeVoss snapped.

"I'm so sorry!" Eleonora whispered, giving Della one last hug before she hurried to join them. She shot a worried look over her shoulder before closing the door.

Della heard the carriage roll away as she cried herself out on the floor. When the tears finally dried up she shivered and stood, going back up the stairs numbly.

If Marien and the duchess saw her as competition now they would likely only make her life more miserable. She simply couldn't bear it anymore. There was no way she could go to the ball to find Roric looking like this. Short of knocking on every manor door in the city she had no way to find him, and she couldn't do such a thing. The things people would say about him if a maidservant went knocking on doors to find him. Della decided she would take Trixie up on her offer. She would leave for Aleece with the troupe in the morning. She stuffed the few remaining belongings she had into a sack. With a sigh, she realized that she had packed the clothes she had intended to change into. Della threw her cloak around her tattered gown and left the house behind without a backward glance. She had to say goodbye to Franci anyway, she could change there. Della felt a twinge of guilt at the fate she was leaving Eleonora to, but she had to hope her sister would meet someone at the ball tonight and secure herself a match. Perhaps it would be whomever she was so excited and nervous to look lovely for. She knew Eleonora wouldn't begrudge her departure, but guilt still pooled in her stomach anyway.

Della moved through the city quickly and clung to the shadows falling in the setting sun. She didn't want to attract attention in her messy state. She took back routes to reach Franci's shop. This time of night Franci was likely in the back room finishing up any projects she had delayed due to the ball. Della made her way to the front door of the shop and knocked on the door.

"We're closed!" came Franci's muffled voice.

Della knocked again, louder this time.

Franci threw open the door. "I said we're—oh, Della! What a nice surprise. I suppose you have all evening free with your stepfamily at the ball."

"Hurry, let me in." Della stepped around her into the shop. She pulled her hood back and turned to face Franci, who was locking the door.

"*Della*. What happened to you?" Franci breathed out, wide eyes taking in Della's ruined state.

"The duchess. And Marien. They ruined the dress. I simply cannot stay there anymore! I won't go back." Della set her sack down on the counter.

"Oh, of course! You don't ever have to go back there! I've told you that so many times." Franci pulled her into a fierce hug.

Della pulled off her cloak and winced when she heard Franci suck in a gasp at the state of her gown.

"I'm so sorry. She ruined it. She had said I could go to the ball if I could find something to wear, but I don't think she ever expected that I could. Marien was all too happy to join in the destruction." Della tried to contain her hair that was spilling everywhere.

"Why those—those—oh! There isn't a vile enough word to describe those two miserable snakes!" Franci spat in anger.

"I only need to change and get some rest before I leave Tamaria for good," Della said tiredly. She slumped against the wall.

Franci frowned. "What do you mean, leave Tamaria for good?"

"Did you see that traveling troupe that came into the city? They're performing at the ball and leaving soon after. They're going to Aleece and they offered to let me go with them."

"Well, thank you for giving me so much time to know I'll be losing my closest friend."

"Oh Franci, I only just decided tonight. I wasn't planning on it until all this happened." Della gestured at her ruined gown.

"Oh Della, I really just want you to be happy. Truly. Though I'll be sad to lose you, I understand how good it will be for you to get away from those ungrateful tyrants. But if you're only going to have one last night in Tamaria, it should be magnificent! You're going to that ball!" Franci tugged Della away from the wall.

"Franci, I'm tired. I only want to rest. Besides, my dress is ruined," Della protested.

"You're standing in a dress shop, Della! Anyway, I may have started on a dress for you when I first heard about the last ball. I always dreamed you'd let me dress you sometime. Besides, you can't let them ruin this night for you! You need to find your Lord Roric and find out what was in that letter."

Della tried to protest further, but Franci was already pulling her into the back room. Admittedly, Della did still want to know what Roric had written to her.

Franci yanked a sheet off a mannequin clothed in a formal ballgown. The gown was a deep midnight blue overlaid on the bodice with matching lace. The entire thing was covered in clusters of silver beading that must have taken hours to sew on.

"Well? What do you think? Do you like it?" Franci gestured at the gown.

"It's so beautiful," Della whispered reverently.

"With no ruffles!" Franci gave her a knowing grin.

"It's far too fine for me. I couldn't possibly wear it." Della lightly stroked the fabric under her fingertips. Her mother's gown was one thing, but this was something worn only by the highest of noblewomen. A position she might have held in another lifetime.

"Nonsense, you inspired this very piece, so it's only right that you should wear it. The way you go on about the stars here some days." Franci shook her head with a laugh.

"The stars? It does look like the night sky. Great Cliffs! Franci, did you actually sew these in true constellations?!" Della exclaimed.

"Yes. I had to buy the strangest sort of map off a traveling peddler as I couldn't really sit outside and sew all night." Franci grinned.

"You truly are a master." Della stared at her friend with admiration.

"Go on, put it on! It's a dress fit for a ball and that's tonight, but the ball won't last forever. You're wasting time!" Franci tugged at Della's tattered clothes impatiently.

"Alright, alright. Great Cliffs, I can undress myself," Della complained.

Della may have been able to undress herself, but she needed Franci's help, plus a few borrowed petticoats to get the gown on properly. Franci carefully braided back just enough of Della's hair to keep it out of her face.

"I could do something more elaborate if you would like, but your head seems a bit tender," Franci offered.

"It's perfect." Della's head *was* sore and she didn't want her hair tugged on any more than it had already been today. She admired herself in the mirror. The gown left her shoulders, collarbone, and neck bare. Her hand touched the hollow of her throat and she felt a pang of regret that she could not wear her mother's pearls.

Franci missed nothing and said, "Would you like to borrow one of my necklaces?"

"Oh, you've done more than enough! This gown is absolutely divine. Besides, I wouldn't want to worry about losing one of the pieces your mother left you."

"You'll look silly without anything around your neck. I know!"

Franci disappeared into the front of the shop. Della could hear her rifling around in bins. She returned a moment later carrying a length of dark blue ribbon and something else in her fist. Franci sat down and dumped the contents into her lap. Della caught the sparkle of silver beads as her friend threaded a needle. Franci deftly sewed a smattering of beads onto the ribbon before holding it up triumphantly. She tied it around Della's neck.

Della touched the ribbon at her throat. "It's perfect."

"I wish I had some shoes for you, but I haven't anything your size and I'm no cobbler. Hopefully no one will look at your feet." Franci frowned at Della's worn boots.

"These will do fine. Unless..." Della recalled the shoes in her trunk.

"Unless?" Franci repeated.

"Well, it probably wouldn't be practical to wear them all night at a ball."

"Wear what?" Franci demanded.

"In my trunk there's—"

Franci disappeared from the room before Della could finish. Della went after her friend, lifting the voluminous skirt in a rather unladylike manner to race up the stairs. She found Franci in the spare room with the trunk open.

"Where in the skies did you get these?" Franci held up the glass shoes. The candlelight set the facets in them sparkling like cut diamonds.

"From the traveling peddler who comes and goes."

"Are these made of glass?" Franci tapped one with her fingernail.

"Yes, I believe so. The fur soles make them surprisingly comfortable, though I haven't walked in them for long or danced in them." Della shrugged.

"Of all the things to buy, why would you ever think to need such shoes?" Franci was incredulous.

"I didn't buy them. He gave them to me." Della pink tinged her cheeks.

"The peddler *gave* you glass dancing slippers? You live the oddest life." Franci shook her head.

"Well, I gave him my lunch and he said he was grateful. He also mentioned no one taking an interest in them, so perhaps they were unsellable. I was expecting him to give me a wooden top or something in exchange for the sandwich, but when he offered these I couldn't refuse as I'd already offended him once before."

Franci gave her an odd look. "Well, put them on and have a look in the mirror, won't you?"

"Oh Franci, the gown is so lovely!" Della twirled and the dress flared out as she spun. She was surprised at how nice she could look after being so disheveled earlier. A pounding knock made her jump.

"Now who could that be? Doesn't anyone realize I'm closed?" Franci threw her hands up in exasperation. She hurried back down the stairs.

Barend's voice floated to Della as she descended the stairs. "Hello, Francesca. Johanna thought she glimpsed Della in a right state earlier, sneaking past our window. Do you know if she's alright? I thought I'd check here first."

"Well, she was a mess, but I think we've sorted it out. See for yourself." Franci gestured towards Della as she entered the shop front.

"Della! You look like a right proper lady!"

"Doesn't she look fit for the ball?" Franci glowed with pride.

"You did fine work on our Della. It's about time she looked like a noblewoman with her blood and all." Barend grinned at Franci.

Della shifted uncomfortably under their gazes. "I should probably get off to the ball. I won't have much of the evening left by the time I get there."

"You're not planning to walk all the way to the castle, are you?" Barend asked incredulously.

"I haven't any other way to get there. I expect all the hired carriages are already taken and I don't have any coin for them anyway."

"Let me take you! I'd be happy to, as long as you don't mind riding in a baker's cart," Barend offered.

"Oh no, I couldn't take you away from Johanna and the baby."

"It won't take long. Johanna would send me right back out to drive you anyway, once I tell her what is going on. We see you as somewhat of daughters to us, and ladies should not be wandering alone at night." Barend smiled at them.

Franci and Della exchanged knowing grins.

"Ones you wish you could encourage towards better ways of living," Franci teased.

"We only wish the best for you, but as long as you are happy we don't mind which path you choose to take." Barend smiled. "So, you'll give me the pleasure of driving you over?"

"Well, alright," Della agreed.

"Wonderful! Let's go." Barend turned to unlock the door.

"I'll see you after the ball," Della told Franci.

"I can't wait to hear all about it!"

"Thank you again! The dress is so lovely." Della dashed in for a quick hug.

"*You're* lovely, Della! Now go before you miss the whole thing!" Franci shooed her out the door with a cheerful laugh.

Della followed Barend the few streets over to his small cottage. He opened the door and ushered her in.

"Johanna dear? I've got Della. I'm going to hitch up the cart and drop her off at the ball!" Barend called before disappearing out the door again.

"Della? Come in here, dear," Johanna called from the bedroom.

Della pushed on the door and it swung inward easily. Johanna was sitting on the bed cuddling a small bundle close to her chest.

"Oh Della! You look perfectly fine! I thought I saw you disheveled, but I've never seen you look so lovely. I suppose all the lords will trip over themselves to get a dance with you tonight. Perhaps one will even wish to court you," Johanna's voice took on a dreamy tone.

"I wouldn't get your hopes up." Della laughed, but she couldn't help thinking of Roric and her stomach quivered with nerves.

"What does your stepmother think of you going to the ball?" Johanna eyed her keenly.

"She isn't pleased, but I intend to avoid her as much as possible." Della edged around the truth of the matter.

"Well, don't let that wretched lady ruin your night. From what I've heard by the gossip, she will take any opportunity to better herself, including tearing down others. I'm happy to see you finally looking like the lady you are. It had better stay," Johanna said sternly.

"I don't intend to return to the duchess' household ever again," Della assured her.

"Good!"

"How is Charlotte doing?"

Johanna's expression softened at the mention of her daughter.

"She's put some nice weight on, though she's still small. She sleeps ever so peacefully, even if it only lasts a few hours at a time." Johanna looked down at the tiny bundle almost reverently. She pulled back the blanket a little and tilted her arms so Della could just see a tiny face poking out.

"She's beautiful."

"I think so too, but it's nice to hear others say it. You never know otherwise, if you only think it because you are their mother," Johanna said as she smiled down at her little bundle.

"Della? The cart is ready," came Barend's voice from the cottage doorway.

"You'd best go. Have a wonderful night!" Johanna told her.

"Thank you!" Della swooped in and gave her a brief, tight hug before leaving.

"Up you go," Barend said as he handed Della up onto the small bench at the front of the cart. He settled in beside her and offered her a lap blanket for warmth.

"Thank you for the lift."

"It's no bother at all," Barend assured her.

"Little Lottie is a treasure."

"Isn't she just? The other day she gave the loveliest little smile in her sleep." Barend beamed.

The ride to the castle was quick in Barend's delivery cart. Della enjoyed listening to Barend as he spoke about his little family the whole way there. He pulled the horse to a stop at the palace steps.

"There you are." He helped her down. "Do you want me to come back to get you?"

"Oh no, I'll find my own way back. You simply enjoy the evening with your wife and child."

"Have a lovely time." Barend nodded when he had climbed back up. He flicked the reins and the horse trotted off.

Della stared at the palace steps for a minute before taking her skirts in her hands and ascending.

CHAPTER NINETEEN

Della walked along the long hall inside the palace. At the end it opened to a grand staircase. She looked over the top railing and observed the large ballroom below with delight. Courtiers mingled in colorful clothing, some dancing in the middle of the room, some sitting at the tables that lined the edges of the room, and some loitered near the wall that held a feast strewn across more enormous tables. All looked merry and delightful. Della grinned as she realized that, for the first time in her life, she was going to be a part of the festivities she should have grown up enjoying. She planned to relish every moment. She delicately picked up her skirts and descended to the first landing. Before she could continue down the stairs to the ballroom a steward grasped her arm.

"Your name, my lady?" he asked her quietly.

"What?" Della tried to pull away, bewildered.

"I need your name to announce you," he clarified, not loosening his grip.

"Oh, that's really not necessary." Della balked, trying to wrench her arm free. She did not want her name announced for her stepmother to hear.

"I must announce you or you will be removed. Only nobility have been invited to attend the ball." His eyes narrowed. The steward nodded to some guards waiting nearby who stepped toward them.

"If you must." Della sighed. She whispered to him and he released her with a satisfied look. She hurried down the stairs, cringing as she heard his booming voice call out behind her.

"The Duchess Adella Caspari of Aleece!" Her mother's name and title, but also her own had her father not remarried.

Heads turned to see the late arrival and Della barely restrained herself from taking the steps two at a time. She had told the steward that she was from Aleece because it was true, and she had also hoped it would help her hide among the unfamiliar courtiers as they assumed she was a foreigner here by invitation for the ball. She realized too late that the foreign visitors would be staying in the palace and not have a reason to arrive late like she had. Della hoped she hadn't just caused trouble for her aunts or grandfather back in Aleece by naming her home country.

Della caught sight of her stepmother weaving through the crowd toward her as she reached the final stair. The woman's face was livid. Della plunged into the crowd on the opposite side from her stepmother, darting around voluminous skirts and behind tall gentlemen. She wasn't used to the crowd like Duchess DeVoss was though, and when she threw a look over her shoulder, she saw the woman catching up. Della glanced around in desperation. There was a man with his back to her, standing a bit apart from the clusters of courtiers around him. She grabbed his hand.

"Dance with me," she pleaded. Not waiting for an answer, she pulled him onto the dance floor where a new song was starting. She heard gasps and whispers titter around her. Della knew she was being forward, but it was the best escape from her stepmother she could improvise at the moment.

"I'm sorry, I only needed—Oh!" Della turned to face him and found herself staring at Roric.

"Della?" His annoyance gave way to surprise.

"Hello." She gave him a shy smile. Butterflies fluttered in her stomach as he lifted his hand to meet hers for the dance. The stars were shining favorably on her tonight. She had come to find him and here she hadn't even needed to search him out.

A smile broke out on Roric's face. "What in the skies are you doing here?"

"On the dance floor? I'm avoiding the duchess."

He frowned and glanced around as they moved with the dance. He spotted the duchess in the crowd watching them. "She looks most displeased."

"Hence my immediate desire to escape onto the dance floor away from her. It makes it rather hard for her to follow me." A smile played across her lips.

"It certainly does." Roric twirled her in several fast loops that spun her across the floor and far away from her step-mother.

Della savored the feeling of being in his arms. They had never danced together before, but his calloused hands held hers and her waist, and it felt strangely natural. She didn't know all the steps, but Roric led her through them with gentle firmness.

"You look magnificent."

Della blushed. "Thank you. You look rather fine yourself."

Indeed, he wore a crisp white doublet that had rows of gold double buttons down it. His boots were a polished black, shining so fiercely they reflected the candlelight. There was even the hint of something gold gleaming in his mass of curls. He was immaculate.

"One must always look their best, just in case a lady of Aleece shows up when least expected." He smiled and twirled her again.

She grinned at him. "If you're trying to make me dizzy, I must warn you that I never get that way."

"I wasn't, but how intriguing to learn of another of your innumerous talents. It seems unfair that you should have them all."

"In reality, it is a curse to be so blessed." She placed a dramatic hand on her chest, then giggled, ruining the effect. She replaced her hand on his arm. "I'm lying. It's quite wonderful, actually."

"Ah, humility, finally a talent you might be lacking." Roric gave her a wicked grin.

Della spoke with mock affront. "Sir! I assure you that I am the most humble person you will ever meet."

Roric chuckled. "You are certainly the most interesting and delightful person I have ever met."

"Thank you, for saving me with a dance," Della told him when the song ended. She made to move away, but Roric held on to her hand.

"Perhaps you can return the favor and save me from all the ladies waiting to pounce the second you leave me alone. Save me with a dance, My Lady."

Della's smile grew. "I'd be delighted to, my lord."

She regretted her decision when the new song started up again. It was a jauntier tune, indicating the dance would be faster and involve changing partners. Her stomach twisted. She didn't want to make a fool out of herself now, not when she'd been having such a wonderful time.

Della bit her lip. She whispered, "I don't know the steps to this one."

"It's not too complicated. Just watch what the other ladies do, and I will guide you through the movements. Worry less about the steps, and more about having fun. It will be alright." He gave her a reassuring smile.

Della nodded, but she was still nervous. She was able to stay with Roric for the beginning of the dance, which gave her time to watch the other girls while she trusted in him to lead her. She had learned the simple arm movements by the time she was spun off to another man, but realized she didn't know what to do with her feet. This lord, a middle-aged man with squinty eyes, frowned at her when she stepped on his feet for the third time.

"Don't they teach you to dance in Aleece?" he grumbled.

"Sorry." Della gave him an apologetic smile that was more of a wince as she stepped on his foot yet again. She had been surprised he remembered what the servant had announced about her, but she *had* arrived late, and he wouldn't recognize her from Tamaria's court. Her dress was also rather distinctive, the silver beaded constellations glittering in the light.

The lord seemed eager to spin her off to her next partner. Della got her footing and looked up, right into the face of Lord Faust.

"Did I hear you announced as the Lady Adella Caspari of Aleece?"

"They wouldn't let me in without giving them my name so I did." Della's chin jutted up defiantly.

He glowered at her. "You're masquerading as a noble-woman."

"I believe they called me *Lady* Adella, which I am."

His hand tightened on hers almost painfully. "You're not a lady."

"I wear skirts, don't I?" Della knew she was being child-ish, but she was tired of explaining herself to this man who couldn't see past the cindersoot.

"Do you think this is wise?"

"To dance? Well, I suppose that depends on my partner. You haven't stepped on my toes yet, so I'd say I chose wisely."

"I meant you coming to the ball."

Della took a deep breath. "I had to see him. I need to know—"

She was whirled away from him and back into Roric's arms, Della blinked up at him. "Hello again."

"Having a friendly chat with Pieter?" Roric's eyebrows lifted.

"Always lovely to speak with him," Della said dryly.

Roric laughed softly. "He means well. He just worries. It's also easier for him to fuss over me than to face his own problems. You aren't the one he should have been dancing with. I do hope I see him back on the dance floor with the correct girl tonight."

Della squeezed his hand gently. "He will find his way."

"I hope so. That girl won't wait forever, and even if she would, mothers do not wait for their daughters to become spinsters." Roric sighed.

"Have many mothers been hounding you for your mar-riage to their daughters?"

"I avoid them too thoroughly to know. Luckily, my mother has been too busy wrangling Freddie into an engagement to focus on me."

"Is that why you thought a Stronghorse might cheer him up?"

Roric started. "You remember that? Yes, he is rather unenthusiastic about this engagement."

"Your parents will make him marry whether or not he wishes it?" Della's hope lingered.

"Yes. It is his duty as the second pr—second son. Though I think he just hates the idea of being married as he wishes to run wild rather than settle down. Our mother hopes that he will fall in love as our oldest brother did, even with his marriage having been arranged as well."

Della's heart fell. His parents would hope for love to grow from an arranged marriage, but still insisted on such a union either way. Could she and Roric find a way, or was it a doomed dream? Perhaps her stepmother hadn't lied to her about the contents of his letter after all.

"I feel a bit faint," Della said as the song ended.

"Perhaps some refreshments would revive you." Roric led her off the dance floor and to the long tables covered in food.

Della popped a strawberry into her mouth and relished the sweet taste. Her stomach grumbled for more food and she realized that she'd been so busy preparing everyone for tonight that she hadn't eaten supper.

Roric grinned. "Try this."

She accepted the small cake with a frown. It was dark brown and she couldn't figure out what flavor it would be. It looked too dark for cinnamon. The top was frosted in a vanilla buttercream that looked delicious, so she took a bite.

"What *is* that?" She looked at him in wonder.

"It's a chocolate cake, though these ones are baked in small dishes to make them sized for the individual."

"I've never tried such a flavor before. It's so rich and sweet."

"You like it then?" Roric peered at her face.

"I think it's the best thing that I've ever tasted!" Della made a mental note to find out what ingredients were required. She would save her coppers to taste such a treat again, and it would be worth every coin.

Roric grinned. "Help yourself."

Della picked up a plate and picked out more fruit, small sandwiches, and two more of those delicious chocolate cakes. Roric added two more to her plate and she smiled at him. He led her to a small table behind a pillar. Della sat and chewed on a slice of fruit while she tried to think of how to ask Roric about his feelings toward her. He had just danced with her through two dances. He had also seemed happy to see her.

"I'm sorry if I caused trouble for you by pulling you out onto the dance floor. I can see several ladies and their mothers staring at you and glaring at me."

"You were much too bold for Tamarian society, but I fear their looks are centered more on jealousy than anything else. I am somewhat of a recluse amongst them and every one of them seems to be hoping to pounce on any eligible man at court." Roric rolled his eyes.

"I may be too bold for society, but am I too bold for you?" Della ventured. She kept the smile on her face even though her heart was pounding in her chest. She had to determine his feelings for her tonight. She had to know before the troupe left.

"I enjoy your boldness. Perhaps too much." He smiled, but it didn't quite reach his eyes.

Now. Della knew she should ask him where this was going now. Her heart was beating so loudly she was surprised Roric couldn't hear it. She gulped, then opened her mouth.

"Would you like to dance?" Roric stood, offering her his hand.

Della placed her hand in his. She could ask him later. One more dance wouldn't hurt. "I'd love to."

Roric led her back onto the dance floor. The musicians played a slow, gentle waltz. Della luxuriated in the gentle way that Roric held her, moving them across the floor in sweeping steps. No matter how this night ended, she would hold on to this moment. She was dancing among courtiers, their equal and his. Tomorrow she might very well be on her way to Aleece with the troupe, on her way to seek out her family and start a new life. She might become a washerwoman or maid, paid fairly for once, but a common woman, not a courtier. She had never truly been a courtier since she set foot in Tamaria and the time for training as one had long passed. Even Roric had admitted she was too bold for Tamarian society. It felt as if there was an answer there, one that she was refusing to acknowledge. So she indulged herself and danced.

"You're quiet tonight. Are you enjoying the ball?"

Della considered his question. "Yes. I hadn't ever worn a ballgown and haven't tasted such decadent food in a long time. I've enjoyed the dancing too. You lead well and I can almost pretend I know every step."

He smiled and spun her, the beading on her dress glittering in the light. "You look like night sky."

"Franci will be pleased to know I wasn't the only one to notice her hard work."

"Plenty of people are noticing it. If she isn't already renowned, she will be after tonight." Roric nodded toward the crowded room where several people were staring at them.

"Are they watching the dance or looking at you?" Della scanned the room. There were too many heads turned their way, moving to follow their path across the dance floor.

He smiled at her. "I think they're all trying to figure out who this gorgeous Aleecian woman is."

Della let out a soft, disbelieving laugh. She was saved from replying by the song ending. Della curtsied to him. She glanced around the room and saw her stepmother fighting the surging crowd. She looked to Roric, who was also frowning as he looked in another direction. Della needed to escape before Duchess DeVoss caught up.

"I think I need to catch my breath from all the dancing."

"Would you like to go outside? There's a stage erected to showcase a performing troupe."

Della nodded, taking the arm he offered her. She noticed more than a few disappointed looks as they retreated toward the back of the room. Several of the large glass doors here had been thrown open to let in the cool night air and people milled in and out. The grounds outside had large pole torches set at frequent intervals, providing plenty of light despite the sun having already retired.

The large wooden stage had gathered a crowd that they joined. A man was juggling torches of fire. Della watched with rapt attention, amazed that he never burnt his hands. He caught all three torches and breathed into the fire, causing it to shoot out in a wide flame across the stage. The crowd clapped and cheered, then gasped as he put the torches in his mouth and swallowed the flame. He bowed and the cheers erupted again.

Roric leaned in. "Is it true that they have stages like this everywhere in Aleece? I've heard troupes such as these perform every night in every city."

"Perhaps in every city, but not in every town and village. Most do have some sort of stage, but the sizes vary. In Delemy there are multiple stages, and troupes that perform every day."

He shook his head. "Tamaria must be positively boring by comparison. No wonder you enjoy the thrill of spurring a horse into leaping a fence."

Several people in bright tunics were doing acrobatics, but Della's eyes flickered to Roric's face. "I wouldn't say boring."

The troupe began singing a song that dragged Della's attention back to them. It was a song she knew well—a ballad about a man who had journeyed far from his lover. He had crossed the Deep Woods and barely survived. He sang out his sorrow of leaving her behind, gratitude that she had not been with him when he barely escaped a dragon, and shame at the fear that prevented him from braving the Deep Woods again to return to her. Della sang along and found tears sliding down her cheeks.

Roric's warm fingers brushed away her tears. "Would you like to walk with me in the gardens?"

Della nodded, not trusting her voice with her throat still thick with tears. They walked away from the stage, the rise and fall of a happier song fading into the background behind them. The gardens weren't far from the stage and had also been well lit with torches. They meandered past a row of peonies. Away from the crowd Della shivered in the night air. Roric quickly unclasped a small, decorative cape. He settled it around her shoulders, and she was grateful for the warmth.

"Thank you."

"You don't need to thank me—I will always meet your needs. You will never be cold or hungry or bored with me."

Della's heart warmed at the look he gave her. She gazed up at the sky and sighed happily. "I'll always treasure the way you can see so many stars in Tamaria. They are so lovely. "

"Exquisitely lovely," Roric agreed, staring at her.

A blush crept across her cheeks, which she hoped was hidden in the shadows of the evening.

"I admit, I'm rather surprised to see you here for more than one reason. I thought you said you would be returning to Aleece," Roric told her as they resumed walking.

"I never planned to return until Eleonora had wed, as they need someone to keep the household running efficiently until then. However, things have escalated and I find myself conflicted." Della fingered one of the roses now surrounding them to avoid meeting his eyes.

"Escalated? Have you gotten yourself into trouble with the duchess?" Concern laced Roric's voice.

Della looked at him. "Did you send me a letter?"

"Yes, I did. Are you in trouble because of that? If so, I am sorry."

"Don't worry about that. It's just that I didn't get to read it and now I never will. What did you say in it?" Della stopped walking and turned to look at him.

Roric stared at her for a long moment, emotions warring in his eyes. "I—"

"There you are! Mother is furious with you for disappearing." A man at least a few years older than Roric came around the bend toward them. They had similar features, but he had a sharper jaw and was a few inches taller than Roric.

"Tell her that I apologize and I'll be back in soon."

The man noticed Della as he reached them. He broke out in a grin. "Ah. *Now* I see why you've skipped out on the party. Hello."

"Della, this is my brother, Freddie," Roric said hesitantly.

Freddie shot Roric a strange look that Della couldn't decipher. It flitted across his face so fast she wondered if she had imagined it. He took her hand and kissed it.

"It's a pleasure to meet the girl my brother insisted didn't exist," Freddie said in a tone of brotherly teasing. Roric's face flamed with embarrassment.

"It's a pleasure to meet a brother I've heard some interesting childhood tales about," Della unabashedly teased him back.

Freddie burst out in a hearty laugh. "I see why you like her. There's not a woman at court I've met who would be so bold. Which is likely also the reason you've avoided introducing her to Mother."

So, he was avoiding introducing her to his family. Was he afraid his mother wouldn't like her or her position?

"She is utterly unique." Roric smiled in relief.

"I'll see if I can hold mother off for a bit longer if you promise to return soon. She's also furious that you refused to dance with any of the ladies she invited here for you tonight, then danced three dances with this mysterious lady from another country. It's nearly midnight and the toasts will start. You're expected to give one," Freddie called as he hurried back to the castle.

"I forgot I have to give a toast," Roric groaned.

Della barely heard him. "Why don't we go inside? I'd hate for your mother to be angry with you."

He hesitated. "I thought you were avoiding Duchess De-Voss."

"I'm not afraid to face her, not anymore. I just didn't want her to stop me before I found you tonight. Roric, what was in that letter?" Della forced herself to keep breathing when all she wanted to do was hold her breath until he answered. Everything hinged on this moment and she could feel it. She could feel a change hovering in the air, but she didn't know what sort of change. She longed for a falling star to wish upon.

Roric's throat bobbed as he swallowed, the sound too loud in the suffocating silence. Della didn't even dare breath, but still he said nothing.

"I think that's answer enough for me." She had only been an entertaining plaything after all. Some bit of fun to be hidden away and then discarded. Her heart ached in her chest where it still pounded from the nearness of him. She cursed her body for the attraction she still felt toward him, even as hurt and betrayal lanced through her. She slid off his cloak and handed it back to him. He didn't take it.

Roric reached for her. "Della—"

A clock began booming out the hour. Della shoved the cloak into Roric's outstretched hand.

"It's almost midnight. I have to go!" She hurried along the path back toward the castle. She needed to get back to Franci's in time to change and meet up with the troupe. Trixie said they would leave around midnight, perhaps one o'clock.

"Della, *please*. Let me explain." Roric quickened his pace to catch up.

Della's heart pounded in panic as she slid back into the ballroom, the clock still chiming. What if the troupe left without her? She started to weave her way through the crowded edges, but found the crowd oddly began to part to make way for her. Perhaps she had been making a ruckus trying to get through so quickly, but she didn't have time to worry about that. Besides, it wouldn't matter soon anyway, as she would be back in Aleece. Della saw a woman grab Roric by the arm out of the corner of her eye, but she didn't stop.

"Theodoric! Where have you been?! You're always disappearing these days!"

That name struck a distant chord of memory, but Della didn't have time to focus on it now. She brushed it away as the crowd stopped parting for her and she had to push her way through once again.

"A moment, Mother, and I promise I'll give the grandest toast you ever heard," she heard Roric say. He broke free, plunging into the crowd after Della.

Once Della had left the ballroom, she lifted her skirts high to move as swiftly as possible down the long hallway to exit the castle.

"Wait!" Roric called behind her as she reached the castle doors. She wouldn't have stopped, but was forced to wait as the servants worked to open the enormous doors. No one should have doors that tall, even in a castle. It was impractical and made it impossible to leave in a hurry.

Della shot over her shoulder, "I haven't the time—"

"I know. I know you need to leave before you're caught here, even if you no longer work for the duchess. A servant at the royal ball..." He trailed off, shaking his head.

"I have just as much right to be here as they do!" Della snapped. She couldn't bear him acting as if she were lesser just because of her position. Why did being a maidservant mean she wasn't worthy of being treated as a lady no matter her bloodline? Her heart was tearing in two. She turned to go through the now open doors.

"A servant cannot live the life of a courtier. There are traditions and rules here. I know in Aleece things are different, but in Tamaria no one would accept you, even if you truly look the part in that dress," he said gently, catching her forearm to stop her from leaving.

Della drew herself up as tall as she could be. "I am a *lady* by birth. More so even than the duchess, whose title she gained from marrying *my* father! Noble blood flows through my veins despite how the duchess, Lord Faust, or anyone else treats me! Despite how *you* are treating me." Della spoke fiercely but hurt crept into her voice at the end.

"You never told me that." He sounded startled.

"That's because I believe a person's value comes from how they behave and treat others, not from their titles. I thought you saw me as more than a servant from the things you said, despite my fallen state. I can see now those were merely flowery words spoken to steal kisses. I was a fool to think that you could see me as a person that you loved, regardless of my title. If you never saw me as ever having more value than a serving girl who was entertaining in private—someone you'd be ashamed of your family knowing even exists—well then, that says more about you than it does of my lack of title," Della said with grim severity.

He looked frozen in shock as though she had slapped him.

"Since you could not love me for the person that I am beneath the cinders that marred my cheeks when we first met, then at least respect me enough to let me go now." Della tugged out of his grasp.

She picked her skirts up again and raced down the steps. Della was already running down to the streets when she heard him calling for her. She glanced over her shoulder as she ran and saw someone pulling him by his arm back into the castle.

She eventually slowed from a run to a brisk walk and realized she had lost one of her glass slippers. Regret filled her, but she couldn't go back. She pulled off the other with a sigh and made her way barefoot to Franci's shop.

CHAPTER TWENTY

I t had been hard to leave. Franci halfheartedly tried insisting that Della stay, but Della had changed out of her
ballgown and gathered her things quickly. She had no time
to debate it with Franci, rushing out desperately fast to try
to catch the troupe before they left. When she had hugged
Franci goodbye it had been a tight, tearful affair.

Della hurried to the edge of town with her small sack
containing a change of clothes and some dried food that
traveled well. She found the performers already loaded into
two vardos with only Trixie waiting outside them.

"You've made it just in time! We thought you might not
be coming and almost left." Trixie opened the door to one
vardo and motioned for Della to climb in.

The vardo had narrow bunk beds built into one side,
three beds high. She'd have to be careful not to bang her
head when she woke in the morning as there wasn't much
space between them. Light snoring came from one of the
beds.

Trixie whistled to the lead driver and leapt in gracefully,
pulling the door shut behind her. She latched it, settling on
a narrow bed as the vardo rocked into motion.

"You can sleep there. Store your bag in one of the compartments underneath so it doesn't slide around while we travel." Trixie motioned to one of the bottom bunks.

In the dim light of the shuttered lantern, Della found three small compartments under the bed, each with a latch to hold the door closed. She opened the first and found it already held someone's belongings. The next one was empty, so she pushed her bag in. She removed her boots and shoved them in too before latching the small door closed.

"Thank you." Della turned back to Trixie, but the girl was already asleep.

Della climbed into the compact bunk and found that it had short wooden slats on the sides to prevent one from rolling out while the vardo moved. Which was good because the bed was so narrow Della barely fit into it laying on her back. She didn't dare turn onto her side and risk falling out over the low railing.

She hadn't changed into a nightgown with the others already in the vardo, and her hand rested on a lump in her pocket. Frowning, Della pulled the item out of her pocket. Her heart twinged as she recognized the handkerchief Roric had given her that night under the stars, where he had held her while she cried. She shook her head at her own foolishness. Della had admitted fears to him that she hadn't even admitted to Franci. The handkerchief in her hand had been washed, pressed, and folded into a neat square. She had carried it in her pocket each day, hoping to run into Roric and return it to him. Della crumpled it in her hand and the stiff embroidery in one corner rubbed her palm. She ran her thumb over the letters there, not bothering to hold it up to the lantern to see it better. She knew what she would find.

TA

T not *R*. She had thought Roric was an odd given name, but it seems it wasn't his name at all. It might be a nickname, or something that he had made up entirely. Della was such a fool to have let herself fall for a liar. She had been so busy protecting her own identity that she hadn't pushed hard enough to discover his. He had known her name, her position, and her residence. She had only known the false name that he had given her. She stuffed the handkerchief back into her pocket. Exhaustion from the entire day swelled up around her and she fell asleep.

As they traveled the troupe stopped at many towns. Each time the performers gave a show, earning money to buy food and other necessities. Sometimes in the poorer villages they would receive stray produce or absolutely nothing, and on those days they used any food they had foraged or caught, occasionally sharing with the villagers who had less. Della even thought she saw Trixie slip a coin into the palm of a little girl once.

Della didn't have performing skills, so she was relegated to singing along to the choruses of songs throughout the performance and holding the collection hat for the crowd to deposit tips. She did cook and mend as much as possible to help repay them for her passage, but they believed everyone must do their part and refused to let her do all the chores by herself. There was a strange comradery in doing such things with everyone together, rather than all on her own as she had grown up doing in Tamaria.

When they entered the Deep Woods and there were fewer towns, they relied completely on foraging and the snares they set up while they camped for the night. Della had already had some knowledge of such things, but learned so much more from the troupe members about the wild mushrooms, berries, and leaves they could eat. They had some dried food, of course, but the fresh food made it last longer and alleviated the monotony of travel fare. Most of the troupe members walked outside the vardos during the day, but they always stopped a bit before sundown to eat the final meal of the day and prepare for the evening. No one was allowed to stay out of the vardos at night while in the Deep Woods. Della heard wolves and other strange sounds that made her glad for the safety of the wooden walls around her. Most nights they would hang a lantern inside and play card games or tell stories for an hour or two before turning in. There was an entire day and night where they were as silent as possible after seeing ogre tracks. Though they managed to avoid running into the creature, everyone seemed to hold their breath until the trees shrank and thinned somewhat as they left the Deep Woods.

The troupe visibly relaxed as the trees thinned a little and they left the Deep Woods. Della herself found her steps feeling lighter and herself sleeping deeper. Though most of Aleece was still considered a forest with towns cropping up in meadows or clearings, the trees weren't as tall and wide. Creatures like ogres rarely ventured into the regular woods where they could be more easily spotted and hunted.

Despite the forested land, towns and cities had still sprung up all over it. As towns grew, the townsfolk chopped down trees to make room for new homes or fields, using the lumber to build houses and shops. The trees did thin closer to the coast, which was one of the reasons the Delemy was at the very edge of the land where it met the sea. Della had smelled the sea before she could see the large stone walls surrounding the capital. Even now within the walls, she couldn't see it. She would have to go to the inner edge of the city or inside the palace grounds to see the ocean properly.

"Do you know what you will do now that you're back in Aleece? You're welcome to stay with us as long as you like, of course," Trixie asked Della as they carried a box of props to The Wings.

All the stages had small buildings called The Wings near them. It was named after the wings in an actual theater, where actors might stash props or await their scenes. The performing stages in the city for troupes held no such side areas and thus The Wings had a few rooms, each occupied by one troupe who had a slot on stage that day. The Wings made it easy for the troupe to keep props nearby without being underfoot and allowed for costume changes, since caravans were in an encampment outside the city walls.

Della pulled open the door of The Wings and the two girls sidled inside before she answered Trixie's question. "I plan to find work as a maid, or perhaps a lady's maid, depending on what is available. Or I will become a laundress if I can't find work as a maid."

Trixie looked at her doubtfully and Della knew why. There wasn't a great demand for maids in Aleece, and even laundress-es were few and far between. Aleeceans were an industrial people, most preferring to do their own work themselves rather than outsourcing, but there were still nobility and those who were too busy running businesses to do the work of a maid in their own home.

"Perhaps you could be a governess," Jenell suggested, having overhead the conversation while bringing over a box of costumes. Della bit back a smile she noticed Felix tripping over his feet to open the door for the tall girl.

Della shook her head. "I don't have enough formal training, having only picked up what my stepsisters were taught in bits and pieces as I did other things around the house."

"Well, we could always try to teach you a song and jig," Jenell sounded a little too optimistic. Della hadn't picked up any of the dancing well enough for it to give a decent performance and, while she could sing, hers wasn't a voice that would cause people to stop and listen. She was better suited for the chorus.

"Thank you. I will do my best while I am with you, though hopefully I will find lodging soon." Della smiled at them fondly. While she enjoyed the troupe, there wasn't a place for her here and she had no desire to perform. For now, she helped them organize props and costumes in the room they had been allotted in The Wings.

Della had tried to secure lodging upon arriving in the city, but with the many travelers and visitors, every boarding house she had tried had been full. She thought of her old manor and her heart ached. She had never had to find lodging here before, having always had her manor or staying with her aunts and grandfather, though most of her aunts had moved away due to marriages in other kingdoms. Some of her aunts were here at all times, there always had to be three in line for the throne. Della knew she should approach them, but her stomach clenched at the thought. What if her stepmother had sent her letters and they truly had been too busy to reach out to her? It was very possible that only Margarete was in the country and had far too much to do as crown princess to answer her niece. Besides, Aunt Margarete was rather stern, the most formidable of all her aunts. Della wasn't sure she was ready to show up unannounced and penniless. What would her aunt do with her? No, Della didn't want to show up like a beggar at the castle doors. She would reacquaint herself with the city and find work first.

The city was smaller than she remembered—the streets weren't quite as large and the shops were a bit shorter. She had only been eight when she was here last. It felt both familiar and strange to her at the same time. The clamor of so many people packed within the walls crashed over her like a wave, but the familiar accent most spoke with had been soothing. Della hadn't realized how much she missed that sound. Through the familiarity and relief, her heart had still twinged when she walked past a dress shop that had two mannequins wearing fine dresses in the window and thought of Franci. One day she would have to bring Franci here to see the styles in Aleece.

"We got a good slot." Felix's comment pulled Della out of her reverie and back to the present.

The troupe had spent the first day in Delemy obtaining permission to perform and auditioning for a time slot to perform on the large stage in the main square. Aleece valued its entertainment, but with so many performers the competition was fierce. Only the best maintained a constant slot here, most were like this troupe and came here occasionally as traveling performers had their own allotment of spots available. The worst performers…Well they were sent to the smaller stages in the less busy part of the city to attempt to get a spot there.

Wendell grinned as he clapped his hands together. "It's almost our turn. Is everything ready?"

Trixie straightened the screen they would use to change behind. "The costumes are laid out."

"Props are set," Felix said.

Jenell peered out the window. "The crowd is as thick as ever."

"Let's hope their coin purses are thick as well." Wendell handed Della a hat to collect tips in and then strode out the door, the rest of the troupe behind him. He leapt up on stage and began to introduce the troupe.

Della stood with Trixie, who wouldn't perform until later. They always collected in pairs so no one was tempted to skim off the top. Della sang the opening song with the whole troupe, most of whom were singing and doing acrobatics on the stage. Della, Trixie, and a few others sang from the ground before the stage. Trixie grinned at her and belted out the words so loud Della almost winced. Coins, flowers, and other offerings from the audience were already being tossed into the hat. Della scanned the crowd, moving to accept offerings from further away as needed.

Her heart skipped a beat when a flash of blonde hair pinned up in the same style her mother had often worn caught her eye. It happened often here in Aleece, where blonde was more common than the Tamarian dark hair that she had grown so used to. She sucked in a deep breath to calm herself, but couldn't help watching the woman anyway. The lady wove through the crowd with the same elegant grace Della's mother had possessed. Though her memories of her mother were few, she at least remembered those small things, her mother's walk and hair. It was painfully pleasing to see this movement that mirrored her dear mother's own grace. She glided so effortlessly through the crowd that it almost looked like the others were moving out of her way. The woman stopped a few rows shy of the front and scanned the far end of the stage. She seemed to be looking the performers over one by one until at last her gaze fell on Della. They both gasped at the same time and the crowd fully parted around the woman.

"Adella?" came her mother's voice in a gasp.

"Mother?" Della whispered in shock at the same time.

The woman frowned. "Mother? Oh! Little Della! My, how you have grown."

The woman rushed forward and yanked Della into a tight hug, oblivious that a hush had fallen over the crowd and even the performers seemed frozen on stage.

"Dear little Della! It's me, Aunt Annalise," said the woman that looked just like her mother.

"*Oh!*" Della shook her head to clear it. Of course! Annalise looked identical to her mother because she was her twin.

"When I overheard the kitchen maid gossiping about having seen a spectator of the late Princess Adella lingering around a troupe in the city, I had to come see for myself. Well, it all makes sense now! I don't know why no one guessed it might be her daughter all grown up."

She released Della and began pulling her away. Della had the presence of mind to shove the hat full of tips into Trixie's bewildered hands as they passed, her aunt not paying attention to the money Della had been holding.

"You must come back to the castle with me, of course! It's wonderful to see you! I didn't know you were planning to come back. Why didn't you write to let us know?"

"I had no reason to believe you would respond to my letters now, after not receiving any responses to them ten years ago." The words slipped out before Della could stop them and she winced. She hadn't realized she had been holding on to that anger. She didn't even know if her stepmother had even sent the letters at all.

Her aunt stopped walking and turned to her. "What letters?"

Della swallowed thickly. "I wrote to you, or at least one of your sisters, every week the first year I lived in Tamaria. I missed my home and my family. Everything was new and strange, and I reached out for some bit of comfort. Not one of my aunts wrote back."

Aunt Annalise's face crumpled a bit, and she folded Della into her arms. "I never received any letters from you. None of us did. We all assumed that was because you were doing so well. Sometimes a new setting can help someone move past their mourning. You were so young and deserved a full, happy life. None of us wanted to remind you of all you had lost. We did receive reports that Duchess DeVoss had settled into a home in Fellsantra with her daughters, collecting the widow's stipend. We knew she could provide for you with that money and waited for you to be ready to reach out."

"She must have destroyed my letters then." Della's heart squeezed from a new wound created by her stepmother's cruelty.

"I'm so sorry, Della." Her aunt released her, linking arms with her as she began walking again.

Della fell into silence. Aunt Annalise continued to chat all the way back to the castle, but Della didn't hear much of what she said, still lost in her own sadness. Della did notice after a bit how a few guards trailed close behind them, but not near enough to overhear, effectively giving her aunt both privacy and protection.

Once they were back at the castle, Aunt Annalise had Della's things collected from the troupe and brought to the room she had the servants preparing for her niece. Della was flooded with gratitude when she opened the bag and found her small pouch of coins had been included and realized the troupe had even added some of the day's wages for the hours she had helped. She wouldn't have expected that, especially after they watched her be carted off by one of the kingdom's princesses.

"What is this? Is this what you wore in Tamaria?" Aunt Annalise clucked in distaste as she picked through Della's threadbare clothing. She frowned and held up a handkerchief. "Why do you have a handkerchief with someone else's initials on it?"

Della snatched Roric's handkerchief back. Aunt Annalise stared at her with startled, wide eyes and Della blushed.

"Sorry." Della balled the fabric square in her fist. "We didn't have a lot of money."

"Oh? The King's stipend for widows wasn't enough? Did your stepmother and stepsisters wear such rags and purchase used hankies? I can't imagine Mariel ever wearing clothes in such a state, vain creature that she is." Aunt Annalise's ever gentle face was briefly marred by a rare anger.

Della looked away to hide the shame bringing pink heat to her face.

"Well at least this is decent. It looks almost like you've never worn it before." Her aunt held up a pale green gown.

The gown was cut in the latest Tamarian fashion and had silver details on the collar, hem, and waist. Pinned to it was a note.

Just in case you have an occasion to wear it. I'd hate for all my hard work to go to waste.

Della easily recognized Franci's handwriting. Her lips tugged into a grateful smile and she silently sent blessings to her friend.

"Well, I'll have a maid draw you a bath and send for the royal dressmaker to have you properly outfitted while you are here. For today, wear this lovely gown," Aunt Annalise instructed her before leaving the room.

The bath felt luxurious. It had been ages since Della had used heated water. Della dunked her hair and rested against the metal back, letting the warmth pull all the tension from her muscles. A maid moved to scrub her, but Della took the washcloth and shook her head.

"I can do it myself, thank you." It would be weird to be scrubbed by someone else after so many years of doing it herself. Even now, she felt oddly exposed. No one had seen her naked body, not even a servant. No matter her bloodline, Della didn't think she could ever get used to it, and didn't see a reason to when she was perfectly capable of doing it herself.

"As you wish." The maid bowed and moved about the room, tidying the already neat items with her back to Della.

Della scrubbed herself quickly. The scent hit her nose and she paused. Roric's face flashed through her mind. "Is this lavender?"

"Yes, my lady. Do you wish me to fetch you a different scent?"

"No, it's fine for now. In the future, would you bring something else? Eucalyptus or citrus perhaps?"

"Of course, my lady."

"Thank you." Della didn't need to be reminded of him every time she took a bath and for however long the smell would linger afterward.

Della let the maid help her with her hair and then wrap the towel around her. It felt so strange to be waited upon. The maid rubbed a pumice stone against Della's palm.

"Oh! What are you doing?" Della pulled her hand back.

"It's to remove the callouses. Forgive me, my lady, if this is too bold, but you have the hands of a maid. It's not fitting for the granddaughter of the King."

Della sighed and held out her hand. She would have preferred to keep them, but she didn't want to make her aunts look bad or rile their anger at her previous situation any further than it likely would be. The maid quickly scraped her hands raw. The remaining pink flesh stung a bit, but it was smooth.

After she was dressed and the maid had arranged her hair, Della went to find her aunts.

CHAPTER TWENTY-ONE

The library in the Aleecean castle was enormous. Della had rarely ventured into its maze of shelves as a child, and even now it was intimidating. It was also the perfect place to hide, and Della had avoided almost every social gathering by spending time wandering the room.

She sat at one of the small tables with a small stack of books and an open tome in front of her. *The Ancestry of Tamarian Monarchy* was her last hope at finding any hint of Roric's noble line. She didn't have high hopes that a book about the royal line would mention noblemen, but it was the last volume the librarian had given her regarding lineage in Tamaria. It would be so much easier if he'd been a prince, but no prince would have given a serving maid so many hours of his day.

Della flipped the last page and sighed. There was the current king and queen, and below them the three princes her step-family had squabbled over so often.

Henrich Adalburg
Frederick Adalburg
Theodoric Adalburg

She sighed, a breeze that sent the handkerchief fluttering toward the floor. Della snatched it up and dropped it on top of the book. T.A. Her eyes flitted to the names in the book. H.A.,

F.A., and T.A. were the initials of the three princes. It—it couldn't be. But Roric had said that he had two older brothers, Henri and Freddie. At the ball, Freddie had said Roric was to give a toast. A toast at the ball honoring Prince Frederick's engagement. It made sense that his brothers would give speeches in his honor. Hadn't a woman at the ball had called him Theodoric? Perhaps she was speaking to someone else, but Roric had answered, hadn't he? Della tried to remember, but she had been so angry and hurt that she hadn't paid much attention to anything besides getting away.

If he was a prince, was that why he hadn't told her where he lived? Why would a prince keep seeing a serving maid? Della had been so surprised at having a future duke out with her and Roric, yet she had been spending time with an actual prince? It was impossible. And yet... Wasn't it also impossible that the daughter of a former princess would end up as a serving maid in another country?

"You can't simply lounge around reading all day, every day." Aunt Margarete's commanding voice made her jump.

Della slammed the book shut on the handkerchief. Della looked at her aunt, next in line to be queen. A silver crown made a depression in her thick, black hair. Aunt Margarete stood ramrod straight, and her red gown clung elegantly to her frame.

"What do you suggest I do then? I don't mean to be difficult, I promise. It's only that I didn't grow up in this life, or even the life of a future duchess. I don't know what to do in a castle." Della sighed.

"We have heard and been angered by your tale of what happened since your stepmother whisked you off in the middle of the night. Indeed, we were furious when you disappeared without warning as a young girl, but I was stuck dealing with matters of state, Tamaria is so far, and we truly thought you would be happiest staying with your sisters." Aunt Margarete's lips tightened.

"Had we known of your misery, we would have rescued you immediately!" Aunt Annalise put in emphatically appearing behind Aunt Margarete. Then softer, "I'm so sorry about that, dear. If we had received even one of your letters, we would have whisked you out of there immediately."

"Be that as it may, your moroseness is clearly not due to justifiable anger toward your stepmother, so I suspect there is something that you have left out of your tale. Since you have decided to omit it, you shouldn't be subjecting us to your obvious bad mood," Aunt Margarete said with an edge to her voice.

Della stared at her in shock.

"Margarete!" Aunt Annalise protested.

"Find something productive to do with your time. You're putting the servants off moping around like this after we've declared you our ward."

"I'm almost eighteen—I'm hardly a ward," Della protested.

"Precisely." Aunt Margarete flashed a triumphant smile. She leveled a pointed gaze at Della before sweeping out of the room.

Della sagged back against the couch and Aunt Annalise came to her, putting her arms around her niece.

"Don't take her words too hard, dear one. She's always been a bit sharp. Even more so now with the strain of running the kingdom while not in full control, as our father hasn't *quite* ceded the throne yet. It has been hard on her. Dear Father doesn't want to put the weight of a kingdom on her, but he doesn't see that she already holds it," Aunt Annalise said softly. She seemed to shake herself. "You really ought to find something to do though. Eighteen is both too young and too old to sit around a castle all day without a purpose."

"The problem is, I haven't a clue what to do with myself. I'm not a duchess and the manor was sold long ago, so I can't go there anyway. No one needs a maid to clean or help the ladies of the house. I *might* be able to find work as a washerwoman, but I do somewhat dread that," Della sighed.

"A washerwoman?! Goodness no! The daughter of a former princess! We would never let you fall so far!" Aunt Annalise looked appalled.

"Well, I can't think of anything else that I could do with the funds I have." Della shrugged.

"We will sustain you as long as you need, funds and all. You can do anything. You could have tutors to learn music, art, history, or anything else. Find something that you are passionate about and do that. It's okay if you have to try new things while you figure it out."

"If I can do anything I wish, I think I may have an idea." Della grinned and strode off toward the stables.

"You- you want to do what?!" the groom spluttered.

"I want to learn to train, breed, and break horses. Preferably Stronghorses, if the opportunity arises," Della repeated.

Oh, the grooms had been happy to let her into the stables, they'd shown off the beautiful creatures with pride. They hadn't minded when Della had said she'd like to brush and help care for the horses. But *this*. Becoming a horse trainer was apparently appalling for a granddaughter of the king. Della was not, however, just the granddaughter of the crown.

"I believe we live in Aleece, a country that prides itself on equality between its men and women." Della tried to keep her voice even despite her rising irritation.

"Yes, but horse breaking is dangerous work! What would the king say if you broke your neck?"

"Perhaps that my chosen line of work is unsurprising, given who my father was."

The groom's fear made him unrelenting and, in the end, Della had to go to Aunt Annalise, who only hesitated long enough to ascertain that Della was absolutely sure that was what she wanted to do. The grooms were given strict orders from her aunt to teach Della in all they could while her aunt sought out a horse trainer to teach her niece properly. All the grooms could really do was go over the care of each individual horse, including one with a special diet. They were all things Della knew, but she was grateful for the time to get to know the vast number of horses kept in the royal stables.

The trainer arrived a week later, while Della was in the stables brushing a horse.

"Are you the noble girl who wishes to become a horse trainer?"

Della whirled around. The trainer leaning in the doorway of the stall wore a green riding outfit that set off their red hair—twisted into a top knot—and green eyes nicely.

"You're a woman!"

"Yes, as are you, Lady Adella Caspari," the trainer said dryly.

Della grinned. Leave it to Aunt Annalise to find a female horse trainer for her niece. "Please, call me Della."

"Good, that was a mouthful. I'm Trainer Roth. I see you know how to properly take care of domesticated horses. We shall progress to taking care of wild horses then." The trainer left the stall.

Della scrambled to close up the stall and put away the brush. Trainer Roth had already left the stables in the few minutes it took her to do so. Della walked outside and found the red-haired woman at the fence of a corral. A light-colored foal frolicked inside.

"Bring him to me." Trainer Roth tossed a halter and lead rope at Della.

Della caught it and entered the enclosure, making sure to secure the gate behind her.

"Hello there," Della addressed the young horse. He tossed his head back and watched her with weary eyes as she approached. She got a handsbreadth away from him when he sprinted away. "It's alright, I won't hurt you."

Della tried again to reach him, but he skipped out of range. The foal galloped in circles around her. Della resorted to running to either side, trying to hem him in. The corral was too wide though, and he always had room to escape. She tried running him down and her hand just skimmed his neck as he darted away again. Della let out a frustrated sound and swiped her now sweaty brow with the back of her hand.

The gate opened and Trainer Roth entered. The foal eyed her suspiciously until she pulled out a carrot. He trotted over, pausing just out of reach. Trainer Roth held her arm in the air as still as a statue. The foal sniffed the treat, then tried to take it. He snapped off the end and retreated, crunching happily. After he finished his bite, he returned for more, this time with less apprehension. Trainer Roth let him take two more bits of the long carrot before she snatched his mane with her other hand. He pulled back, but remained too focused on the carrot to try hard to escape. She gave him the treat and used her now free hand to slip on a halter, fastening it quickly. She had tied the lead rope onto the halter prior to putting the whole thing on him, and held it firmly now that he had finished the treat and began to fight harder to get away.

"You can exert all the effort you want and get nowhere. If you are resourceful and kind, you will find success much faster. One never succeeds for long by bullying others without ever giving a reward. It's the same when working with horses. It is best to start with a kind, but firm hand," Trainer Roth said.

"I didn't know we could use treats." Della fought down the urge to roll her eyes. Had she known Trainer Roth would arrive today and what would be required of her, then she would have stocked her pockets with carrots or apples.

"One must always use every resource that is available. It is better to use intelligence to work more efficiently than to work harder in order to compensate." Trainer Roth rotated so the anxious foal could run circles within the confines of the rope.

"I will bring them next time."

"Those are words of any trainer who let a horse elude their capture, throw them off, or seem impossible to train. Do not let me hear them again. You must always be prepared for anything."

"You have made your point." Della bit the inside of her cheek to keep from saying more.

"I can see that I have." Trainer Roth pulled the rope to bring the foal in closer. Tired now, he only gave one halfhearted jerk against the rope when she laid her hand on his neck. "See how I let him tire himself out? Before he was letting you do that, waiting until he had to skip out of reach. Horses are faster than us, but you can be more resourceful and use that to your advantage. Come, get to know him and let him grow used to you."

Della stood beside the woman, who handed her another carrot. Della held it out and this time the foal barely hesitated before taking the treat. He let Della stroke his neck while he munched happily.

"What's his name?" Della rubbed his muzzle.

"That is for you to decide. He shall be your first task. Befriend him. He's too young to ride yet, but horses are much easier to train when they already trust you. Freshly caught full-grown horses are much harder to train than a foal who was fed treats and has already come to accept your touch." Trainer Roth smiled.

"I shall name him Alion then, if we are to be friends." Della patted his flank.

She smiled. He was her first challenge to overcome in her new life. It was a life where she was the one in control for once, making decisions to ultimately become the woman she wanted to be. She hoped her parents would be proud.

CHAPTER TWENTY-TWO

D ella pulled her horse from a trot to a slow walk as
they rounded the bend. Her childhood home had
been hidden by the Aleecean trees until that moment. As
she grew up, her family had enjoyed the cozy seclusion that
the woods had offered. Even when they had ventured into
the city proper for longer than a day, they had stayed at the
castle overnight rather than a noisy inn.

With the grand manor before her, a wave of emotions
washed over Della. Joy at seeing her last true home again,
nostalgia as memories flooded her mind, and an odd ache
at the thought that her father would never return to her
here. It left her feeling oddly displaced. She pulled her horse
to a stop on the cobblestones before the large steps. She
and Aunt Annalise dismounted, as did the guards that had
accompanied them.

"Wait out here please," her aunt told the guards.

Della lifted her skirts as she walked up the steps with her
aunt.

"Here, dear." Her aunt pressed something into her hand.

Della looked at the object in her palm. It was a house key.
She fitted it in the lock and swung the door open. "For some
reason I had expected it to creak."

"I had it maintained. I hoped one day the duchess might return." Aunt Annalise smiled softly.

Della wrinkled her nose as they stepped into the house. "Why on the Great Cliffs would you want her back?"

"Oh! Don't use such common language, dear," her aunt admonished.

"Sorry. I wasn't exactly brought up as a lady."

"You forget I knew you used such language as a child, too. I thought you would grow out of it, but I see you haven't."

Della's cheeks warmed as her aunt saw through her flimsy excuse. The truth was the rough expression reminded her of Tilya and her father, so she had kept it in her vocabulary.

Della glanced around the sitting room. The furniture and paintings had all been covered in sheets to prevent the dust from ruining them. It was a kind gesture, one that implied its residents were merely on holiday for the season and would be returning. It also gave a strange, ghostly appearance to the house.

"Be that as it may, you are a duchess. The *true* Duchess Caspari. You misunderstood me before. Your stepmother has no right to this house. I suspect that's the reason she fled so quickly. Once the time of mourning had passed, her title of duchess would have been removed in lieu of the title duchess regent until you became of age. At that point, she would lose the title and rights to the estate entirely. I realized when you spoke of the manner being sold that you didn't know your own inheritance, but I was so thrown off by your notion of becoming a washerwoman that I completely forgot to correct you." Aunt Annalise gave her a wry smile.

"*What?*" Della stopped short.

"It's unsurprising that your stepmother wouldn't have told you of all this. I just hadn't realized that you were too young to have learned about the rights of succession in Aleece." Her aunt sighed.

"I know the line of succession. The throne goes to the oldest regardless of gender unless they wish to abdicate, becoming a duke or duchess. They may do so as long as a younger sibling agrees to take their place and there are at least three princes or princesses in line for the throne," Della recited automatically.

"Yes, everyone learns the *royal* line of succession from a young age as part of their history lessons, but you would have learned as you got older how title and estate succession outside the royal family works. The title of duchess was your mother's as she exchanged princess for duchess in order to marry your father. Therefore, the title was not your father's, but rather he became a duke consort by marriage. We tend to bypass the word consort out of respect, which is why you never hear anyone referred to that way. With your mother's passing, your father technically became the duke regent, though everyone was so used to simply calling him the duke that we didn't bother officially exchanging the title. We also loved him and Adella so dearly that we didn't intend to ever revoke the title of duke even after you became the duchess. We assumed you would likely marry and move to your husband's home, or if you wished to stay here, we would have simply granted your father new lands. Perhaps that was a mistake on our part given how things progressed, but at the time we could not have foreseen it." Aunt Annalise shook her head regretfully.

"So did that make my stepmother duchess regent by marriage?"

"No. In truth it was an oddity. Your father should have been duke regent and your stepmother duchess consort, a title only granted to both until you were of age. When you became duchess, they would have lost their titles. We never anticipated the new marriage or how muddled it would make everything. After your father passed, we did send a missive to let your stepmother know we would change the titles as you got older."

"So, essentially...my stepmother has no title?" Della almost laughed at the irony. She had forced into servitude by a woman with no title, when all the while Della was the true duchess. No wonder her stepmother had forced her to serve as their maid! If she had grown up a noblewoman, Della might have uncovered the truth.

"Yes. Either as duchess regent or duchess consort she had no true rights to the title of duchess beyond raising you." Aunt Annalise trailed a hand along a windowsill.

"That clever minx! She is living in Widow's Court in Tamaria under the title of duchess!" Della exclaimed.

"Yes, we did assume she might have done such a thing, especially after she tried to sell the manor and we put a stop to it. She was quite upset to learn about the inheritance of titles." Aunt Annalise shook her head. "Once she left our country, her title wasn't really in our control, though we did consider writing to the king of Tamaria. Then Odelia pointed out that the king's stipend would ensure you and your sisters were taken care of, and that it can only be received by a noblewoman, so we all agreed it would be better not to ensure her title was stripped. Besides, there was nothing for her to do here but remarry and as she had already been married twice, coupled with two daughters and a stepdaughter in tow... It seemed unlikely. We could have easily sent for you, our dear niece, if we revealed the truth, but how could we leave your step-sisters and stepmother to poverty at the same time? We thought you were happy, especially with two sisters. All twelve of us have leaned on each other through hardships and know well how sisters can lift each other up. We ultimately deemed it best to leave you be. Had we known... I wish it had been different for you. Oh, how I wish we had rescued you from her. I'm so sorry, Della." Her aunt's eyes shimmered with silver tears of regret.

Della said the only thing that might be able to justify it for both of them. "In truth, I don't think they could have managed without me."

She felt a twinge of guilt though, as she thought of her stepfamily trying to manage now. Was Eleonora playing the role of servant? Della pushed those thoughts aside when her aunt spoke again.

"You certainly are capable. You even managed to rescue yourself—a feat that included crossing the Deep Woods!" Aunt Annalise said with admiration.

"It's not like I did it alone. I was traveling with a troupe in their caravan. I'll always be grateful to them for providing me with a way home. I could never have crossed the Deep Woods otherwise."

Aunt Annalise grinned. "Which is exactly why they have been rewarded with a permanent spot in the rotation of the main stage here. They did something we failed to do—they brought you home to us."

Della's smiled back, but turned away quickly so her aunt didn't see it falter. She pretended to examine a portrait of her parents that hung on the wall. Was she home? She wondered what Roric's home looked like, then quickly banished the thought. She wandered from room to room, feeling strangely empty as she walked through the deserted manor.

"It must feel odd, to be here without them. I know I feel the loss of each sister who has moved on to a new life in one way or another, though we try to see each other when we can. Even I am only visiting for a time, and soon I'll return to my husband."

"It does seem like it would be rather lonely to be here without anyone else," Della admitted.

"Well, you can stay in the castle all you like! If you should wish to live here, we can certainly hire a full staff to keep it bustling as well. You really ought to socialize with the court too. You may find friends to invite over for tea or parties."

"I don't know about all that, but the stables and pastures here would serve me well if I can become practiced in my father's line of work," Della said thoughtfully.

"I hope his name will lend you some prestige in this new endeavor. My sisters and I will support you however we can."

Della smiled. Her aunts had already helped by financially supporting her and finding Trainer Roth.

"Thank you. I plan to work hard and earn my own reputation in time. That and some financial independence, so I won't be a strain on you forever."

"You have some fortune left. We set it aside when Odelia noticed how quickly it was dwindling under your stepmother's care. As for working hard, I can see that you will. You already are. I know your parents would be proud."

Della felt her heart swell with pride. Her father would indeed be proud. He had so often let her watch as he worked with the horses that he bred and trained. He had even let her help with the smaller tasks of brushing them down, feeding them, or walking them around the pastures to show them off to potential buyers. She liked the idea that her mother would be proud too. Her mother certainly hadn't been concerned with titles, so her daughter becoming a horse trainer likely wouldn't have displeased her the way it would the mothers in Tamaria. Though her mother had valued love above all else, she even gave up being a princess for it. Della's heart ached as she thought of Roric. She couldn't help it if he didn't love her enough to see beyond the cinder girl, though. Her mother hadn't cared that her father was a horse merchant, only that he loved her and she loved him.

"Well?" Aunt Annalise prompted.

Della's cheeks flushed. "Sorry, I was lost in my thoughts."

"I suggested you stay at the castle for at least part of the week to meet members of court. Even if you don't want to host, it would likely help you to form some acquaintances or friendships in order to grow your business here. You'd be surprised how much of the interactions at court are not for social reasons. Political scheming is what Adella used to call it." Humor gleamed in her eyes.

"I suppose that would be logical. But Aunt Annalise, I've never been to court beyond running around as a child. I wouldn't even know where to begin!"

"Well, that can be easily remedied. I'll get a governess for you, and you can practice with me as well."

"I'm a bit old to have a governess." Embarrassment flooded Della. Most children finished with such lessons years ago. By her age, women were only taking lessons of the few skills they chose to study in depth for the rest of their lives, such as playing an instrument or learning a trade, not learning court etiquette. Thank goodness she had been old enough to have learned to read and write well, along with math that she had used many times when bartering.

"Nonsense! You're never too old to learn, and there's nothing wrong with catching up on the things you should have been taught. It will help you immeasurably to become the duchess you were meant to be. Sometimes misfortunes blow us off course, and just because you have found yourself back on the correct route, that's no reason to not plug the hole in your ship. It will only be to your advantage," her aunt's soft voice was almost stern for once.

"When you say it like that, it sounds silly for me to not take the lessons."

"One should never be embarrassed to seek out knowledge. I'll even find the most discreet governess and have her stay here in the manor while she tutors you. That way, none of the servants at the castle will gossip. Though first, we'll have to find you a cook, maid, and butler. Probably a lady's maid as well," Aunt Annalise told her cheerfully.

"That sounds expensive and unnecessary." Della raised her eyebrows. She didn't want to hire unneeded help just to flaunt her new status. That was something her stepmother would do, but not her.

"Nonsense. It's nothing like the staff we have at the castle. It's probably less than you should have, but to start it will do. As Margarete said before, we've made you our ward for the time being anyway, so don't worry about it cutting into your inheritance." Aunt Annalise waved a hand.

"That's not what my concern was, but very well. May I ask for a specific person as my lady's maid?" Della asked.

"Of course! Write down her name and I'll have one of my ladies-in-waiting inquire after her."

Aunt Annalise linked arms with Della and led her out of the manor, back to their horses. Della felt much more cheerful as she swung up onto her horse. Things were finally falling into place.

CHAPTER TWENTY-THREE

Della breathed in the sea air as she rode along the Aleecean beach. The dappled gray mare made the uneven sandy way feel as smooth as a paved road. The ebb and flow of the waves was soothing to Della. This beach had become her escape to alleviate the restlessness she felt at court. Despite her lessons, she still felt stiff and awkward around the nobility. She was grateful to her aunts for taking her in, but she felt out of place here. Her days in her manor were filled with working the horses, her current gray mare was the first of what she hoped to be many acquisitions. Florentina had a gentle nature, but was untrained—a perfect starting place for Della and Trainer Roth had agreed.

The horse trainer had brought some of her own untrained horses to show her what to do and for her to practice training now that she had befriended Alion. Trainer Roth seemed pleased with her quick progress despite her sternness, having declared Della to be a natural after her first week of training. Della had decided to purchase Florentina to keep as her personal horse, partially to remind her of her first true success. She rode Florentina down to the beach often to give her exercise and to escape the court.

At the sound of sand-muffled hoofbeats, Della glanced behind her and saw a rider speeding along the beach toward her. She twisted back around and purposefully pretended not to see them. She hoped it wasn't a servant sending for her, as she didn't want to return to the castle just yet. When she heard them pull up behind her, she let out a sigh.

"I was hoping for a slightly more enthusiastic greeting, but given the circumstances, I suppose I could have expected worse."

That familiar voice startled her, and she yanked the reins a bit too harshly as she commanded the horse to turn around. The mare snorted but obliged by turning her to face the man.

"Roric. Or rather, Your Highness," Della's voice was practically a sneer as she flourished a mock bow from the saddle to hide how she was trembling.

Roric sighed. "Della, is that really necessary?"

"I'm pretty sure the bow is required when addressing royalty from Tamaria."

"I meant the jeering." He sighed again. "I'm sorry that I've hurt you to the point that you feel the need to add such a bite to your words."

"I get the feeling you're only apologizing because my station has changed," Della said coldly.

"I'm apologizing because I truly mean it and because I want you to actually listen to what I have to say." Roric ran a hand through his hair in frustration.

Della's fingers twitched at the memory of running her hands through his silken hair. Her hands tightened on the reins so hard her knuckles turned white.

"There's only one thing I need to hear. Are you, or are you not here because you've discovered I am not simply a servant?" Della asked callously.

"That certainly makes things easier, but—" Roric raised his voice to a shout as Della spurred her horse away from him at a gallop, "—it's not why I'm here!"

The horse galloped away from Roric and back toward the castle. Della's blood pounded in her ears along with the hooves of the racing horses. Florentina was fast, but she was no match for a Stronghorse. Noa's speed allowed him to quickly overtake them despite Florentina's head start. He reached over and caught her horse's bridle, pulling them both to a halt.

"Would you just listen, woman?!"

"I don't see any reason to." Della yanked on the reins. Roric lost his grip, but Florentina had also had enough of the abuse and sat down. Della yelped in surprise as she tumbled from the horse's back and landed in a cloud of sand. Her cheeks heated and she was grateful no one else was around to see, or her fledgling reputation as a horse trainer would have crumbled. She scrambled up to find Roric at her side. Della shook out her skirts, noticing with some discomfort that her fall had forced sand into various areas under her clothing.

"Della, Tamaria isn't like Aleece. A prince cannot court anyone he wishes, even if he is third born." Roric held out his palms like she did when trying to placate a skittish horse.

"You seemed happy enough spending time with me, despite your country and your mother's rules. Was it exciting for you? Breaking the rules to have a bit of fun. Did you even stop to consider that you were playing with the feelings of someone whom you thought was only a lowly servant girl? If you thought there was no chance for us, then you should have left me in peace!" Della scratched angrily at the sand beneath one sleeve.

"Della, I wouldn't have sought you out for a bit of fun. There were enough girls at court who would have been happy to be a prince's plaything had I ever wished to be such a man, which I have not. I'm telling you with all sincerity that my feelings for you have always been real."

Della laughed bitterly. "Then why treat me like a dirty secret that no one could ever know about? Your brother, Freddie, said at the ball that you had told your family I didn't exist when they suspected you were seeing a maiden!"

"It's precisely because I cared for you that I couldn't tell anyone. If we were discovered they would have kept me from you! I knew it was impossible, but I wished to see you as often as I could. I've become quite besotted with you. I was delighted when I found out you weren't a servant because it meant that my mother couldn't oppose my courtship of you," Roric answered.

He took a step toward her, but Della stepped back under the pretense of gathering Florentina's reins.

"So you... You hid me so you could keep seeing me, not because you were ashamed of me?" Della tried to fight the tiny bit of hope beating in her chest. She wasn't ready to give up her anger just yet.

"Yes. I never wanted to hurt you. I knew I should stop seeking you out. It was an impossible situation—I, a prince and you, a servant. It could never be. But when I met you, it felt as though I'd found a piece of my soul that I hadn't known was missing. Every day I was away from you felt like having that part of my soul ripped away. It was an anguish I couldn't help wanting to stop, and you were the only balm that soothed it.

So yes, Della, I sought you out even when I knew I shouldn't, that it would only end in devastation, at least on my end. I sought you out, and I tried to store up each tender moment with you, hoping it'd be enough to keep me from shattering in the years I'd spend aching to hold you once more in my arms. Can't you see how finding out you should have held a place in court changed everything? It ratified the hope that I found I'd dared to have even in such a futile situation. It meant I had a chance to be with, *truly* with you forever, if you'd have me. If that is not enough for you to know that my intentions, that my love for you is true, then ask me right now to renounce my crown. I will do it. I don't care about your title or mine. All I care about is you." He took another small step toward her. This time she didn't back away.

Della swallowed hard. "You would give up your crown for me? And be what, exactly?"

"Whatever you wished. You're a duchess—we could be nobility. Perhaps we can pick up some sort of trade, like wood carving, or be merchants. We could simply take whatever inheritance I have and travel the world." He winced. "Assuming my mother doesn't convince my father to revoke that upon giving up my crown. Though my father could likely be persuaded to give us some money, or at the very least Freddie would happily siphon us some."

Della laughed at the thought. "You would do it, wouldn't you? The odd prince who helped a maidservant with her chores. Terribly, I might add."

"I drew up the water just fine and dried the dishes well." Roric's face held mock indignation.

"I suppose one might be more forgiving when considering you had faced down a descendant of the cockatrice." A smile tugged at Della's lips.

Hope sparked in Roric's eyes as he took another step toward her.

"I supposed I hadn't ever considered the possibility that you kept our meetings a secret to make more of them possible," Della conceded, returning to his earlier declaration.

"Seeing you was all I ever wanted." He stepped close enough to brush some sand from her hair. When it fell down her face, he swept it away from her cheek and left his palm resting there. Della found it hard to breathe. Her heart thundered wildly in her chest.

"So... you truly care for me?" Della hated the vulnerability that leaked into her wavering voice, but Roric smiled.

"One might even say love," he assured her softly before closing the space between them.

His lips met hers in a tender kiss and his other hand found her lower back to press her closer. Della's arms encircled him as the kiss deepened. They kissed until one of the horses snorted and they broke apart, laughing. Della couldn't tell if the heat in her cheeks was a blush or a delighted flush. Roric cleared his throat.

"Well, I suppose we should ride back to the castle. We have much to discuss, but we will risk rumors if we stay out here unchaperoned," he said.

"Oh, *now* you've decided we must be chaperoned?" Della teased, one eyebrow quirking up.

"I did try to bring Pieter along. Though now that I may court you properly, I intend to do everything the right way. I won't let anything tear us apart again, and rumors do have a tendency to do that—at least where a prince is concerned."

They mounted their horses, but enjoyed a leisurely pace back to the castle.

"So, how did you find me?" Della asked him as they rode.

"I sent Pieter to talk to Eleonora—neither of us thought approaching the imperious duchess would be best—but she was too nervous to say anything. She directed us to your dressmaker friend who said you had family in Delemy. She told me to inquire after Adella Caspari. Of course, Pieter asked the royal scholars after the name to see if it matched any nobility. He was furious when they told him it was the name of a deceased princess." Roric rubbed his neck and frowned at the memory.

"He didn't want you to come after me. He thought it was another trick," Della stated, unsurprised.

"Yes, but I had already left under the guise of vanquishing a new ogre infestation, one that I had hinted was getting dangerously close to the regular woods beyond than the Deep Woods. I might have embellished some rumors. Pieter assumed you had merely used the name thinking no one in Tamaria would notice and, well, since none of us did, it would have worked. I asked if there were any recorded duchesses with the name. I thought the duke must be the king's cousin and it wouldn't have been odd for him to name his daughter after his cousin's child they had lost as a way to honor her. Pieter and I were both quite shocked to find out it was a princess who had given up her title to become a duchess and also had a daughter named after her.

"I altered my men's course for the capital after receiving his letter with that information, thanking the stars for my good fortune. I knew my mother couldn't possibly fight our marriage if you had royal blood, or at least that my father would allow it, which would be enough. Mother's going to be furious that I traveled all the way here on an unannounced trip, chasing after a girl she's never heard of, that I initially courted as a servant."

Della made a face and Roric gave her a helpless shrug. She supposed he couldn't control his mother's thoughts and feelings on the matter, but only his own actions, which had brought him across dangerous land to find her.

"Pieter also wrote that he had sent the name Caspari to Cheval, the horse trader. That last name and a Stronghorse named Reynart recalled his memory of your father, who it turned out was quite the renowned horse trader that had kept his trade even after becoming a duke through marriage.

"All of these things aligned with what you had told me previously, except for you being a servant. However, your friend had implied that the duchess had forced you into a position below your station. So, I came to Delemy and made inquiries. I was directed to your old house first, not knowing you'd be at the castle." Roric shrugged as if he hadn't just defied his parents and longstanding traditions to search through two countries for her.

Della realized she was staring at him so she said the first thing that came to mind, which was to correct him. "It's not my old house, it simply is my house. I was too young to understand it, but I had inherited the title of duchess from my mother, not my father. The Duchess DeVoss technically isn't a duchess at all. So, my family bestowed the title, lands, and estate upon me at my return."

"Duchess Della. It does sound lovely." Roric smiled. He nudged his horse close enough for them to hold hands.

"Prince Theodoric Adalburg," Della tested the name out. She grinned mischievous. "I haven't made up my mind about that one."

"Well, you can continue to call me Roric. I didn't give you a false name, that was my nickname as a boy. Though I hope you will at least come to like the surname. I'd like you to have it, if you will have me," Roric told her, rubbing his thumb across the base of her finger where a marriage ring would sit.

"A prince and a duchess who was formerly a servant? Where would we live?" Della laughed, but it had a nervous edge to it.

"Wherever you wish. My castle. Your manor. The estate my family will likely grant me once I marry. I also saw some interesting vardos throughout my travels. We may have to ensure we only have two children and perhaps one dog if we live in such small quarters though." Roric grinned.

Della really laughed this time. "Do you mean that? Truly?"

"Well, I might make you compromise on the vardo. I think I could only live in one for a few months out of the year. But the rest of it, yes. *You* are my home. I don't need a castle, a crown, a title. Wherever you are, let me be there too, because if I am not, then I am lost."

Della lifted her face upward and he was already leaning toward her. She kissed him, speaking with her lips, though not with words. One of her hands slipped behind his neck, the other rested against his chest. Roric's hands buried in her hair as he deepened the kiss. A contented sigh slipped from her lips, breaking them apart just barely. He chuckled against her mouth, pulling away slightly.

"Am I to take that as a yes?"

"Yes, Roric, I will marry you. *After* you court me properly, and in a very public matter."

Roric laughed against my mouth again. "Yes, Della. I will treat you as I should have from the very beginning, My Lady. You will shine among all the court as I stand at your side."

Then he kissed her again, and the sun had shifted to a new position overhead before they made their way back to the castle.

CHAPTER TWENTY-FOUR

"Oh Della, there you are!" Aunt Annalise said, as Della and Roric stepped into the hall. She paused, appraising the young prince.

"This is Prince Roric of Tamaria," Della said quickly. "Roric, this is my aunt, Annalise."

Aunt Annalise frowned. "I don't recall that name among the three princes of Tamaria."

"Formally I'm known as Theodoric. Some close to me call me Roric," Roric clarified.

"I see." Annalise smiled, eyes twinkling.

Della blushed.

"I have a letter for you, Della. It was sent to your manor, but since you are currently here, one of the servants sent it over for you."

"Thank you," Della said.

She took the letter her aunt held out and immediately recognized Franci's script addressing the letter to Della.

"Do you mind if I read this now?" Della asked Roric, who shook his head.

"Come, let's go in the parlor here." Aunt Annalise led them to a nearby room.

Aunt Annalise and Roric sat down across from each other, talking quietly while Della stood by the window. Della opened the letter and read it quickly. Della felt a wave of gratitude as she read Franci's letter. Her friend had tried to warn her that Roric was coming after her, in case Della didn't want to see him. Though a laugh slipped out at the timing. The letter hadn't reached her before Roric, but the courier had certainly tried. They had left it at her manor—it wasn't the courier's fault she hadn't been there. Della sat beside her aunt on the settee.

"Was it something important?" Aunt Annalise asked.

"Franci tried to warn me of Roric's arrival." Della smiled.

Her aunt's smile faltered. "Warn you?"

"We had a falling out," Della explained. "I may have run off during a ball."

"I tried to follow when she left the ball, but my brother stopped me. I had a speech to give for Frederick and his betrothed. I had duties I had to attend to as a prince before I could follow my heart. These months apart, I cursed myself for not casting it all aside in that moment. I knew when I went to speak with Della the next morning and she was gone that I had chosen wrong." Roric was looking at her aunt, but leaned forward to cover Della's hand with his own.

"I left that night. The troupe that performed at the ball was the one that let me join their caravan back to Aleece. They were leaving soon after midnight and it was my best chance to return."

"I had Pieter—my cousin—ask her stepsister about her, though I didn't know she was her stepsister at the time. She wouldn't say anything in front of her family, and Pieter didn't push her as I would have. I do believe he quite likes the girl. I should have gone, should have been there to push for answers, but I didn't want to get Della into trouble with the duchess if she truly was her maid. All she told Pieter was to ask the dressmaker."

Aunt Annalise raised her eyebrows, but she looked like she was fighting a smile.

"Franci is my dearest friend. Eleonora knew she could tell you the truth about me."

"Why didn't you tell me from the beginning? I could have courted you properly at the start."

"I was wearing clothes fit to be a servant. My hands are calloused in a way no noblewoman's should have been. You would have laughed at me or thought me mad. Besides, I didn't think I would catch your eye. My stepmother would also have flayed me alive." Della shrugged.

Roric sighed. "You're right. I believed you immediately when you said you were a servant. I likely wouldn't have believed you if you had told me the truth and I would never have sought you out, thinking you were scheming or mad. Although you were wrong to think you wouldn't catch my notice."

"You two have a rather interesting tale," Aunt Annalise observed.

Della looked away, embarrassment tinging her cheeks.

"My dears, in my opinion it is better to have to fight for your love than to fall into it. One can easily get up and walk away from a fall, but it is not so easy to let go of a treasure you have worked to obtain. The best love stories are like a rose—beautiful, but also covered in thorns which can prick or protect." Aunt Annalise smiled at them.

"Does this mean you approve of this match?" Roric sounded a little nervous.

"I do indeed. Margarete and Father will too. We all will, so long as Della is happy and well taken care of. Though this time I will expect regular letters to be delivered untampered with so that we may ensure it."

"Of course! You know I wrote to you. Perhaps the couriers did not wish to brave the Deep Woods so many years ago." Though Della suspected that was not the case, she didn't want to cast blame without proof.

"Perhaps." Aunt Annalise's mouth pulled into a tight line as if she, too, thought it was unlikely.

"I think we are all doubtful on that, but one thing we will never doubt is the kindness and grace Della extends to even those most undeserving of it." Roric squeezed her hand.

"Indeed." Aunt Annalise was smiling again.

A maidservant entered and whispered in Aunt Annalise's ear. Aunt Annalise clapped her hands together once, and a smile lit her face.

"Send her in, please."

The maidservant bobbed a curtsy at the order and left the room. Soon after, a plump woman, mousy brown hair now fading to gray, entered. Della stared with wide eyes for a moment, her heart filling with joy.

"Tilya!" Della dashed to her old nursemaid and flung her arms around the woman.

"Oof." Tilya wrapped her arms around Della and chuckled. "I see time has not taught you to walk across the room like a lady."

Della drew back, gratitude shining in her eyes. "Thank you for coming."

"I heard you want me to be your lady's maid."

"I would so love it if you would be, though I understand if you don't wish to."

"Little Lady, I would do anything for you. However, since I was released from my position by Mistress DeVoss, I found a position as a housekeeper. I think in my older age I'm better suited for such a thing. Your lady's maid should be young as you are—someone who will gossip about the court and giggle over men with you." Tilya shot a pointed glance at Roric standing not too far from them.

Della's face fell, but she nodded.

Tilya tucked a finger under Della's chin and lifted her head to meet her eyes. "Chin up always, Adella Caspari. I'd be happy to come on as your housekeeper if you'd like."

"Oh yes! Yes, please do, Tilya. That would make me so happy."

A thunk sounded as two manservants deposited a trunk on the floor of the room.

Della raised an eyebrow. "You already brought your things?"

Tilya smiled and shook her head. "No, Della. Not my things. Those are yours, the things your mother left you that I smuggled out before that witc—*woman* could get her claws on them."

Tears threatened Della's eyes once more, spilling out as she flung her arms around Tilya and hugged her again. Someone coughed. Della let go and turned.

"Aunt Annalise, Roric, this is my childhood nursemaid, Tilya."

"We've met, though it has been many years," Annalise said.

Tilya bobbed a curtsy. "Your majesty."

"You must have been much kinder than the nursemaids I had, to have earned such a tender reunion." Roric smiled.

Tilya arched a brow. "I don't suppose you were the picture of innocence as a boy and easy on your nursemaids?"

Roric's face heated slightly, and he looked somewhat chagrined as he gave a small shrug, palms up. "I might have caused a bit of trouble, though Freddie was certainly the worst of us in that regard."

"And who are you to my Della?"

"Oh! I'm sorry, Tilya. I didn't properly introduce them. This is Prince Theodoric Adalburg of Tamaria, though I call him Roric. He's my...betrothed." Della stumbled over the last word, blushing fiercely.

"Betrothed? My, how you have grown. Your mother's gowns will likely fit you now."

Della looked at Aunt Annalise. "Do you mind if I—?" She gestured at the trunk.

"Of course," her aunt replied.

Della went to the trunk and opened the lid. She didn't know whether to weep or cry as a familiar scent, somewhat musty with age, reached her nose.

"I put the sprig of lavender in there to keep away the smell of mothballs. I remembered how your mother would put those flowers under your pillow to help soothe you as a toddling babe." Tilya had come up behind Della.

Della touched a hand to one of the skirts. Her mother's things. She had something of her mother's once again. She would treasure the items in this chest forever. Her hand moved to a large jewelry box sitting on a pile of dresses. She opened it and tears streamed down her cheeks as she smiled.

"Oh," Della breathed as she touched a necklace.

"Your mother had a fondness for pearls. I put one of those necklaces in your trunk when you left, but you can see she had several strands."

Indeed, there lay at least three pearl necklaces in varying lengths and thickness amid other pieces of sparkling jewelry. Della still ached as she thought of the necklace she had lost in Tamaria, but the sting of that loss dwindled with all she had gained today. It wasn't the small wealth sitting in that box, but the distinct style her mother had possessed showing clearly in each piece. Vague memories filtered into her mind as she remembered the way her mother wore certain dresses and adornments. Such memories were more precious to Della than any ring or necklace.

Della wiped at the tears on her cheeks. "Thank you. You've given me more than you know."

But when she met her former nursemaid's eyes, she thought the woman just might realize exactly what she had preserved and given back to the young girl that she loved.

CHAPTER TWENTY-FIVE

Della felt oddly more exposed on the return trip through the Deep Woods, despite being surrounded by dozens of guards. While she traveled with Roric in the carriage for most of the day, there wasn't room to sleep in the carriage and the guards traveled on horses, so everyone slept in tents at night. As the wind pushed against the fabric letting strange sounds trickle in, Della longed for the wooden safety of the vardo. To make matters worse, she was the only lady in their camp, so she slept in her tent alone. Tilya had offered to accompany her, but Della didn't want to put the older woman through the difficult journey, and she needed someone to look after her manor while she was away. Della regretted only when she lay awake at night, ears straining to discern if the distant sound of footsteps were from the patrolling guards or prowling creatures. The lack of sleep made her exhausted, but somehow her mind still kept her awake each night with thoughts of monsters ravaging the camp. She tossed and turned, and ever awaiting the reluctant creeping of dawn.

"Are you alright?" Roric asked her on their fifth day of traveling.

Della shifted as the carriage jostled her. "My sleep has been...troubled. I do not like traveling through the Deep Woods."

Roric nodded in agreement. "There are many tales and signs of strange creatures here. It can be unsettling."

"I know it's silly since we are constantly surrounded by guards, but alone in my tent every sound is frightening," Della admitted.

"If you cannot sleep at night, at least try to rest while we travel in the carriage. Let the daylight and my presence chase away your nightmares," Roric assuaged her fears.

Della leaned back against the plush cushions. They were rather soft.

"Perhaps I will rest my eyes, just for a few moments," Della yawned as she spoke, eyelids already fluttering closed.

Sometime later the carriage jerked to an abrupt halt, causing Della to smack her head painfully against the wall. She opened her eyes and rubbed her head as she sat up. She opened her mouth to protest the rough stop, but Roric lunged across the carriage and covered her mouth. He met her eyes and put a finger to his lips. She nodded and he dropped his hand.

"They've sighted an ogre," Roric whispered. He leaned back and lifted the curtain with two fingers. "We've halted and are hoping to keep quiet enough that we escape notice while it passes. You can still breathe though."

Della let out a breath, only realizing that she'd frozen so completely with terror when he mentioned it.

One of the horses let out a nervous whinny. Roric tensed and Della winced. Roric looked over at her and gestured for her to sit next to him. She stepped across the carriage silently until she nestled in beside him. He wrapped an arm around her, pulling her into his side. Della relaxed as she breathed in his scent. She couldn't tell if her heart was racing from fear or from the nearness of Roric's body. She almost laughed at herself for still responding to him in that way while in such a situation.

A roar ripped through the silence. The clang of steel and horrible crunching sounds rang out. Roric let go of Della and removed his sword carefully in the small space. Around them, soldiers yelled as they joined the fray. Horses neighed in distress.

"There's more than one of them," Roric breathed.

"What?" Della felt the blood drain from her face.

The carriage door was yanked open. It fell backward and hung at an odd angle, ripped off the top hinge. A massive leering face looked in at them with deep-set eyes, large ears, and leathery skin. The ogre opened its large mouth in a wide grin, revealing pointed teeth.

"Out the other door. Now!" Roric shouted as he stabbed at the beast.

Della yanked open the other door and tumbled out, barely managing to keep upright as the ogre shot in a hand after her. Della stared as Roric's sword sliced at the ogre's reaching arm. A deafening bellow had her head snapping to the right where a ring of soldiers engaged another ogre. Upright, the beast was taller than two men with long arms that could reach much further than their swords. Its legs were thick as tree trunks and ended in stumps with wide, blunt claws rather than toes. Della watched it swing an enormous club at soldiers who dodged and ducked around that blow before jabbing back with their own weapons. The sounds of battle to her left drew her attention to a third ogre attacking soldiers with its bare hands. Della gulped.

"Run, Della!" Roric yelled.

He climbed out of the carriage behind her. The ogre he'd been fighting clutched its arm and roared in pain. Della knew she should run, but fear froze her in place. Noa burst into view, unsaddled, but bridled. She galloped toward Roric, who sheathed his sword to swing up onto her bare back. He plucked Della off the ground and tossed her up behind him.

"Hold on tight!" he commanded as he steered his Stronghorse toward the woods.

Della's limbs obeyed this time as she clung to Roric with all her might. She buried her face in his back and tried to gain a decent grip on the massive horse with her legs. Her dress was not meant for riding and though she should have been embarrassed that it had bunched up around her thighs, she was merely grateful for the extra hold her bare calves gave her. Della heard the sounds of a rampaging ogre in pursuit as the Stronghorse raced further into the Deep Woods, away from the path and the ogres. They dodged trees and leapt over brambles as they evaded the ogre that pursued them. A tree flew past them, smashing into their path and forcing them to head deeper into the woods. Another tree crashed into their way.

"It's herding us," Della realized in shock.

"It can't be! Everyone knows ogres are stupid," Roric balked at the idea, though Della knew he wasn't discounting it.

A third tree flew into the way ahead.

"The trajectory—that tree went further past us because the ogre is gaining on us. It was forcing us to change paths to slow us down so it could catch up," Della said in horror. She threw a look back and the ogre met her eyes with a sickly grin.

"Primitive, but effective," Roric said through gritted teeth as he steered Noa around the fallen trunk. "I suppose they could be slowly evolving."

"One had a club. That shows signs of intelligence to think to carve or break the wood down into that shape," Della pointed out.

Another small tree whipped by them, branches knocking into Della's back and sliding her precariously to the side. At that moment, the Stronghorse was forced to jump over a large thicket and the impact from the landing threw Della to the ground.

"Della! Are you alright?" Roric called, pulling up short several feet away.

The ogre roared as it crashed into the thicket. Della scrambled to her feet and ran. Sheer terror gave her strength as she fled. Roric yelled and pulled out his sword. He rushed past Della, still astride his mount, and swung at the ogre. Della kept running. She broke out of the trees and onto the riverbank. She slowed to a stop and tried to catch her breath as she watched anxiously for Roric to appear. Della could hear him shouting as he fought the ogre.

Rustling sounded and her head snapped to the right to see another ogre stepped out of the trees. Blood streamed from several wounds on the beast. It must have been one of the others that had attacked their company. It limped as it prowled toward her. Perhaps she could outrun it. Della ran, but she only got a few strides before a giant hand wrapped around her body. The ogre's fingers couldn't close all the way, but before Della could wriggle free the beast flung her. The breath whooshed out of her as she bounced painfully along the ground. She scrambled to stand, but it grabbed her skirt, tearing it as it flung her in the other direction. Della cried out when her shoulder connected with a rock as she rolled. She panted and tried to blink away the spots that had burst in front of her eyes.

When her vision cleared, she saw the ogre staring at her with the expression she had once seen on a cat that was toying with a mouse. She had gone into a shop and when she'd come out, that cat was still playing with the desperate and exhausted mouse as though the amusement it gave was better than the meal itself. If ogres thought like that, even her death could take agonizing hours. But Della did not wish to die, and she certainly wasn't going to go down without a fight.

Della felt for the rock she had rolled over and pried it loose from the ground. She stood quickly, trying to anticipate the ogre's movements as it advanced on her. She flung the rock and dove to her right, rolling across the ground away from the ogre. Della got to her feet, but she looked back as the ogre let out an angry cry. The ogre held a hand over an eye as it roared. It swiveled its head, fixing her with a furious, one-eyed glare. It lurched toward her.

"Help! Roric?!" Della yelled. "Help!"

She screamed as she was knocked to the ground by a massive hand. The ogre grabbed her leg and began dragging her on her back into the woods. Della scrambled for anything on the ground that could help her. She pulled up handfuls of sandy dirt and small pebbles, which she quickly let drop back down. Her right hand found purchase on a rock, and she tried to pry it free with both hands. It held firmly, but it also pulled Della to a halt. The ogre looked back and grunted. It gave a mighty tug, painfully pulling Della loose as the large rock also came free of the ground. Della thrashed abruptly, yanking her leg free. The ogre lunged forward, but she rolled inward toward it. The beast stopped in surprise as Della sprang up next to it. She used all her strength to smash the rock into the ogre's knee—the knee of the leg it had already been limping on. She smashed its knee again as the ogre cried out. Della swung a third time, but the ogre slapped her away with the back of its hand, flinging her back to the of the edge of the forest.

Della groaned as she landed, her hip smacking into a tree trunk. Still, she forced herself up and tried to run. The leg the ogre had dragged her with screamed in protest and her shoulder and hip seared with pain. Della gasped as she moved her injured limbs, but forced herself toward the river. Maybe the ogre wouldn't follow her if she flung herself in. Of course, she didn't know if she had the strength to swim, but staying on land right now seemed to hold certain death.

A loud thunk had Della screaming and sprawling on the ground. New pain flared from the back of her knee. She looked behind her and saw a rock on the ground beside her. The rock she had used to smash the ogre's knee. It had thrown it back at her. A hysterical laugh bubbled up from her at the thought that she had taught the ogre that. That these primitive creatures could learn, were learning and adapting, even as they fought.

Twigs snapped and the ogre limped out of the trees, dragging one useless leg. Della forced herself to her hands and knees and crawled toward the riverbank.

"Anybody...help, please," Della had meant to yell, but it came out as a gasp.

A large, firm hand clamped down on her leg again. Della's strength gave out and she couldn't fight the ogre's grasp. The river splashed nearby and Della closed her eyes, listening to the sound as she awaited death.

The ogre roared and released her. Della's eyes flew open. Roric was there atop his Stronghorse, slashing at the beast with his sword. He held a dagger in his other hand, using it to stab when he had to parry the ogre's blows on his longer blade.

"Della!" Roric sent a panicked look in her direction.

Della sat up. "I'm alright. Watch out!"

His glance toward her had cost him. The ogre sent him flying off Noa's back and rolling across the ground, blades flying in different directions.

"Roric!" Della screamed, forcing herself to her feet. Her leg almost buckled beneath her, but she shifted her weight onto her other leg and limped toward him.

Roric still lay flat on his back, eyes glazed and completely winded. Della tried to run, tried to will her injured leg into working enough to reach him in time. The ogre got there first. Della lunged for him and her knee buckled. She hit the ground hard, still several paces away.

"Roric!" Her scream was a sob. Out of the corner of her eye something glinted in the sunlight, but Della couldn't look away from the man she loved.

The ogre raised a mighty hand as Roric struggled to sit up. A whinny rang out and Noa reared up behind the beast, striking it with her powerful hooves. The ogre bellowed in pain and turned, swinging an arm that sent Noa skipping out of range. Roric rolled just as the ogre whirled and smashed down a fist directly where he had been lying. Roric scrambled to his feet and ran toward where his sword lay near a tree. Della realized it was too far away and the ogre's legs were too long—it would be on Roric again before he could reach his sword.

She looked around in desperation, searching for another rock or anything she could throw. There, glinting in the sunlight, lay the dagger Roric had dropped. Della snatched it up and tried to position her hand around it the way she'd seen troupe members do when throwing at a target. She aimed for the ogre's center, hoping if she missed, the creature was large enough that she would still hit something. A prayer to the stars left her lips as she hurled the dagger with all her might. It struck the ogre's side and the creature howled in fury. The ogre lurched toward her, Roric now forgotten.

Della tried to rise as the beast lumbered across the ground to her, but her body screamed in protest and she swayed on her knees. The ogre's face split into a menacing grin as it reached an arm out toward her. Then its face went wide with surprise. The ogre looked stupidly down toward its middle where a sword had broken through. The beast clutched at the blade, then roared and let go as its palm split open on the sharp edges. The ogre swayed, then toppled over, hitting the ground with a mighty crash that shook Della's bones. Roric stood panting behind the creature. He hauled out his sword and severed the ogre's head to ensure it was well and truly dead.

Roric's eyes found hers and he ran to her. Della tried not to cry out as he lifted her into his arms, but a moan still escaped her lips. From Roric's grunts as he carried her, he had unseen injuries as well. He lifted her onto the Stronghorse, then swung up behind her and cradled her as gently as he could while they rode bareback through the woods toward the soldiers. Guards on horseback found them before they could reach the road.

"Your Highness! You're alive." The relief was evident in the man's voice.

"That I am, Captain Alders, though not for lack of effort from the ogres." Roric's face was grim.

"Borst, go tell the others that the prince and the lady have been found. Regroup where we were attacked," Captain Alders ordered one man, who broke off from the group and galloped away.

"Were there any casualties?" Roric asked the captain as they rode together, the other soldiers falling in to flank their prince.

"We lost three men that I know of. Others are being treated and I'm not sure the extent of all the wounds sustained. We killed one of the ogres and the men chased off the other. The third had followed you before anyone could disengage from the battle. We were unprepared for such an attack. I take full responsibility," Captain Alders said solemnly.

Roric waved that away. "No, I will not hold you accountable for any losses. You and your men fought well. Our ogre defense tactics were never strategized for more than two ogres at once. We were unprepared because the training regiment set by the crown did not account for such a possibility. It is on our heads, not yours."

Della admired the way Roric took responsibility even when Captain Alders had offered himself up as a scapegoat.

"I shall discuss this with my father when we return and we will make improvements to our strategies," Roric promised.

"You should know that the ogre seemed to learn from me as we fought," Della told him.

"What?" Roric and Captain Alders asked at the same time.

"After I attacked its knee with a rock to weaken it, I ran, but it threw the rock back and hit me behind my own knee. It was quite efficient at felling me," Della admitted grimly. "It hadn't used a rock prior to that, only beat me with its hand before dragging me. It also seemed to gain...enjoyment from letting me try to escape and then dragging me back."

"That is concerning. Thank you for telling me. Captain Alders, make sure you question the men to see if any of them noticed such adaptations while they fought with the ogres," Roric commanded.

Captain Alders was gaping at Della. "Do you mean to say that you fought with an ogre on your own?"

"She held it off bravely, and helped me take it down," Roric said proudly.

"That's impressive." Captain Alders looked her up and down as if he had never seen her before.

"It had incapacitated me. I wouldn't have survived without you," Della protested

"It almost killed me as well. It was through your bravery and resourcefulness—at the risk of your own life—that bought me the time to slay the beast. You were attacked by an ogre, battled it, and lived to tell the tale. You are truly a wonder, Della my darling," Roric insisted.

"And you are my brave prince, who came to my rescue just when I needed you the most." Della meant the words in more ways than one.

CHAPTER TWENTY-SIX

Della breathed a sigh of relief when they reached Fell-santra. The encounter with the ogres had forced them to leave several soldiers behind in the first town beyond the deep woods. A messenger had been dispatched to send for more physicians than the small town had, but Roric was hopeful that all his men would live.

"We are home." Roric picked up her hand and gave it a squeeze.

"My heart has found its home in you." Della smiled at him.

He ran a hand through his hair. "We fought off ogres, now we just have to conquer my mother."

"Roric, are you nervous?!"

"The ogres were exhilarating, but Mother...Well she might have had plans to marry off all of her sons to princesses. You mean more to me than any princess could, but I'm not thrilled to have to tell my mother I've undermined her plans. My father rules the kingdom and my mother rules the house. I don't think I've ever crossed her intentionally," Roric confessed. He ruffled his hair further.

Della took his other hand in hers to stop his nervous habit. "Nothing has been announced. You can still change your mind."

"Never." He squeezed her hands tightly.

"If it goes horribly, I shall rescue you. Marrying a duchess in Aleece grants you the title of duke consort, I'll have you know." Della's lips twitched despite her effort to hold back a grin.

Roric let out a laugh. "We might need to go further than the next country over to escape my mother's wrath. Don't worry, I'm sure she will come around. Or at least my father will, and he will temper her. He always smiles in satisfaction when he sees my brother, Henrich, and his wife look at each other with love. I'm sure Father favors love for any who can be afforded it, and as the third prince, surely I can."

"Your father sounds wonderful." A bit of the tightness in Della's chest eased.

"I think you will get along swimmingly with him," Roric agreed.

The carriage rolled to a stop. Roric gave her a wry grin as the door swung open. He jumped out of the carriage and turned to help her down. She was expecting him to offer his hand, but he grabbed her waist and swung her down instead. She let out a delighted laugh and he grinned.

"Theodoric! You've arrived." A man who looked so much like Roric and Freddie that he could only be their oldest brother, Henrich, came down the castle steps.

"The scout said you'd be here soon." Prince Frederick strolled over. He dropped his voice, "You'd better come inside quickly unless you want the entire courtyard to hear you get a tongue lashing."

Roric groaned as he led Della up the gray stone castle steps. "So, Mother knows I'm here already?"

A tall, well-dressed woman that was standing just inside the doorway spoke in a worried tone, "She's waiting for you in the sitting room."

Henrich wrapped his arms around her and Della realized she must be his wife.

Della took in the castle entry hall. Tables holding vases of flowers were scattered along the hall. A long rug in the royal colors of navy blue and white covered most of the floor. The gray stone walls were draped in portraits and tapestries. Navy curtains framed each window.

Roric led her to a sitting room near the entrances, his brothers following with that mixture of curiosity and dread one has for a sibling who has angered their parent. Della's heart pounded wildly, and she briefly wondered if she could stand to live in a place where she had to walk on eggshells yet again, palace or not. She suddenly longed for her manor with the familiarity of Tilya and horses.

Roric pulled her into a tight embrace. "Don't fear. I won't let you be disrespected. Please give me a chance to work things out. If I can't, if you are unhappy here, then we will go. Just promise me that if you wish to leave, we leave together."

Della pulled back and looked into his eyes full of sincerity and love. She nodded. Roric squeezed her hand once before walking into the sitting room. Della paused before the doorway, unsure if she should go in or not. Roric had already crossed the room to where his mother was glaring out the window. Her brown hair was pulled up into a lavish bun that was encircled by an enormous crown.

"Hello, Mother!" Roric said a bit too cheerfully.

She whirled around. "Oh no you don't! You don't get to smile at me and then expect me to forgive you. It was bad enough that you took off leaving a note saying you were vanquishing ogres—which you lied about—"

"I didn't lie. I simply didn't find the ogres and had to continue on further to search for them." Roric grinned.

"Don't even pretend like you were looking. You were chasing after some girl that hadn't even been to court and Pieter tells me was a servant in that awful woman's house!"

"Even you agree that Duchess DeVoss is horrible, so it is conceivable to realize that she married the girl's father for his title and then forced the girl to labor for free so she couldn't be competition on the marriage market. Della is lovely, so the woman's fears were warranted there. Also, we did, in fact, find and fight with not one, but three ogres, which is why my return retinue was so much smaller."

"What?!" The queen looked her son over, ensuring he still had all his limbs. She cupped the scabbed over gash on his cheek. "If you hadn't gone after that girl this wouldn't have happened."

Roric stepped away from her. "Mother, enough. I love Della, and I'm going to marry her. She is the Aleecean Duchess Adella Caspari, so her pedigree is not an issue. I know that you want to blame her for my actions because that is easier than believing a child you raised would go against your wishes, but know that my actions are mine alone. I came here to introduce her to the family and gain Father's and your blessing, but I will not have you being spiteful towards her. You will offer her respect and politeness if not love. If you cannot, then we will elope and live out our days in Aleece or traveling the world."

Freddie sucked in a breath and muttered behind Della. "I don't believe anyone has ever spoken to our mother that way."

"Theodoric! You cannot speak to your queen in such a way! You don't get to come in here and make demands after disobeying me!"

"I don't find asking you to be courteous to my betrothed to be a demand. However, if you will not, then we will leave. I won't stand by and let her be insulted whether through words or actions. I want to continue to spend time with my family and get to know hers, but I will not bring her back here if any of you are rude, and I won't return without her." Roric squared his shoulders.

"I see. Well, I suppose I would want your father to do the same for me. Perhaps you have grown up more than I realized. You couldn't have made it easy for me and fallen in love with a princess?" She gave an exasperated sigh.

"I heard she has royal blood. Her mother was one of the fifteen princesses in Aleece some time ago." Freddie strolled into the sitting room, stopping beside Roric.

"Twelve. There were twelve Aleecean princesses," his mother corrected automatically. "Frederick, I don't remember sending for you."

"It's lovely to see you too, Mother." He winked.

"You two will be the death of me. The disaster that happened with Henrich's betrothal, Theodoric consorting with servants, and Frederick kissing a corpse in the woods." The queen massaged the bridge of her nose.

"Hey now, she wasn't dead. I said she *looked* like a corpse at first, but then I realized that she was indeed alive. I wouldn't have kissed her otherwise. What better way to wake her from sleeping than a kiss from a prince?" Freddie looked completely unruffled.

"That is exactly why I knew I had to secure your betrothal the moment you returned."

"She has a point. You almost died," Henrich said as he strode in and stood with his two brothers.

The queen raised her eyebrows. "Are you all here to plead Theodoric's case? Three against one isn't fair."

"Would you rather we continued to eavesdrop from the doorway?" Freddie grinned.

The woman standing with Della whispered, "I think we'd better go in now."

She linked arms with Della and they walked in together. The queen's imposing eyes raked over Della, who reminded herself to breathe as she dropped the girl's arm and swept a perfect curtsy. Roric moved next to Della, wrapping an arm around her waist. The queen's lips tightened.

"Welcome, Duchess Caspari, to the Tamarian castle."

"Thank you for having me."

"My son left me little choice."

"Mother," Roric warned.

The queen held up a hand. "Peace. I am queen, I will speak my mind as I see fit. However, I will be polite. You are welcome here, Your Grace."

"Please, just call me Della. Adella was my mother's name, and I don't need such a formal title as Your Grace. I am Aleecean, after all." Della laughed a little nervously.

"Call me Freddie then. I keep trying to get everyone to, but since I came of age everyone else refuses except Theo—or Roric, as you call him." Freddie grinned.

"This is my eldest brother, Henrich, and his wife, Nicolette." Roric gestured to them.

"A pleasure to meet you." Della curtsied to the crown prince and princess.

"It will be so nice to have another girl around." Nicolette's voice was a soft, musical sound.

"The rumors are true, then," a booming voice said from the doorway.

Della turned and saw a tall man with salt and pepper hair entering the room. His fine clothes included a heavy cape and his head was topped with an enormous crown of gold and red velvet. Della's eyes widened and she dropped into her deepest curtsy yet.

"You may rise, child." The king's voice was kind. He looked her over and shook his head with a smile. "Seeing you explains it all. Golden hair and eyes of the sea. No wonder my son has fallen for such a beauty."

Della blushed at the praise. No one ever complimented her looks.

"Father," Roric protested.

The king raised one eyebrow. "Are you contesting her beauty? I wouldn't recommend that if you fancy her."

"Of course not!" Roric choked.

"Don't have such fun with Roric now that he's finally shown interest in someone, Father. You might frighten her away, and then what would we do with the recluse?" Henrich spoke up.

The queen looked like she thought that might be the better scenario, but the king only laughed.

"Quite right, Henrich. Welcome. Perhaps you can help straighten out some of the mystery and rumors from the truth of your life. Let us walk together so that I might get to know the woman my son cares for." The king took Della's hand and patted it before tucking it under his arm.

Della threw a glance at Roric, who shrugged apologetically.

The king led her out of the castle to a private garden. He stopped at a bench. "Let us sit. I am getting old and you, my child, are limping."

"We encountered some ogres on the road back." Della winced as she settled on the bench. Her injuries still ached.

"You were injured by one?"

"Yes. Roric saved me from one, but then another found me. It seemed to enjoy hurting me and letting me try to escape. Though that extra time saved my life, it was rather painful."

"That's terrible luck to encounter two together. It is also disturbing to hear it enjoyed playing with you. I shall have to talk with my knights about it and perhaps revise their fighting tactics."

"There were actually three that attacked our group together. Roric said the same thing—that you would be creating new strategies for fighting against them in larger groups."

"Three?! That is truly concerning. Hmmm." The king looked contemplative. Then he examined Della. "You call my son by his childhood name. He must trust and care for you immensely, then."

"I'm not sure that's the reason. I didn't recognize him when I met him, having never been to the Tamarian court. He gave me that name knowing I wouldn't be able to discover who he was from it." Della shrugged.

"Theodoric generally avoids being anywhere near the ladies of court, despite his mother's best efforts. If he sought you out, it's because he cares for you."

"Oh, I know he cares for me—he crossed the Deep Woods to find me. I just don't know that it meant anything for me to call him his childhood name."

"If he hasn't asked you to call him anything else, then I'd say he likes that you are the only one to call him that now." The king touched a rose on the bush beside the bench. "Tell me about yourself, Duchess Caspari."

"Please, just call me Della."

"Della then. You have already told me much with just that."

Della wondered what that could be. "I hope it conveys something auspicious."

"Were Theodoric crown prince, I would say it was not. However, as the third son, finding someone who cares for him and not just the title of princess is welcome."

Della smoothed her dress as if doing so would smooth out her nerves. "Wouldn't it be the opposite? You wouldn't want someone who only wishes to be princess married to the crown prince?"

"Henrich needs someone who knows she will become queen one day. This kingdom needs that. You ask to go by a nickname rather than your formal title and name, which tells me you are not seeking to be seen with a crown on your head and all eyes upon you. You are with Roric despite feeling uncomfortable with that. As he is unlikely to ever be king, I am glad that he has found someone who loves him for who he is. Henrich did not have that luxury but has still managed to find love in his arranged marriage, for which I am also glad." The king turned his kind eyes on her.

"Does that mean you approve?" Della's stomach quivered. She wasn't sure if she was supposed to ask a king such questions.

"I do wish that Theodoric had spoken with us before asking for your hand in marriage, but at this time I don't see any reason to stand in your way. His mother will take a bit more cajoling as she dreamed of each of her sons marrying a princess and had her sights set on one who would inherit her own kingdom for Theodoric, but I think she will be happy that he will not live so far from us if the two of you do marry."

"Do you love her? The queen, I mean." Della's face flushed with heat. Did she really just ask the king that? "I—I mean, forgive me. I only ask because my parents loved each other very much and I—"

"It's alright. I know that Aleecians view marriage very differently than we do here in Tamaria. Our marriage was one of practicality, but I loved her at first sight. The queen took some convincing—a few years of it." He chuckled. "But I would say we have something one might call love between us now."

Della smiled and fingered a rose to the side of her. She inhaled the floral scent swirling around her. She decided that her home, wherever they decided to live, would have a patch of lavender that she could breathe in whenever she wished.

"How is it that you and Theodoric met? I can't fathom a way that a maidservant and prince would bump into each other, especially if you served Duchess DeVoss whom everyone avoids like a disastrous plague."

Della snorted.

The king sighed. "I should probably not say such things about those in my court, but that woman has tested my patience more than any other."

"I understand. She tends to have that effect on those who encounter her." Della tapped the rose. "I met your son when he was thrown from his Stronghorse and I caught her running wild."

"Is that so? My son failed to mention that particular detail." He shook his head. "And yet it still bonded with him."

"Perhaps Noa recognized his heart beyond his ignorance in her care. We are all ignorant about something. I have the barest experiences of court and would rather avoid it altogether, yet I know I must if I am to be with Roric, so I shall seek to adapt." Della bit her lip. Would he think her unfit after admitting that?

To her surprise, the king nodded. "Those are wise words for someone so young. Many are too lost in their prejudices to recognize what they themselves lack. As for everyone being ignorant about something, I believe I now understand that my son pushed to expand the widow's stipend because of you."

Della blinked in surprise. "He did what?"

"I know my sons. Though it was Henrich who approached me, he would not have pushed to expand the widow's stipend. He is the heir to the throne and wouldn't risk asking to allocate more money to extend it to all peasants. That could deplete the royal treasury far too quickly. Henrich also seemed reluctant to ask, which usually means it was something one of his brothers cajoled him into bringing to me. Frederick is far too concerned with finding a way out of his impending marriage to bother with others and such a request is not something I would expect from him. I would not have expected it from Theodoric either, as he is somewhat spoiled by his mother. One of his greatest flaws has always been acting with no thought of how it would affect others as he has never had any true reason to need to. However, he has been acting differently as of late. It is a change I approve of. As you are the only recent change in his life, I must assume that is why my son has had a change of perspective."

Della couldn't stop the smile that spread across her lips. "I can't believe he asked you to do that."

The king tilted his head, a knowing look on his face. "Men have waged war over a pretty face. The combination of beauty and intelligence is powerful."

Della blushed at the compliment, unsure how to respond. So instead, she asked him a question. "Are you going to do it?"

"Expand the stipend you mean?" At her nod, the king continued. "I am letting Henrich choose how he thinks the request should be handled."

"Has he told you what he will do?" Della bit her lip. She shouldn't be questioning the king. She was a terrible courtier.

The king's eyebrows rose. "You are tenacious. From what I understand, he has been drafting a proposal to present to the royal advisors, devising a plan for sums that match their late husband's previous income. There are not enough houses in Widow's Court to move them all there, nor would this expanded stipend be given to any commoner whose husbands did not die in war."

Tamaria was not at war and had not been for some time. This would not help many new widows outside of the nobility. However, it might encourage future kings to prevent war due to the extra cost of losing their men. Della said aloud, "It is progress, an improvement upon the current stipend."

"Should it be passed."

"Should it be passed," Della agreed.

Roric appeared in the gardens then. "Father, Mother has requested that we all take lunch together today. Della and I have been on the road for weeks and need time to clean up."

"Your prince comes to rescue you again. Though I hope you have realized that I am less of a dragon than one might assume." The king rose and helped Della up.

"It was a pleasure to talk with you." Della curtsied.

"With you as well. You have given me much to think about." The king strode off.

"Does that bode well or ill?" Della asked as they headed back toward the castle. She was looking forward to a long, hot soak in the bath.

"Father looks satisfied. He isn't nearly as hard to please as Mother. I think even Mother will come around once she gets over her ruined plans and comes to know you. It's impossible for anyone who knows you to not care for you." Roric smiled down at her.

Della smiled back, but her heart lurched. She knew someone who knew her and did not love her back. Someone she would have to face again.

CHAPTER TWENTY-SEVEN

The bell on the shop door tinkled as Della walked into the familiar space. Her eyes scanned the room, searching out those familiar black coils. Women crowded the store, gossiping around her as Della worked her way through them.

"I heard the youngest prince went to Aleece. He did dance all night with that Aleecean girl."

"Well, *I* heard he was off hunting ogres in the Deep Woods."

"What an awful thing to do! Can't they have knights do that sort—"

"—think the pink is prettier than the blue. Besides, Anna just got a new blue gown."

"You're not suited to pinks, my dear. Wouldn't it be nice to match—"

Della made it to the other side of the room and slipped through the door that led into the workroom in the back. She shut the door behind her with an audible snick.

Franci spoke as she whirled around. "You can't be back h—Della!"

Della grinned at her friend. "I think I just might be allowed back here, actually."

Franci laughed. She dropped the bolt of fabric she was holding and rushed to fling her arms around Della. The two girls clung to each other, laughing and crying.

Finally, Franci pulled back. "What are you doing here? Did you finally realize your dream of working in a dress shop?"

"You know that isn't why I'm here." Della laughed again.

Her friend blew a wayward curl out of her face. "I can hope, can't I? So the prince found you then?" "He did. I received your letter as well. Thank you for sending a warning."

"I wasn't sure if you'd want to see him or not." Franci bit her lip.

"I didn't, but he found me anyway."

Franci huffed out a breath. "I shouldn't have told him about your family! It's just that I knew you had liked him—he explained he was the Lord Roric you'd met–and he had your other strange shoe as proof. I didn't want your role here as a serving maid to be what prevented you from love. I should have known after how you came rushing back from the ball that it was more than just a lover's spat."

Della laughed at Franci's glower and held up a hand.

"It's alright, Franci. We spoke and worked everything out. We are betrothed." Della gave her friend a shy smile.

"Truly? Oh, Della! That is wonderful! Wait, he didn't force you into it, did he? We can get you out of it."

"No, Franci, he didn't force me into it. Though I only agreed with the caveat that we have a long and very public courting beforehand. I want to make absolutely sure we will love each other forever before I marry him. We also need to figure out which country we will live in, or if we will go back and forth. Those are not things I wish to find out *after* I've already wed. Though it does mean I will be spending time at court, which means I will need plenty of dresses."

Franci squealed with excitement. "I shall make you a dress in every color and more! You look lovely in almost every shade. Oh! Then there will be the wedding gown. Don't worry, I won't make you look like a frosted cake."

Della laughed again. "Yes. Well, you can wait on the wedding dress for a while. Let's focus on the everyday gowns. I have also come into my inheritance, which means I can finally pay you what your designs are worth."

"Nonsense. You are my dearest friend. You shall receive the cost of the dress and nothing more."

"But I must pay you for your time!"

Franci waved a dismissive hand.

Della sighed, resigning herself to finding a way to sneak in the correct amount.

"You could wear your strange shoes to your wedding as well." Franci's eyes glazed a bit as if she were already designing a wedding gown despite Della's protests.

"The glass slippers?"

Franci looked at her. "Yes, though I don't think they are actually glass. I tested one of my needles against the bottom and it didn't leave a scratch. You'd have to have a jeweler confirm it, but I suspect since they are dwarvish made that they are actually crafted from diamonds."

"Diamond slippers! Do you really think so?" Della's mouth had dropped open and she shut it with a snap.

Her friend nodded. "I've heard rumors of mountain dwarves making things from gemstones, though this would be the first time I'd ever actually seen it."

Della briefly wondered who that peddler was, and if he had realized the true value of what he had given away. She would have to take the shoes to a jeweler and then try to find the peddler again if she could. Della would compensate him fairly if it was true. Diamond slippers for a bride—what a thing to wear! She smiled at the thought.

"There is one more thing I'd ask of you, Franci."

She arched a brow. "What is it?"

"When I do get married someday, will you be one of the maids who attend to the bride?"

Franci's face broke into a grin. "Of course, Della! I'm sure the maids of the bride will have very flattering dresses."

"If you design them, I'm sure they will be. Thank you."

"Anything for my dearest friend, my sister—"

"—in all but blood," Della finished.

"I must get back to the shop, but we will talk again. Soon." Franci held Della's gaze.

"Very soon, don't worry! I will tell you everything now have time to take tea without it being in secret."

"As you should have always had."

Della touched Franci's shoulder. "I know. Thank you for helping me in all the ways you have. I will forever be grateful. If there's anything I can do to repay you—"

"I was just looking out for you as friends—sisters—should. Although," Franci's lips quirked up into a mischievous smile, "if you managed to convince the queen to buy one of my gowns, I wouldn't mind."

Della laughed. "I will see what I can do."

"Come back to visit." Franci led her to the door.

"As often as I can." Della grinned.

They stepped back into the front of the shop and Franci gave Della a little way as she was swept away by customers. Della just grinned and made her way outside. Her heart was warm as the sun on her face as she walked. Roric had sent her in a royal carriage, but she had exited it on the outskirts of town, not wanting to draw unnecessary attention to herself. Their betrothal hadn't been announced yet—Della had wanted time to reunite with people and share the news herself first, and the queen had been happy to delay, though Della thought the woman might be starting to soften.

The scent of freshly baked bread made Della's stomach gurgle. She slid into the baker's shop and found Johanna behind the counter.

"Good afternoon," Johanna called cheerfully.

Della strode over to the counter. "Hello, Johanna."

"Della! What are you doing here? We haven't seen you in months! Franci said you'd returned to Aleece. That awful woman didn't have you locked up in her cellar again, did she?"

"No, Franci was correct. I did go back to Aleece, but I've returned. You'll be happy to hear that I'm betrothed."

"Betrothed! By the skies. Barend! Barend!" Johanna jumped up and came around the counter. She pulled Della into a hug so tight that Della's face was smashed against her shoulder.

Barend's voice came from the doorway to the back. "What is it? Johanna, who are you suffocating?"

"Oh." Johanna released Della. "It's Della. She's come back to us."

Della waved at Barend.

"Have you decided to live with Franci and work in her shop, then?" Barend peered at her.

"Likely she's planning to live with her husband and start a family." Johanna beamed.

Barend blinked. "Husband?"

"I don't have a husband yet. I'm betrothed, but we plan to have a *long* courtship first." Della looked pointedly at Johanna, who put her hands on her hips.

"If you're betrothed, there's no point in wasting time."

"His mother might disagree with you." Della's stomach clenched with nerves at the thought.

Johanna waved a dismissive hand. "Oh, posh."

Barend frowned. "Who is this man?"

"I call him Roric." Della winced. She knew they would be excited, but it still felt awkward to share such news. "You know him as Prince Theodoric Adalburg."

Johanna's jaw dropped. "You're betrothed to a prince?"

"How in the skies did you meet the prince?" Barend's frown turned confused.

"Didn't you take her to the ball being hosted by the royal family?" Johanna elbowed her husband.

"You can't get engaged to a man you met at a ball once!"

Della laughed. "I didn't meet him at the ball last month. Well, I did, but I knew him before that. I wouldn't accept a betrothal from a man I just met! Even if he did search for me across two countries."

Johanna's brow arched up. "I expect you to explain that."

"I will. But first, do you have any sticky buns?" Della's stomach grumbled again.

Johanna went back around the counter. She took a plate out of a cupboard and pulled a sticky bun from the box on the counter. She slid the dish toward Della, who plunked a gold coin onto the counter.

Della took an enormous bite and sighed happily. Cinnamon and vanilla melded together in her mouth. "You two make the best baked goods I've ever eaten."

"This is too much, Della." Johanna was frowning at the gold coin in her hand.

"Consider it a start toward repaying what I owe you. Did you think I didn't know you charged me less than the other customers and snuck in more food?"

"The prince is paying for this?" Barend raised an eyebrow.

Della shook her head. "I have my own inheritance that I reclaimed in Aleece. I'm an official duchess now."

"Lady Della." Barend winked and she rolled her eyes.

"There's no need to call me that. Just Della has done nicely all these years, and it will continue to do so."

A cooing babble drifted up from behind the counter. Johanna bent and lifted a bundle into her arms. Della realized they must keep a cradle back there for the baby.

Johana lifted the baby to face Della. "Look, Lotte. That's our friend, Della. She's a duchess now, but she's going to be a princess. Can you imagine that? You'll be friends with a princess!"

Della smiled at the cooing babe. "You look like a princess, Lotte."

"You do too." Johanna smiled at her.

Barend rounded the counter and put his arm around his wife. Della thought they looked like the picture of happiness, standing there as a family. She wondered if she and Roric might look like that someday too, with a baby of their own in her arms. A clock chimed the hour and she started.

"Oh dear, I have to go." Della stuffed the last of the sticky bun into her mouth and wiped her hands on her handkerchief.

Johanna handed the baby to Barend and put her hands on her hips. "Now wait just a minute! You haven't given us a proper explanation about anything."

Della gave her an apologetic smile. "I'm really sorry. I will come back in a day or two. We can have a nice, long chat then. For now, I can't be late for tea with the queen."

"The queen!" Johanna's eyes widened.

Barend waved Della off. "Go, then. We will be here when you come to call again."

"And you'd better tell me all about the royal family. Honestly, Della, you are always surprising me." Johanna came over and tugged her into a quick, tight hug before shooing her out the door.

Della's heart was full as she made her way back to where the carriage was waiting. She had missed her friends. They had become her family in her years in Tamaria. Roric had said he would even live in a caravan, and though she didn't think that was a true possibility, she thought she might be able to convince him to live between both countries. Perhaps they could even have a safer path forged through the Deep Woods. Maybe putting up a wall around the path? She would ask him, and they could think of solutions together.

CHAPTER TWENTY-EIGHT

A few days after her arrival in Tamaria, Della received an invitation from Eleonora to take tea with her at Duchess Faust's residence. She had assured Della that her stepmother and Marien would not be present.

Eleonora was sitting by Lord Faust when Della and Roric walked in. Della's heart warmed at the sight of Eleonora's smile radiating her happiness. Eleonora hadn't noticed her yet and turned her head to say something to the woman on her other side.

"That's Duchess Faust, Pieter's mother," Roric whispered.

The three noticed them and stood. Eleonora rushed over and took Della's hands in hers. She gave Della a pleading, tearful look.

"Oh Della! Please forgive me for everything. I'm so sorry for the way I treated you. I never wanted you to be a servant, only a sister." Eleonora burst into tears.

"It's alright. I know you didn't. You tried to be kind and were reprimanded for it, yet you still continued."

"But I should have fought against my mother harder! I knew it was wrong! I was weak, I was a coward!" Eleonora sobbed.

"If you had fought, you would have only been punished further. It's okay, I forgive you. I never held it against you." Della gave her a reassuring smile.

Eleonora took a shuddering breath and dropped Della's hands to mop at her eyes. Lord Faust handed her his handkerchief, which she accepted with a grateful, hiccupping laugh.

Guilt coiled Della's stomach at what she had left Eleonora to deal with by returning to Aleece. "Besides, I left you too. I'm so sorry. I wanted to wait until you were married, but I just couldn't stay."

"Please don't ever feel guilty about that. Loyalty through hardship is one thing, but loyalty while enduring cruelty is something else entirely. Mother saw you rising up and she would have done anything to tear you back down. I was so afraid for you. It was a relief to find you gone that night, much as I knew I would miss you." Eleonora gave Della a sincere smile.

"I hear I am to address you as Your Grace now." Lord Faust looked uncomfortable.

"Della is just fine." Despite the words, Della stared at him with her chin held high and he stared back unrepentant.

"Pieter, you look like you're staring down a bear, not looking at a future princess." Duchess Faust maneuvered around her son, fluttering nervously.

"I think he would prefer the bear," Della said dryly.

"I wouldn't think so!" The duchess looked shocked.

"I would," Lord Faust confirmed.

"Pieter!" The duchess and Eleonora gasped out at the same time that Roric growled it.

"It's quite alright. He has disapproved from the beginning. Seeing me here is like salt to his wounds." Della waved them off. "I'm glad you found the courage to pursue Eleonora despite her mother."

"She is worth it." Lord Faust pressed a kiss to Eleonora's hand.

She gave him a tender smile in return. "It probably helps that Pieter ensconced me here and has forbidden Mother to visit without a formal invitation."

"That woman was forcing you to do household chores! A lady of your standing should never have to—" he broke off at Della's sardonic expression.

"One must wonder if you would have found the courage to pursue Eleonora if she dressed in rags with calloused hands," Della observed.

"Della!" Roric protested.

This time Lord Faust held up a hand against the protests. "Her point is a fair one, even if it stings. I am humbled to say I would not have. I would have missed out on the finest pearl for the sake of reputation. For that, I know I owe you an apology, as well as the utmost thanks for saving her from the life I would have failed to extricate her from had you not taken the brunt of it all these years."

Della evaluated him, then nodded once. He returned the gesture.

Roric glanced between them. "Is this war finally at an end then?"

"It is," Lord Faust said.

"We shall have peace," Della agreed.

Duchess Faust smoothed her dress. "Good! I'm not sure what all happened, but Pieter can't be rude to a future princess. I simply won't allow it!"

"Nor would I have him if he disparaged you." Eleonora shot him a fierce look as she laid an arm around Della. Lord Faust gave an almost imperceptible wince.

"All is well between us," Della assured them.

"Then let us sit and enjoy the tea before it grows cold!" Duchess Faust clapped her hands and the servants entered with the tea things.

Della enjoyed the hours of talking and laughing with her sister and soon to be family. Eventually Eleonora and Lord Faust took to a corner, chatting quietly together. The duchess sat down next to Della.

"She seems happy. I'm so glad," Della said.

The duchess rested her teacup on its saucer. "She does indeed. He does too. I honestly thought he'd be forced into marriage out of duty as he turns his nose up at every girl who approaches him. I admit her mother does worry me, but she seems to be held in check for now."

"Eleonora is nothing like her mother, if that's one of your fears." Della sipped her own tea.

"That does ease my concerns somewhat. However, everyone knows she wants to marry her daughters off to the wealthiest men she can, and Pieter is the highest one can go. Excluding his cousins, the princes, of course." The duchess stirred in another spoonful of sugar.

"Eleonora doesn't care about that. She has done as her mother asked, but has always dreamed of finding love. I knew she fancied someone, but she kept it to herself, not even telling me. She wouldn't have wanted her mother to find out it was the future duke, lest she push Eleonora at him. Eleonora wanted love to grow naturally with someone, no matter their title."

"Do you think the woman will interfere now that Pieter is obviously enraptured?"

"No. She is likely pleased, even if disappointed that she didn't orchestrate it herself. She wouldn't risk the match by irritating Lord Faust. I believe she will hold her peace. If anything, I'm sure Roric could stop her from being a nuisance, but I get the feeling your son has things well in hand. I doubt he would have approached Eleonora without a plan."

"Oh, that's wonderful to hear! Roric, my, I haven't heard that name since he was a boy." The duchess patted Della's knee with a smile and Della blushed.

"Della, if you still wish to attend to your other business, we should be going," Roric said.

"Oh, yes. I lost track of the time. Thank you for having us. I had a lovely time."

"You must come again," Duchess Faust said.

"Yes, please do!" Eleonora hugged her.

Roric led Della out.

"Is it proper in Tamaria for Eleonora to be living with the Fausts?" Della asked once they were in their carriage.

"It is uncommon and not the best situation for gossip, but considering the alternative..." Roric shrugged.

"Do you think Eleonora could stay with me in the castle? I don't want to ask your parents for that if it would be too much, but if it would help those two, I would love to be able to offer that."

"I will discuss it with my father and see what he says. It would make sense since she is your sister. You are always searching for ways to help others, My Lady. I love that about you." Roric laid a hand on hers.

Della smiled up at him. They rode the rest of the way in companionable silence. When the carriage stopped, Della's stomach flipped.

"You know you don't have to do this."

Della pulled her hand away from his and wiped her sweaty palms on her skirt. "I really do."

"I could do it for you. Or we could write to them from afar."

"I have to face this. They need to hear things from me and I have answers I want that even their silence will grant me. I know how to read them. I also—" she paused and gulped. "I just need this."

"Alright. I'm right here with you."

Della exited the carriage before she lost her nerve, forgetting yet again to let the footman help her down. She might never get used to such things. Roric emerged and laid a comforting hand on her waist. Della stared up at the enormous residence that housed her torture for several years. Her heart pounded and she took a breath to steady herself. It didn't help.

"Della—"

She strode up to the door. The footman knocked. Della shifted anxiously while they waited. Time stretched out into agony though it may have been only a few minutes before the door opened. Marien stood there. Della noticed a few stains on the girl's gown.

"I suppose you've come here to gloat!" Marien said sullenly. Her eyes darted to Roric and she bobbed a quick curtsy.

"No. I came to talk."

Marien moved aside and gestured roughly at them to enter. A few guards moved to follow them into the house.

Della held up a hand. "We don't require protection here."

"We'll be alright." Roric shut the door on their disgruntled faces.

They followed Marien across the entrance hall and up the stairs to the sitting room. Della's heart thudded in her chest as she walked the familiar route. It was strange to be in this house once again. She told herself she was safe, that Roric was here, that nothing bad would happen to her anymore. Her muscles still tensed with each step.

"We have guests."

"Who is it? Oh!" Duchess DeVoss' face went white as a sheet before she regained her composure. "Please sit down, Your Highness, Your Grace."

Della did not curtsy, but she sat. Roric took a seat next to her.

"Are you happy that you weaseled your way into the palace?" Marien asked through her teeth. Della knew her stepsister was thinking she had taken everything that could have been Marien's.

"Marien, I never meant to—"

"Marien! Don't use such a harsh tone with your stepsister." The duchess flashed a nervous smile. Della thought she saw a pulse of fear in the woman's eyes.

"My betrothed hasn't come here to punish you, though I advised her to, and offered her a plentiful choice of options," Roric said harshly.

Della placed a placating hand on his arm. "Dear, please."

"Very well. Perhaps I'll wait in the entrance hall. One of us is not so gracious and quick to let go of their *rightful* anger." Roric strode across the sitting room. He paused in the doorway, shooting meaningful glances at her stepmother and stepsister. "Call for me if I'm needed."

Silence coated the room like smoke, so thick one could almost choke on it.

Della needed to acknowledge what she had done because it had hurt them, even if she had felt it necessary to flee because of how they had wronged her. She broke the silence first. "I understand that I did exactly what you were afraid of, Stepmother. I left in the night and returned to my homeland."

"You left us in a terrible lurch! We came home from the ball and had to undress ourselves, not knowing when you would come back. We had to make breakfast ourselves and do everything!" Marien groused.

"I gave you everything and you abandoned us."

"Everything? You gave me everything?" Della asked incredulously.

"You had clothes on your back, a roof over your head, and food to eat." Duchess DeVoss sniffed.

"Let us put aside the facts that my clothes were worn and small, that I kept everything under this roof clean, and that I prepared all the food you spoke of. I would have happily done those things if I had still felt a part of the family. If I had been made to feel appreciated. All I ever wanted was love. My father married you to give me a complete family."

"I already had a family."

Her stepmother's words felt like a slap. Della blinked twice as her eyes pricked with tears. She hadn't known heartbreak could come in so many different forms. "Then why did you marry my father?"

"We were starving. Marrying your father offered us a way out. That's all he and you ever were. Now here I sit, a duchess, with one daughter engaged to a duke and another to be married off soon, I am sure."

Della looked past her own hurt to the woman before her. The duchess wore her pride like a shield. It was all she had left.

"Did you never love him?" The thought had never occurred to Della.

"I married for love once and it was enough to learn the destruction that comes from such a match."

Della felt a flash of pity for the woman. Eleonora had told her that her father had died from an illness that had ravaged their village. Della was suddenly grateful that Roric would have the finest doctors to attend him should he ever fall ill. She had given him up for herself once, and she did not think she could do it again. She wasn't sure if she would be brave enough to open herself up to another man after such an incident either.

"If you thought what we did was so awful, then why did you never fight it? You cleaned and ran wild. You were always wild. You wouldn't have made a decent courtier and you'll be the worst princess this country has ever seen!" Marien lashed out with her tongue, looking as if she wished she could claw Della to pieces instead.

Della recoiled from her stepsister. She knew she would be a terrible princess—she had said as much to the king. Still, Roric loved her and she loved him. The king had assured Della that she would be properly educated, but that she would not be required to make any decisions that would affect the kingdom, or even any decisions about anything at all, unless she wanted to.

"Marien, despite what your stepsister did being heinous, hold your tongue," Duchess DeVoss snapped.

"Perhaps what I did was wrong. I shouldn't have left you without any way to fend for yourselves. However, if any of you had helped me, then you would have known how to get by just fine." Della gritted her teeth.

"I did the best I could." Duchess DeVoss sniffed again.

"The best you could? Really? Did you distribute the household chores amongst us all so it would be equal and done quickly?"

"I—"

"Did you get down on your hands and knees to scrub the floors so that your *three* daughters might each have a chance at a decent life? If you weren't going to remarry, I see no reason why you couldn't have done that. Before you suggest you needed to step in as governess, I can assure you that you could have taught most things while cleaning or cooking so long as we were all in the same room as you." The words poured out of Della in a torrent.

"I clothed you! I kept a roof over your head! Did you care about any of that? No! You just wrote sobbing letters to your aunts about how much you missed them! I saw our money dwindling and I knew we needed you to do your part, you ungrateful wench!"

Della's stepmother flew up from her seat, arm high in the air. Della caught it and a look of icy shock splashed over the woman's face. Della tightened her fingers.

"Careful, stepmother. I have claimed my rightful title as Duchess Caspari in Aleece. I am also engaged to a prince who would not let you go without repercussions if you struck me," Della said coolly.

The woman paled and yanked her arm away as if Della's touch had burned her.

"I didn't come here to threaten you." Della sighed. "It's rather the opposite. You see, I don't want you to live in fear of me. I only came to say that I've moved past everything that happened here. Or at least that I am working to do so. We may be considered family by law, but I won't be in your lives any more than perhaps to be seen from a distance at whichever social events we all happen to attend. I will afford you all the politeness your status allots you should our paths cross again as I do not intend to revoke your false title. However, I ask that you do not approach me or ask any favors of me. Ever." Della held her chin high and her shoulders squared.

"I see. How...gracious of you," Duchess DeVoss repeated the word Roric had used as if it pained her, though she looked somewhat relieved.

Marien just looked on sullenly.

Della stood but paused. "The letters to my aunts. You never sent them, did you?"

Her stepmother gave one tight, almost imperceptible nod. Della nodded sadly. She had already concluded as much.

"I must be going. I will be taking Reynart with me."

Duchess DeVoss opened her mouth to protest, but Della held up a hand.

"You do not ride him, nor do you know how to care for him. You kept him only for what he could offer you, without ever intending to give anything back to him. I cannot, in good conscience, leave him here." Della paused, swallowing against the lump in her throat. "And he is the last connection I have to my father. He comes with me."

The duchess said nothing, not even to argue.

Della looked over the woman she had hoped would one day grow to love her. Her stepmother may have withheld any scrap of kindness, but Della would choose to be like her father, not this woman. "There is one other thing I wish to say. Should you ever find yourself wishing for my forgiveness, know that it has already been given."

Her stepmother looked stunned. For the first time in her life, Della saw Duchess DeVoss with her mouth slightly ajar, frozen in shock. Marien wasn't even looking at her as Della bobbed a small curtsy and for once left that sitting room feeling dignified.

"I have a present for you at the castle," Roric told her as they left the manor that had both broken and forged Della.

"What is it?" Della clutched his arm as they walked, excitement banishing the anxiety within her.

"I said it was a surprise!" Roric chastised her.

Della ignored him. "Is it a horse?"

Roric feigned a long-suffering sigh. "It might have hooves."

"It is a horse!" Della cried in delight.

"Not just any horse."

"Roric, did you find me a Stronghorse?!"

"She's a feisty young thing, though tall. You can keep her *if* you can bond with her," Roric teased.

"If I am not her person then I shall gladly give her up in hopes that she may find the one who is."

"How could you not be, with a heart like that?"

AUTHOR'S NOTE

When I decided I wanted to rewrite Cinderella's story, I first formed the basic idea of how I wanted to go and then I read every copy of the tale that I could get my hands on. I was struck by the original version's ending where she frankly forgave her family. That was the true grace and pure goodness of Cinderella shining through. I decided I wanted that too. I didn't want her to seek for vengeance as there are already so many versions like that, but rather for Della to keep that original kindness from the tale. However, I also wanted to modernize it by having her also set boundaries with them. Eleonora was as kind as she could be and not toxic, so their relationship stays and gets to grow. Della's stepmother and Marien were intentionally cruel, so Della lets them know that they will not gain anything from her in her new position, and that though she won't be cruel to them in turn, she will also not be friends with them either. Politeness is all they can expect from her. Della forgives, but doesn't forget. She has learned to set healthy boundaries.

I also realized when working on the second draft that I rarely wrote Della in the manor with her stepfamily. That is because, as those abused in their own home will understand, that place is a place of fear and misery for her when they are there. To keep the tale lighthearted, and because escape is the desire of those who have gone through such trauma, Della actively seeks to run errands that will keep her out of the place that gives her anxiety. The original draft had fewer undertones of the abuse, but after writing the dedication during the second draft, I knew I had to be true to Della and my own history, and add more of it in, while still keeping it cozy and light.

Another thing to consider is how different people respond to trauma. Most people think of fight or flight, but there is also the fawn response where you freeze like a deer caught in the headlights. Many people wonder, why don't they just move? Why don't they run? But sometimes trying to make the decision is so scary that it's easier to stay frozen. That is what happened to me. I planned to leave for several years before I actually did. Even the day that I left, I went back and forth between sobbing and feeling horrible, and giddy laughter. The friends that were helping me move asked me multiple times if I was alright with genuine concern. I almost put everything back and just stayed, even though staying would have been the worst decision and leaving helped me almost immediately. Della gets caught up in that too, where she stays longer than she should have without exceptional action. She is frozen not wanting to make waves, afraid of the consequences, all while recognizing that leaving is truly the best decision for her.

With regard to naming the Stronghorse race, I found I loved when foreign words translated into something so obvious. People have done it time and again throughout history, making it a realistic option. It helps that it made me giggle doing it, despite knowing some will criticize me for such an obvious choice—after all, that was the point.

Acknowledgements

I cannot believe that in all the years I have been writing stories, this is my first published book! Despite executive dysfunction, fear of both succeeding and failing, being a mother to two young children, and a host of other obstacles, I finally did it. Little five-year-old me, middle school me, high school me, you can all be proud that I finally accomplished our lifelong dream.

I want to thank my husband for going on this journey with me. I sprang it on him earlier this year that I had written two books last year and wanted to publish this one this year. He has been adapting to the life of being married to an out of the closet writer who treats writing like a full-time job, despite not making a cent from it yet (though if you are reading this, I've sold at least one copy—unless I donated it to a library). So thank you, my love, for all your support in this endeavor and always.

To my darling girls, I hope you have been taught how to set boundaries from the beginning. Don't worry, if I ever pass on, I know that you are mischievous enough to chase away any wicked stepmothers before your dad could ever marry one.

I also need to thank my dear friend, Kayla Eshbaugh, who inspired me to chase my dreams by publishing her own books.

She answered countless questions, gave advice, was the first person I told that I was writing a story to publish. She did all that, and was a beta reader, and even put this beautiful cover together from photos I chose, all while writing and releasing five novels and a few novellas this same year. Thank you for being such a lifesaver. Don't ever forget that you are amazing.

Sabrina, my wonderful writing buddy, thank you for all the talks. You have been so supportive and helpful, and answered so many of my random questions. Thank you for all the cafe meet-ups, cheerleading, and fun at writing conventions.

Thank you to Cheyenne, my editor, for catching spelling errors, missing descriptions, and confusing phrasing, to name a few.

To all my readers, thank you for taking a chance on *Beneath the Cinders*. If you ever wish to chat, feel free to reach out via social media or my email.

About the Author

Alice has been writing stories since she learned her letters in kindergarten. When she wasn't writing, she was making up stories in her head. Next to writing, she loves reading and doing jigsaw puzzles. She lives in Utah with her husband and children. While Alice enjoys reading a variety of stories, she prefers to write happily ever afters since books were always her escape. *Beneath the Cinders* is her debut novel.

Printed in Great Britain
by Amazon